I walked a few yards on up t 

f something burnt on the ev

I turned to look at her a it my eye.

"Look out!" I yelled as a e bushes behind her.

I recognised it instantly from Julie Maynard's memories. Mother turned. The creature raised its club up over its right shoulder and advanced on her. A moment's hesitation then mother ran towards me. The creature sprang after her; God it was fast, and the path so narrow that I could do nothing until she was past me. It tripped her as she reached me. She went down and I launched myself at it as it swung the club.

It caught me on the left shoulder. My arm went numb, but I hit the creature solidly in the chest with my full weight. It fell backwards, dropped the club and rolled on top of me, scrabbling for my throat with sharp claws. I grabbed one claw with my good hand and tried to pull it away. The acrid burnt-tyre stink of it filled my nose. I pulled my head back and butted it as hard as I could in its ugly monkey face. It shrieked, but the grip on my throat did not loosen. Blood pounded in my head and the edges of my vision started to go dark.

There was a thump. It shrieked and released my throat. I sat up holding my neck, my heart beating wildly. Mother dropped the club and knelt beside me. There was no sign of the ape-like creature. I took my hand away from my neck and looked down; my fingers were covered in blood.

"Are you alright?" she asked. "What the fuck was that?"

ISBN 978-1-950565-76-4

For information address Crossroad Press at 141 Brayden Dr., Hertford, NC 27944
A Mystique Press Production - Mystique Press is an imprint of Crossroad Press.
www.crossroadpress.com

First edition

SHADOWS OF FAERIE

BY MARTIN OWTON

ACKNOWLEDGEMENTS

Many people helped me to get this story to version you hold and I will doubtless have forgotten some. I like to recognise the members of the T-Party Writers of London, Rushmoor Writers, Patrice Sarath, Fran and Rupert Dore, Charles Phipps, and my agent Ian Drury.

I'VE ALWAYS KNOWN I'M SPECIAL.

Every kid says that, of course, and in a sense it is true. Most of them grow out of it as they get old enough to discover the world shits on you like everyone else. It shits on me too, but I'm still special.

My dad came from somewhere else.

Not another country, but another world. One that is joined to this one in a way I don't understand. He's one of the Otherfolk.

I've never met him, at least not that I'm aware of.

But he left me with something.

I know things about people as soon as I touch them. Big things mostly. The things that really matter to them, things they don't tell people. Things I don't want to know about them. Even a brief skin-on-skin touch can do it; brushing past someone in a crowded room, standing at the bar trying to get served.

I don't play rugby.

I try to avoid touching people. I wore gloves all the time for a while; people thought I was weird and that was worse. I've got used to cutting my own hair; I really don't want to know what my barber is thinking, at least the dentist wears gloves.

It wasn't always like that. Before the hormones kicked in and my voice broke I was just another kid with a single mother. Pretty common around the Waterside and New Forest where I grew up. Guess my dad liked 'em young; mother was only eighteen when I was born, a real looker too, and still is. She kept men at arm's length after I arrived; just me and her for a long time. That was OK by me; I didn't want to share her. Kept telling me I was special, but not telling me about my father. Can't say I blame her. I wouldn't have kept a secret like that when I was a kid, not that anyone would have believed me. I made her tell me when it happened first. I got some of it by just grabbing hold of her.

It didn't creep on me gradually. I was two months short of fifteen when I knew with shocking, almost explosive, clarity that Danny Lewis had nicked a motorbike and interfered with his little sister and really actually hated me. Then it happened with Melanie Croucher. After that I stopped touching people.

I've always wondered about my father. I'd love to meet him, get to know him and find out more about that other place. Could he live up to my dreams of him? Probably not, but I'd like to find out.

CHAPTER 1

It was after six when I left the lab. Later than usual because Prof ripped into one of the Egyptian lads for not drying his solvents properly and wouldn't let him go. I hurried down Welbeck Avenue hungry and annoyed at my Wittig reaction which wouldn't go to completion. I intended to warm up a portion of the chilli I'd cooked last night then get back to the lab and try the reaction again with a different base. The house was dark and the front door locked. I was a bit surprised because Karen was usually back by now. I opened the door, put on the hall light and went upstairs to my room. Karen's door was ajar. She's normally really careful about that; we all are. We all lock our rooms. Rule one of sharing a house in a dodgy area of Southampton.

"Karen." I called out and pushed the door open, thinking maybe she had fallen asleep. Silence. I switched on the light and went in.

Karen was curled up on the bed, her bare back turned to the door. Seeing her naked I pulled back, but then the wrongness of it all struck me.

"Karen." I called out louder. She didn't move. Then I saw the blood soaking her blue duvet cover.

I touched her and a vast wave of fear rushed through me. I saw him standing naked over me, the knife in his hand. I screamed at the white hot bite deep in my side. He laughed and his voice followed me as I fell into a black hole filled with pain.

I collapsed onto the worn beige carpet and pain vanished as the contact was broken.

I just made it to the bathroom to throw up.

The police showed up as quickly as you'd hope they would. Two uniformed constables in a patrol car first, then the plain-clothes a few minutes later. I stayed down in the kitchen clutching a cup of tea I couldn't bring myself to drink. Greg and Chloe, my other housemates, showed up in the middle of all this and were briskly told to come back later by one of the uniformed guys.

My tea was pretty nearly cold by the time the plain-clothes came to talk to me. She was brown-eyed blonde girl of around thirty, five seven, no makeup, hair pulled up tightly in a Croydon facelift, brown leather jacket and shapeless sweatshirt worn over tight-fitting jeans.

"Charlie Somes? I'm Detective Sergeant Wickens." She held out her hand.

I declined to shake it.

"Contact dermatitis," I said. "One of the chemicals I work with has made my hands really sensitive."

"OK." There was a touch of estuary English in her voice. "You found Karen? Do you feel up to answering some questions?"

I nodded. She took a notebook out of the pocket of her jacket and flipped it to a blank page.

"Let's start with your details. You're a student?"

"Postgraduate student of chemistry. I'm halfway through my PhD."

"Karen was a chemist too?"

"Yes. First year of her PhD, but in a different group."

"And you were friends?"

"Yeah, you know. Share a house with someone, you get to know them pretty well." True enough; Karen was one of the very few who knew about my talent. Greg and Chloe didn't.

"Nothing more?"

I shook my head. "She used to have a boyfriend back in Leeds. He's the one you want. Name's Robert Evans." His face was flaring in my mind. "Big scary bastard. Wouldn't take no for an answer. He was stalking her."

"Slow down, let me get this down." She scribbled away at the notebook and I waited, figuring out the best way to tell her.

"She told me about him. I saw him once when he came here.

Not the kind of guy you'd forget in a hurry. Six foot five, long black dreadlocks, tattoos down his arms, pierced eyebrow and bottom lip. Carries a knife with a white bone handle. Stabbed her with it then raped her."

I had to close my throat then to stop from being sick again. She scribbled away then put down her notebook.

"Hold on. My boss needs to hear this." She slipped out closing the door behind her and returned a moment later followed by a bulky six-footer with broad shoulders, big broken nose and thinning dark hair. He looked like a rugby player, prop or maybe hooker; definitely a forward.

"Detective Inspector Brown." His accent labelled him as local. "My sergeant says you know who did it."

"Yeah." I nodded. "Robert Evans. Ex-boyfriend. Stalker. Wouldn't leave her alone. Nutter."

He looked at me for a moment. Guess I passed whatever test it was. "Get the word out there for him," he said to Sgt. Wickens then turned back to me. "Don't leave the country. We'll need a full statement from you."

They both left the kitchen. Through the door I heard Sgt. Wickens radioing Evans' description to the control room. I looked at my watch; twenty past eight. It seemed likely to be hours before I could go up to my room. I couldn't go to the gym because my kit was upstairs so I decided to go back to the lab. There would be people working there until midnight and it was somewhere I belonged that wasn't here. Sitting here in the kitchen with nothing to do but think about what had happened was just bloody morbid.

"Where are you going?" asked Sgt. Wickens as I opened the front door.

"Dunno." I shrugged "Back to the lab maybe." She looked at me as if I'd farted. "Not all students are useless wasters. Postgrads really have to work."

She had the good grace to look slightly ashamed. "I know. I've got a degree too. I'll need you to come down to the station and make that full statement. Leave me your mobile number."

I gave her my number and walked out, glad to be away from the house. It was raining and I hadn't got a hat, but I wasn't tempted to go back for one. I tried to phone my mother on the way but only got her voicemail; she was probably working. I left a brief message saying I'd call again. I didn't want to worry her.

I lasted about ten minutes at the lab; time enough to break two flasks so I left before I did some real damage and went up to The Stag's Head, the union bar. I bought a pint of London Pride and sat at a corner table. There was no-one there I knew. I watched the people chatting, drinking and playing pool and tried so hard to not think of Karen, to wash the memories out of my mind and utterly failed. I left my beer unfinished and walked out into the rain not really knowing where I was going.

Sgt. Wickens phoned the next morning and asked me to come down to the Civic Centre police station. I was feeling a bit light-headed as I'd barely slept once I got my room back, and that sleep was filled with vivid dreams of Karen's death. I said I'd come right away. The Professor frowned with annoyance when I told him where I was going and made it clear he expected me to make up the lab time, as if my being there since six didn't count at all.

I took the bus down to the centre of town and sat wondering about how someone could end up in Robert Evans' state of mind. It was a complete mystery to me, but then I'd never been in love.

I gave my name at the desk at the police station and had barely sat down before Sgt. Wickens appeared to take me through to an interview room. She was dressed more formally than yesterday in a dark skirt and pale blue shirt that didn't suit her; the blue making her face look washed out under the fluorescent strip lighting.

She pointed to a camera mounted high on the wall. "Just so you know, this will be recorded, video and audio."

I looked up at it. "Do I need a lawyer for this?"

"If you really want one. But I emphasise, you are being interviewed as a witness."

I thought for a moment about calling up the students' union helpline and asking for a lawyer, but figured I'd be in for a long wait if I did. Anyway, she was right; I was only there as a witness.

"Let's get on with it," I said, pulling out a plastic chair.

She took a seat across the table from me and put her bag on the floor. "Just identify yourself for the camera, please," she said.

I looked up at the camera again. "Charlie Somes."

"Detective Sergeant Wickens. Now Charlie, can you take me through the events of yesterday? Start around midday."

"I had lunch in the tearoom at the Chemistry department, after that I worked in the lab until the group meeting at four with the Professor. That finished about ten past six. I walked from the lab down to the house. Takes about ten minutes so that would be around twenty five past when I got there."

"Did anybody see you in the lab between lunch and four?"

"Yes. I work in an eight-man lab. Everyone else was working and they'll all have seen me. I used a couple of the instruments in the afternoon so the system will have a record of those. Why do you ask?"

"Just routine. Carry on please."

"The house was dark when I got there. I unlocked the door, switched on the light and went upstairs. I noticed Karen's door was open which was unusual so I went in. She was dead on the bed. I phoned the police and the rest you know."

"You named Robert Evans as her killer, why?"

"Well, he's the odds-on favourite. She told me about him after he showed up and creeped everybody out. He was her boyfriend when she was at Leeds. He got kicked out at the end of the second year, but stayed in Leeds and hung around with her just pissing around, smoking a lot of dope. When she was trying to work for her finals, he wouldn't give her the space she needed so she kicked him out. He wouldn't take it, kept phoning her and turning up. When she came down here she thought she was rid of him, but he carried on."

"Had she done anything about it?"

"I know she had an appointment to see someone at the advice centre recently, but she didn't tell me what the outcome was."

"The advice centre?"

"At the Students' Union."

"OK. I can check that with them. So we've established she was your friend and close enough to talk about past relationships. How close were you? Was she your girlfriend?" She looked me directly in the face as she asked.

The question surprised me and I took a moment to answer. "No. We just shared the house."

"And did you want more?"

"No. She was nice enough, but not interested." Not true; she had made her interest very clear and something would have happened but for the obstacle of my gift. I remembered her words exactly. *You've got to do something about it, or you're going to be a loser all your life.* My unkept promise to do something was less than a month old.

"Do you have a girlfriend right now?"

"No. What's this got to do with anything?"

She gave me a long hard look. "What I'm trying to understand Charlie is what you told me yesterday. You said that Karen had been raped, and described the knife she was stabbed with. But she had been dead for at least two hours when you found her, so I'd like to know how you knew that."

The realisation that I'd told her that hit my stomach like an icy fist. She watched flinty-eyed as I struggled to put my thoughts in order.

"I'm waiting, Charlie."

There didn't seem to be any alternative to the truth.

"I could tell you, but you won't believe me."

"Why? Are you going to lie to me, Charlie? Try me. I've heard a lot of unlikely stories."

I looked her straight in the face.

"In a way it's simple enough. She told me what happened."

"When?" Her brown eyes narrowed. "She died somewhere between three and four o'clock. You didn't find her until nearly half six. If you're going to bullshit me then I'm going to nick you and we'll do it the hard way."

A knock at the door interrupted. Detective Inspector Brown took one step into the room and beckoned to her.

Her lips thin with annoyance, Sgt. Wickens grabbed her bag and stood up. She leaned forward towards me.

"Think about it, Charlie," she said. "I'll be back soon."

I sat there at the bottom of a well of shit. I'd told her the truth, she didn't believe me and now I was screwed. I could prove I wasn't there when Karen was killed, but she'd keep digging. It would get back to Prof and then any chance I had of getting a decent reference would die a sad lonely death. Only last year he threw someone out when they got busted at a festival for coke. Even if I was ultimately cleared, that sort of suspicion hangs around forever.

Maybe a week would have been long enough to think of something tell her, but the hour before she came back in was nothing like. I was going to have to take a big chance.

"Have you thought about it, Charlie?" She sounded more pissed-off than ever. I stared at her and spotted the tell-tale yellow stains on the fingers of her right hand.

I looked up at the camera. "Do you want to take a cigarette break outside?"

The hard look in her eyes softened slightly. "Yeah. Why not?"

She didn't take me out the way I'd come; rather she led me through the corridors until we reached the parking area and then up the slope to emerge beside the main entrance to the Guildhall. We walked the short distance to the park. She stopped by a bed of newly-flowered daffodils, pulled out a pack of cigarettes from her bag and lit one without offering one to me.

She took a draw of the cigarette. "What's the story then, Charlie?"

"Like I said. She told me what happened."

"I already told you I'm going to nick you if you bullshit me. We can go back in right now if you want."

"This is the tricky bit." I took a deep breath and prepared for her disbelief. "I have the Sight. If I touch people skin to skin, I get a lot of knowledge about them and what they're thinking. And it works for dead people. I touched Karen and that's how I know. Give me your hand."

To her credit she didn't interrupt me, nor did she walk away. She just stood there, took a long drag on her cigarette.

"Oh yeah? Let's see then." She held out her hand out. "I think you're bullshitting me, Charlie, and I don't like bullshitters."

I hesitated. I'd never deliberately tried to read someone before. Could I do this?

She fixed me with cold eyes, her hand still outstretched. There wasn't a milligram of sympathy in her stare; she was waiting for me to fail.

"This had better be good, Charlie."

Heart thumping, I reached out and took her hand.

A torrent of information frontloaded with scepticism, memories and feeling flooded my mind like a fire hose in the face. Usually I recoiled from this but I closed my eyes and forced myself to reach into it, to focus, analyse and select.

I don't know how long I stood holding her hand but her cigarette was burned down almost to the filter when I opened my eyes.

"Watcha got, Charlie?" She dropped the cigarette butt and ground it out. There was a hint of amusement in her face. I wondered where to start.

"Sharon Patricia, Patricia for your mother's mother. Age twenty nine, birthday second of October, one sister Sandra. You slept with your last boss, but you don't fancy your current boss." There was lots more I could have used, including what she'd like to do with me if she got my clothes off which was a big surprise.

I thought she handled it well; if someone I didn't know had a load of detailed knowledge about my life I'd have been freaking out, but she just smiled at me pursing her lips and looking at me through narrowed eyes. I guess she had a lot more practice at hiding her reactions than I did.

"That's a good trick, Charlie. But I've seen stage magicians do it just as well. You need more than that."

"You're worried about your father because he drinks too much and doesn't take care of himself. You've argued with your sister about who should look after him."

Her smile didn't change. "Keep going, Charlie."

"You had a dog called Kipper who died when you were twelve. You cried so much that you missed a week's school."

Her smile broke then, just for a moment. Then the narrow-eyes returned.

"Right! Let's see what you can really do."

She took me back down the slope to the parking area, fished a set of keys out of her bag and opened up an unmarked blue Fiesta.

"Get in."

I did as I was told. She started the car and dived into the one-way system. We went down past the station and headed out through Shirley, cutting through residential roads to avoid the traffic. She drove fast, changing gear often and didn't talk.

I figured out where we were going when we crossed Winchester road.

"We're going to the General, aren't we?"

"Clever boy," she said. "Now I see why you're doing a PhD. You sure you want to go through with this?"

"Sure." I wasn't, but the alternatives looked ugly.

When we got there she made straight for the staff parking area, flashing her warrant card to the security guard who raised the barrier for us. She parked on the end of a row and we walked briskly towards the main block.

"Where are we going?" I asked as we headed away from the main hospital entrance.

"You'll see," she said.

We reached a plain door in the windowless brick wall of an outbuilding. She pressed the call button of the intercom box beside the door.

"Detective Sergeant Wickens, Hampshire Police," she said. There was a buzz and the door fell open.

Once inside she led me without hesitation down a short corridor to an office. She left me in the corridor as she had brief conversation with someone in the office. She came out with a middle-aged Asian technician in blue scrubs. We walked around a corner; a green sign at the end of the corridor read Mortuary in white letters. Should have known straight away; a knot of tension wound up in my stomach as I remembered the agonising flood I had received from Karen.

The technician unlocked the double doors and held one

open for us. The room beyond was dimly lit with a floor of cream tiles and smelt odd, part disinfectant part something else musty and decayed. I wished I had a thicker sweatshirt; it was damn chilly.

The technician consulted a large ledger on a high table beside the door and then walked over to the wall of refrigerated cabinets. He rolled a large metal hoist out of the way and consulted a pink sheet of paper inside a transparent plastic folder hanging from the shiny metal handle of one of the doors halfway up the wall. Satisfied, he opened the door and pulled out the shelf. On it lay a body wrapped in a pale blue sheet, dark stains below the abdomen area. He unwrapped the sheet.

"Keep the face covered please, Sanjay," said Sgt. Wickens. He looked at her questioningly, but did as he was told then retreated to the door.

"Brought in this morning." Sgt. Wickens turned back to me. "You said you can read dead people," she said quietly so Sanjay would not hear. "Tell me what happened to him."

Shivering slightly I approached the corpse, Sanjay watching me intently; perhaps wondering if I was going to throw up in his mortuary. I laid the palm of my right hand on the shoulder; it felt like a leg of lamb straight out of a butcher's cold room.

The stream of information wasn't the rush that I'd got from Karen—I guessed that this guy had been dead rather longer—but it was there. Reaching for it was like swimming through cold dark water. I forced myself to dive deeper then the pain hit me. An ugly snarling face filled my mind as fists and feet smashed into my body. I went down and the blows continued, harsh voices laughed as I spiralled downwards into darkness.

"That's enough, Charlie." Sgt. Wickens' voice and her hand on my arm pulled me back. I opened my eyes and stared at her uncomprehendingly; my mind still filled with fear and pain.

"Watcha got then?" Not much sympathy in her voice, obviously she thought I was putting on a show.

"Yeah. Just give me a minute. What happened?" I sucked in a deep breath and tried to stop my head spinning.

"You were standing there touching him for a couple of minutes then started to sway. I thought you were going down."

"That long? I had no idea, didn't seem like it."

"OK. Let's get you out of here then you can tell me the story. Sanjay, we've seen enough here," said Sgt. Wickens to the technician who was still staring at me. He replaced the sheet and slid Alan's body back into its frigid cell as I walked slowly out of the room supported by Sgt. Wickens.

"You okay? Not gonna get sick on me?" I guess it would be pretty inconvenient to her if I folded up right there as well as looking dead suspicious.

"I'm okay. I just got caught up in it. They didn't give the poor bastard a chance."

"Right. You can tell me about it in a minute. Let's get you sat down."

By the time we reached the little office my head had stopped spinning and I was beginning to feel embarrassed. I sat in the chair and Sgt. Wickens squatted in front of me, examining me closely; brown eyes still just as hard.

"I'm fine," I said. "Do you want to hear what I got?"

"Damn right I do."

She retrieved her handbag and took out a notebook.

"What ya got?" She perched on the desk, pen in hand.

"His name was Alan Wilson. He worked for the Council Housing Department, lived with his mother in Shirley. He was gay. He went up to the common looking for sex. It was something he'd done before. Three men attacked him, knocked him down, kicked him. He didn't know them. Skinhead haircuts. Dark jackets, boots. One of them had a tattoo of a spider's web down his neck from his left ear. He was worried about who's going to look after his mother." The last part closed up my throat and brought a rush of tears to my eyes.

"Is that everything?"

I nodded. She finished writing and closed her notebook

I wiped at my eyes, the sadness I had felt was fading and anger was replacing it.

"He was just a harmless guy. He did nothing to deserve what happened," I said, my throat still half closed.

"Not many of them do," said Sgt. Wickens, just slightly gentler.

"You stay here." She took out her mobile and went out into the corridor closing the door.

I sat in the office staring at the green-painted wall and a huge pile of shit heading my way. She wasn't going to believe me and was going to go out of her way to fuck me over. I didn't even look up when she came back in.

"An Alan Wilson was reported missing by his mother this morning at ten o'clock." Her voice was studied neutral, like the speaking clock "I checked with the Housing Department. He works there, but they haven't seen him today."

I looked up at her. The flinty sheen was gone from her eyes replaced by a quizzical look.

"Wash your hands and let's get out of here," she said. "I'll buy you coffee."

The way Sgt. Wickens drove it didn't take long to get to Shirley, just long enough to make a decision. She took me to a café at the top end of the High Street and bought me a big mug of coffee and a muffin. We sat at a table for two like old friends.

"I want to do something," I said. "Use what I can do to help catch them."

"Why's that, Charlie?" she said, her voice warmer and softer than I could have imagined half an hour ago.

"The bastards that killed Alan Wilson enjoyed it and they'll do it again. Someone's got to stop them and make them pay." I was suddenly angry; the memory of Alan's suffering surging through my mind. "I couldn't do anything to help Karen, but maybe this time I can."

"I'm glad you said that, Charlie, 'cos I feel the same way. You've already helped me and I was hoping you'll carry on. I'll make it worth your while." Her smile was a more knowing one.

I thought again about what she'd like to do with me if she got my clothes off, and wondered if that was part of the deal. A scary, but rather interesting idea, and another reason to learn to control my gift and keep my promise to Karen.

"You won't tell anybody else about it?"

"Who'd believe me?" True enough.

"We've got a deal then." I looked at her over the rim over my coffee mug. She really was quite pretty when she smiled.

CHAPTER 2

"There's counselling, of course, but I've always found the best way to get over something like this is to really dig in to the science. Lose yourself in the chemistry for a few weeks."

I didn't think there was anything I could say in reply to that except "Yes Prof." It's hard to go against the man whose reference will utterly determine your future.

I wondered what trauma he had suffered in his life that he had survived by digging in to the science? A paper rejected from The Journal of Organic Chemistry perhaps? A grant application refused? That's the story of my teenage years and frankly, I found his suggestion callous and insulting.

I went back to the lab where everyone's sympathy and veiled curiosity filled up most of the afternoon. There was certainly plenty of science to dig into as a key step of my synthesis failed and I had to pretty much go back to the beginning.

Greg and Chloe were sitting at the shabby kitchen table when I got to the house. It was half past six; it felt like a whole lifetime had passed in the last twenty four hours.

"Charlie. Are you OK?" Chloe leapt up from her chair and gave me a big hug - cloth on cloth contact, no problem. Her eyes were red and puffy which didn't go well with her magenta hair.

"It's been a fucking tough day, but I'm still standing," I said when she released me. "How are you?"

"Feel like shit," said Greg. "Want a cup of tea?"

I nodded and he flicked the switch on the kettle.

"We were talking about what we should do," said Chloe.

"About what?" I asked.

"Finding somewhere else," said Greg.

"I don't think I can live here knowing what happened to Karen," said Chloe.

"I'm with you on that," I said. "But what about the notice clause in the contract? Two months' notice, or two months' rent. I don't think Mr. Patel is going to just let us walk away even with what's happened. No way can I afford to hand over two months' rent."

"We'll go and see him tomorrow," said Greg, passing me a mug of tea with the teabag still floating in it. "See what he says."

Given our landlord's past record of fixing faulty stuff I didn't think we had a chance.

I opened the fridge to get the milk. Karen's shelf was another reminder.

"What do we do about Karen's stuff?" I asked.

"Her room's locked," said Greg.

"There's her food in here." I said.

"I wouldn't eat it," said Chloe. "You can have it if you want."

"I'm not going to eat it," I said. It just didn't seem right. "Dump it then."

"But it's like we're throwing away part of her memory," said Chloe. I didn't think I had an answer to that so I concentrated on my tea for a while.

"We're going to eat in the Stag's Head, then go to the Film Society," said Greg. "I just want to get out of the house."

"They're showing Conan the Destroyer," said Chloe. "You should come."

"It's a nice thought, but I don't fancy it. I'll probably go to the gym. Anyway it's nowhere near as good as the first one." I'd seen them both with mother when I was about twelve.

"Don't say that," said Greg. "I haven't seen it."

"Sorry mate," I said feeling guilty.

"Is your boss giving you any time off?" asked Chloe.

"What do you think?" I said. "He said I should bury myself in the science for a couple of months to forget about it."

"Really?" said Chloe. "My boss has given me a week off and is making me go to counselling."

Chloe's a Psychology PhD student; her boss is a woman and fits the stereotype.

Chloe headed upstairs to repair her make up. I sat across the table from Greg drinking my tea.

"How does someone get to the point where they can do something like that?" said Greg. "Sometimes life makes no fucking sense."

"I don't know. He must have been OK once for Karen to get involved with him."

Just then my phone rang. It was my mother. Greg went upstairs to give me space to answer it.

"Charlie. Sorry it's taken me so long to call you back. I was on a nightshift. How are you?"

I thought about everything that had happened in the last twenty four hours and decided it couldn't be put into one phone call. "There's been a lot going on. I need to see you. I'll tell you about it then."

"How about Sunday? Is that soon enough? I'm on nights until the weekend."

"I thought you weren't going to do nights."

"I need the money, Charlie. Will I see you Sunday then?"

That suited me well enough; plenty of time to get my thoughts in order before I talked to her.

Greg and Chloe clattered down the stairs on their way out. I waved goodbye and said goodbye to mother. I went upstairs to get my gym kit passing the locked door to Karen's room.

"I'm going to do something about it," I said to her memory.

In the event I decided I didn't want to be around people and went for a run instead, hoping to tire myself out enough to sleep. It must have worked because I don't remember hearing Greg and Chloe come back.

I went into the lab early to rebuild my synthesis. The first few steps were well-documented procedures, but about twenty times the scale that I usually work on. That can make life interesting, for example you have to be much more careful keeping reactions cooled if you don't want to lose the lot. Monitoring the reaction through the day gave me plenty of time to think. Alan Wilson's last moments were still raw within my mind and wouldn't allow me to reconsider my decision.

When my phone rang in the middle of the evening I didn't recognise the number. I nearly let it go to voicemail, but curiosity got the better of me.

It was Det. Sgt. Wickens.

"You said you wanted to help. You got an hour?" There was an edge of urgency in her voice.

"Yeah. Why?"

"Want to meet a skinhead with a tattoo on his neck?"

"Yes." No hesitation. Greg and Chloe were out and I didn't like being in the house alone.

"Pick you up in twenty minutes."

She was early; her car, an Astra this time, pulled up outside the house seventeen minutes later and I hurried out to meet her. She looked like she was dressed for a night out; sparkly low-cut top, tight white jean though now I questioned that. s and her hair up. I took a moment to appreciate her different look.

"Stop staring and get in."

I did as I was told and she pulled away before I'd got my seatbelt on. We zipped through the Friday night traffic going down towards the river.

"We picked up Evans," she said. "Caught him trying to get on a ferry in Portsmouth. He'd cut all his hair off but he's a bit too tall to hide. He's confessed the lot."

"Good!" The relief flooded through me. I hated the idea that he might have got away. "What'll happen to him?"

"Life sentence, minimum fifteen years."

"Doesn't seem like enough."

We crossed the river at Cobden Bridge and headed into Bitterne, a part of town I knew only from a name on a bus route. She parked across the main road from a fairly large building that looked like an old hotel; the sign along the side proclaimed it The Bitterne Park. We got out and she locked the car.

"Is that where we're going?" I asked.

"That's it. Come on." She swung her bag over her shoulder and walked towards the hotel.

The bouncers on the door barely looked at us as we went in. The bar was almost shoulder-to-shoulder packed with young people; about half of them looked underage. I knew there wouldn't be any decent beer to be had. Det. Sgt. Wickens stretched up on tiptoe to look.

"They're still here." She smiled tightly. "Over there."

She took hold of my arm and towed me through the crowd then turned and pushed herself close to me.

"The group sitting at the table just over my shoulder."

I looked past her at the group and one face leapt out at me. Det. Sgt. Wickens caught me around the waist and turned me around.

"Don't stare at them. Now is that him?"

"Yes. For sure."

"Good. OK, let's get out of here."

"No. Hold on. I want to get a touch of him."

"You sure?"

"Yeah. Maybe I can get something useful from him."

"OK." She dug into her bag and pulled out a tenner. "Get us drinks. I'll have a Diet Coke."

I took the money and worked my way to the bar doing my best to avoid any skin contact, but one bare-shouldered girl turned as I moved past and I caught a blast of mindless half-drunk boredom. I was right about the choice of beer on offer so I bought a bottle of Staropramen for myself and let the barman dump the change on the counter before I picked it up.

By the time I got back, Det. Sgt. Wickens had moved to stand almost beside the door to the Gents toilet.

"He's going to have come past here sometime soon the rate he's putting the lager away," she said as she took her Coke. "You stand there and look at me. I'll keep an eye on him."

It was no hardship to stand there and look at her, even though we had to keep moving out of the way of people heading for the toilet. She smiled back at me, her gaze flicking over my shoulder every few seconds. It was hot and almost too noisy to talk, but I was enjoying myself; tonight I was going to make a difference.

"OK. He's moving."

I took a long pull from my bottle and flicked a look over my shoulder. Tattoo boy was pushing his way towards us. He was shorter than I expected, about three inches less than me, but much stockier; his shaven head seemed to spring directly from his heavy shoulders. I was planning some kind of brushing contact, but he caught my eye as he approached.

"Whatcha looking at?" he grunted.

"Sorry mate," I said, suddenly scared by his physical presence.

He grabbed my chin, pushing my head back. Through the pain I got a torrent of emotion—mostly anger—and thoughts.

"You wanna go outside?" He snarled, pushing his face close to mine so that I could smell his evil breath. I should have been scared, but I was too busy analysing the rich data stream for something that would damn him. A space had opened around us, but then Det. Sgt. Wickens was there pushing her warrant card in his face.

"Fuck off, Darren. I know who you are. You wanna get nicked, just carry on."

He let go of me and stared at me for a long moment.

"I'll remember you." Then he pushed his way past and went through the door to the toilets as the bouncers appeared through the crowd.

"Got what you wanted?" asked Det. Sgt. Wickens.

"Oh yeah. Like reading the headlines on a newspaper."

"Let's get out of here then."

I finished my lager in two swallows as we manoeuvred our way to the exit.

I was sweating despite the cool evening, my hands shaking and clammy from the adrenaline, my own supplemented by Darren's. We didn't speak until we were clear of the smokers hanging around in the car park.

"So did he do it?" Det. Sgt. Wickens asked.

"Yes. And enjoyed it, and is thinking about doing it again when the investigation has died down. I can give you his two mates and the girlfriend's flat where he's stashed the gear he was wearing." I massaged my chin feeling light-headed and pretty pleased with myself.

"Great." Her smile lit up her face. "My boss is going to love this."

We reached the Astra, Det. Sgt. Wickens unlocked it and we

got in. She pulled out her notebook and I gave her everything I'd got from Darren.

"You going to be able to use this without bringing me into it?" I asked.

"No problem. We'll be acting on information received. We do it all the time."

"So Darren's going down?"

"If he did it, then forensics will find something. Then he's going to be going away for a long time."

"What happens next?"

"We'll be paying him a visit just as soon as we can get a warrant. And if you're right then I'll buy you dinner."

"Sounds like a deal to me."

I was evaporating down the last fractions from my purification column in the late afternoon when my phone rang. This time I recognised DS Wickens' number.

"I owe you dinner, Charlie. What are you doing tonight?"

"Nothing much," I said, a great warm glow spreading through me at the thought of tattooed Darren spending the next fifteen years in Parkhurst.

"What do you like?"

"I'll eat anything."

"I know a good Italian in Shirley."

"That's fine by me."

"I'll pick you up at eight."

I scooted out of the lab at about six, ignoring the dirty look one of the post-docs gave me. I needed time to shower, wash my hair and iron one of my few decent shirts.

Then what? Just thinking about it made me twitch. I remembered the thoughts I had picked up when I first read her and had a feeling I knew how she intended the evening to go, but what was going to happen when I touched her? Undoubtedly I would be deluged with her every thought and feeling. How would I handle it? It wouldn't be like the few seconds reading her. If I didn't cope the evening would be a disaster, and I couldn't think of any strategy to deal with it. I remembered the one and only time I'd been naked with a girl, when I was a first year. It was at a party, at her house I think, and I was pretty drunk. She was very experienced, the piercings should have given me a clue to that, and fascinated by my virginity. I'd been determined that I would go through with it, but when her thoughts hit me I drowned in the flood of comparisons with her previous lovers. At her thought of 'now he'll never forget me', I realised I'd been collected and lost my erection completely. I got no sympathy, just anger and frustration. She pushed me off and put on her clothes without a word. I saw her with someone else later that night. I got the most drunk I've ever been at that party.

Maybe if I hadn't spent so long running away from it, I'd be able to handle it by now. I toyed with the idea of texting her to say I couldn't make it, but that just seemed too sad.

Still, worrying about it was only going to make it worse, and maybe I was wrong anyway and all I'd get offered would be a plate of spaghetti bolognaise.

DS Wickens was early. I had barely finished my shirt and my hair was still damp when she rang the doorbell. Greg answered the door and called up the stairs. "Charlie! There's a babe here to see you."

Greg gave me a big dirty grin as I came down. He wasn't wrong about DS Wickens though; she looked lovely. Her hair was loose and curled to her shoulders; she was nicely and subtly made up with dark cherry lips and just a hint of eyeshadow. It was a mild evening so she had on a light cream jacket over dark blue dress which exposed a fascinating glimpse of cleavage and finished at mid-thigh.

She smiled sweetly at me. "Are you ready, Charlie?"

I remembered to breathe and gasped out, "Yes."

"Come then." She turned in the doorway. "I hope you're hungry."

She'd brought her own car, a year-old dark blue Mini, this time. As she drove she told me that I had been right; Darren's kit had been in the girlfriend's flat, blood-stained trainers and all.

"That was really good, Charlie. My DI is well pleased."

"Glad to do anything to help. I hope it's a little consolation to his mother."

I knew Roberto's, the restaurant; I had walked past plenty of times after looking at the prices on the menu. A pleasant smell of cooking garlic and basil greeted us as we entered and the manager showed us to a table in a quiet corner leaving us with menus and the wine list.

"Are you a red or white man, Charlie?" She smiled again with a twinkle in her brown eyes that had me thinking I'd been right about her plans for the evening.

"Whatever. I don't know a lot about wine. I'm more of beer drinker."

"I'm only having one glass so have what you want."

I ordered a bottle of the house white on the basis that any good restaurant should have a decent house wine, and I didn't want her to think I was taking the piss by ordering something really expensive. There were certainly some pricey wines on the list.

A waiter brought the wine and took our orders. She poured herself a glass of wine and passed the bottle to me.

"So why chemistry, Charlie?"

"Cos some parts of it just come easy. I mean, it's a huge subject, but there are some bits that I can just do. The stuff I'm good at, the transformations, there's no one best way of doing things so there's always scope for finding your own way."

She looked at me over her glass. "I have no idea what you're talking about, but I can see you're fascinated by it."

"Yeah. It's like you can be an artist rather than a scientist. There's still space for a bit of magic, and that's what I love. When something works for the first time, that's what makes it worth it."

"So is Southampton a good place to be doing this?"

"Oh yeah. One of the top ten in the UK."

"I had no idea. So where will this take you?"

"You know, I'd love to have my own research group. But more realistically I'll probably end up in the research department of a drug company. I'm completely dependent on a good reference from my boss whatever."

The starters arrived, she refilled my glass and we carried on talking. By the time the main courses arrived, I realised we'd been talking for half an hour and it had been easy and natural.

Of course the fact that I knew what she thought of me made me considerably less nervous than I would otherwise have been. Her smile more than hinted at an extended evening.

It was nearly half past ten when she paid the bill; we had talked for over two hours without any awkward silences and without mentioning my Gift.

As we stepped out of the restaurant she slipped her arm into mine—cloth on cloth contact, no problem.

"Fancy another drink?" she said. "My flat is just around the corner."

"Love to," I said, savouring her closeness.

She drove us the short distance to her flat—the upper half of a house in Atherley Road near where the old Dell used to be. It was a small flat but tidy and nicely decorated; all beige and lemon yellow with curtains that matched the carpet, quite unlike the student flats I was used to. I sat on the sofa while she hung her jacket on a hanger on the back of the door.

"What do you want to drink? There's wine in the fridge or I've got vodka and mixers."

"Wine's good." I'd already drunk most of the bottle of white wine at the restaurant so the vodka sounded like a bad idea.

She fetched a bottle and two glasses from the kitchen, but instead of pouring put them on the table beside the sofa and sat down beside me, close enough that I caught the flowery smell of her perfume. She looked at me for a moment, the pupils wide in her brown eyes.

"Would you be able to read my mind if I kissed you?" she asked with a sly grin.

"Yes." I grinned back at her.

"I'll try not to shock you too much then," she said then leaned forward and kissed me.

I tried to relax and enjoy it as she ever so delicately nibbled at my top lip, but the torrent of thoughts and emotions overwhelmed me. At the front was the raw heat of her desire, behind that her memories of every man she had ever kissed and pain from someone who had hurt her. The inevitable comparisons drowned my enjoyment. One hand started unbuttoning my shirt, on one level I was delighted but her touch brought more thoughts and memories. I couldn't help myself. I had to pull back before I lost myself in it all.

She raised her head but left her hand on my chest; I caught a full blast of her confusion which just made it worse.

"Shit no!" I lifted her hand and the river of information ceased when I released it.

"What's wrong Charlie? I thought we could have a bit of fun."

"It's the fucking touch thing. I can't turn it off." To my embarrassment I thought for a moment I was going to be sick. "I'm getting everything. Every memory of every man you've ever kissed. I can't compete with your memory of Tom, no matter how much I remind you of him."

She sat back and looked at me as if I'd slapped her. I thought for a moment she was going to cry.

"Oh Charlie," she said so quietly it was almost a whisper. "But what do you do? How have you done it before?"

"I've only done it once. It was horrible."

"Oh my God!" She nearly laughed but held it back. "I had no idea. How old are you?"

"Twenty four."

Then she did laugh. "Jesus, Charlie. You've got to get a handle on this, or you're never going to have any fun." She reached down, took a cigarette from the pack on the table, lit it and sat there looking absolutely gorgeous. "How've you managed?"

"Like any other guy without a girlfriend." The urge to throw up had receded, but now my groin ached from the undischarged sexual tension.

"That's sad, Charlie. You've got to do something about that."

Hard to disagree with that.

"Do you want some wine now?"

I nodded and she poured.

"Got any ideas?" She stubbed out her cigarette in the ashtray. "Know anyone else who can do this sight thing?"

"No. Not in the real world. Maybe Gandalf could explain how to handle it."

"Or Yoda."

"Yeah. But if he did I'd never understand it."

We both laughed and I relaxed. I think that was the moment that she stopped being Det. Sergeant Wickens and became Sharon.

Sharon offered to get me a cab but I refused; it was a mild night and I had plenty to think about on the walk home. I reached a conclusion too, though not an entirely comfortable one. I realised who was the one person who might be able to teach me how to handle my Gift; my father.

Clearly there were some difficulties with this. Such as I had never met him and had no way of contacting him. I suspected my mother could find him though.

Now I get on OK with Mum, mainly because I don't live with her anymore. I know she's proud of me, particularly since I got my first degree, and our relationship has gotten easier. I'd like to keep it that way, but she doesn't talk about my father.

I could just grab hold of her and scoop the memories out of the data stream, but really who wants to trawl through their mother's memories of her sex life? Besides, he might well talk to her when he wouldn't talk to me. I needed her to introduce me, and that meant persuading her to open up about him. I'd need to be very careful with how I approached that.

It was half past midnight when I got back to the house and there was no sign of Greg and Chloe. I went to bed and it took me a long time to get to sleep as I turned things over in my mind; no startling revelations occurred to me.

I didn't see them the next morning either, but then I was up early, earlier than psychology post-grads get up anyway. Only about half the postgrads work on a Saturday so the department was quiet. I kept my phone within reach in case Sharon called but she didn't.

Greg and Chloe were waiting for me in the kitchen when I got back grinning like a pair of Cheshire cats in a toothpaste commercial. It was good to see them back to form after what we'd gone through.

"What's her name, Charlie?" asked Chloe.

"Where'd you find her mate? She's gorgeous," said Greg.

I've known these guys a while. They're the closest friends I have, so I knew that there was no way I was getting away without telling them at least some of the story.

"Her name is Sharon, she's twenty nine and she's in the police."

"So you're a toy boy now," said Chloe, her grin even wider.

"How long have you been seeing her?" asked Greg.

"Last night was the first time."

"Are you seeing her again?" said Chloe, running her hand through her shoulder-length magenta hair. The roots were showing her original brown, I wondered which colour she would go with next.

"I hope so."

"About time you got yourself a girlfriend," said Greg. "We've been worried about you."

Had I got myself a girlfriend? I wasn't at all sure about that; Sharon didn't seem to fit the description that Greg and Chloe had in mind.

"Worried about what? That I was gay?" There had been a few people who had made that mistake; embarrassing all round.

"No. We never thought that," said Chloe. "It's just that you were never interested in any of the girls I put your way."

That wasn't exactly true. I just hadn't known how to overcome the touching issue and, fearing more embarrassments, hadn't dared confront it. I rather doubted many of the girls Chloe had introduced me to would have handled it as well as Sharon. It was slightly surprising that Chloe had never spotted my aversion to touching people like Karen had, but then Chloe had never given the slightest indication of fancying me.

"Let's not get carried away with this," I said. "It might not go anywhere."

"Let's hope it does," said Chloe. "It's time you had someone nice."

"Amen to that!" I was wondering how to change the subject when Chloe's mobile trilled; she got up to answer it and I silently thanked whoever had called her.

"Best of luck, mate," said Greg. "Be great if something good comes out of all this shit. There's a decent band on at The Hobbit, you want to come?"

"I can't really afford it." I know it sounded a lame excuse, but I had too much on my mind to feel sociable.

"Bollocks mate. It's Saturday night. You're not allowed to sit in and be miserable. I'll buy you a pint. Come on."

CHAPTER 3

It takes forever to get out to my mother's place by bus and I used all that time to consider what I was going to say to her. I'd been thinking about it for the last four days, but still hadn't made up my mind if I was going to tell her everything.

The small towns and villages of the Waterside slipped by with a few woods and fields between them, until we reached the refinery where drab suburbia took over totally. I got off the bus at The Langley Tavern and from there it's a ten minute walk. Mother's cottage must have been pleasantly rural when my great aunt lived there; now it just looks lost among an estate of new houses.

I knocked on the door and waited.

"Coming." Mother's voice sang from behind the door. A moment later it opened, mother stood there wearing an apron over jeans with holes at the knees and a Motorhead t-shirt. With her still-dark hair piled up and wearing her old clothes she certainly didn't look as if she had just come off a week of night shifts. The delicious smell of roasting lamb followed her, 'Don't Fear the Reaper' played in the background.

She put her arms around me, careful to not touch skin, and hugged me.

"Come on in, lunch will be a few minutes yet. I thought you might appreciate a good meal."

We went through into the kitchen.

"So what brings you out here?" she asked as she put the kettle on. "You sounded like you wanted to talk about something."

"Guess so. I've had a hell of a week. Actually Monday was OK, but it all kicked off on Tuesday and I'm still spinning."

"What's been happening?" She passed me a mug of tea. I waited for her to sit down before continuing.

"My housemate Karen was murdered on Tuesday."

"Fuck! Charlie! No!" Mother very rarely swore in front of me. "What happened?"

"Crazy ex-boyfriend knifed her in her room. I found her when I got in from the lab. I touched her." Just speaking the words brought her pain and fear surging back into my mind.

"You mean it works on dead people?"

I nodded, my throat closed by the strength of the memories.

"Oh, Charlie. Was it very bad?" She reached a hand towards me for a moment then drew it back.

I nodded again, closed my eyes and clutched my mug of tea trying to push the memory from my mind.

When I opened my eyes she was looking intently at me, eyes wide with concern.

"I can't go on like this. It's getting stronger," I said after a few deep breaths. "I've got to learn how to handle it. I can't be a freak for the rest of my life."

She looked at me and shook her head. "I don't know how I can help you, Charlie."

"No. But maybe my father can." I held my breath waiting for her reply. I hadn't intended to ask about my father this soon, but the window had opened.

I watched her as she thought about it feeling my heart thumping. I didn't know what I was going to do if she refused.

"Are you sure, Charlie?" she said eventually. Relief flooded through me; at least she hadn't just said no. "You're not still angry with him?"

"No, I'm not. I'm past that and I don't know what else to do. But if I ever want to have a normal relationship with somebody then I have to do something."

"Have you met someone then?"

"Yes. No, well maybe." I didn't really want tell her about Sharon yet. "The point is there's no chance of it going anywhere right now, so I have to do something."

"Yes, you do. You've been running away from it for too long. I'm just not sure that seeing your father's the best thing."

"Why not? Do you think he wouldn't help?"

"That's quite possible, but what concerns me more is what he might think of as help could make things worse."

"What do you mean?"

"I'm really proud of you, Charlie. You've got your life going somewhere. Getting involved with your father could threaten all that. I don't want things to go back to how they were when you were sixteen."

"How? You think he'll fill my head full of otherworld stuff, and I'll just pack in my PhD to go off with him? That might have been true when I was sixteen, but not now. I'm going to finish my synthesis."

"You don't know him. He wanted to take you with him when you were a baby. I wouldn't let him. I didn't want to let you go."

It is possible my mouth dropped open in surprise. "You never said."

"I couldn't tell you for years. You wouldn't have handled it. This is the first conversation we've had about him when you haven't been angry."

I sat there in silence trying to get my head around it all for a couple of minutes. Mother got up to see to the roast.

"So can you still find him?"

She bent to take the joint out of the oven and didn't answer until she had the roasting dish on the draining board.

"Yes, I think so."

A nasty suspicious thought crept into my head. "You still see him don't you?"

She looked at me over a pan of steaming carrots, a challenge in her eyes. "Sometimes."

I wasn't proud of the surge of...what?...Jealousy?...Anger? that pulsed through me. She must have read it in my face.

"I'm allowed a life too."

Only a few years ago I'd have risen to that; today I had the sense to change the subject.

"Does he ever ask about me?" I said without looking at her.

"Sometimes."

"And what do you say?"

"That you're growing up to be a fine young man and I'm proud of you."

So he was still interested in me; that sounded fairly promising.

"It's time to get the dinner on the table," she said. "Let's eat and I'll think about it."

I laid the table while she made the gravy then we sat down. Normally I can't get enough of mother's cooking, but the feeling of betrayal that still burned me had stolen my appetite. I just about cleared my plate and refused more; mother looked sideways at me but said nothing until the end of the meal.

"Leave the plates," she said. "I'll sort them later. You look like you need some mindless violence. Want to kill some zombies?" She grinned at me. "I've got the Playstation set up next door."

We went into the snug little sitting room where the PS2 was plugged into the TV. Mother fired up Resident Evil 3 and we dived into the zombie apocalypse.

She was right; it was just what I needed. We played for a couple of hours and I lost myself in concentration. When we finished, I felt wrung out; I'd blown away over a thousand zombies and that feeling of betrayal.

"You're out of practice." She had beaten me comfortably.

"I don't play these days. I don't get time."

"Glad to hear it. I used to worry about you spending so much time playing when you were younger."

"I suppose I did play a lot back then." As I didn't have any friends then it was hardly surprising; it wasn't a great time to look back on. I could have made a crack about her having bigger stuff to worry about these days, but chose not to; instead I went to put the kettle on for a cup of tea before I went back to town.

"I'll call you in the week," Mother said as we waited for the bus. "I'll speak to your father and see what his reply is. I'm not being obstructive. I just want to be sure he's not going to do something that'll make things worse."

The bus rumbled into view and she hugged me carefully around the chest.

"It's been good to see you."

I sat on the bus thinking about what she had said and that cold sick feeling of betrayal crept back over me. It had simply not occurred to me that she might still see him. Perhaps now it was easier to understand why she had had so few boyfriends, at least that I knew about - though now I questioned that.

It nagged at me all the way back into town. Despite her having agreed to speak to my father I felt let down. I couldn't get beyond the fact that while my mother hadn't actually lied to me, it felt like it. I was glad we hadn't got around to talking about Sharon. I didn't think mother would be too keen on me using my talent to help the police; she'd always told me to keep it quiet.

The pissed-off feeling stayed with me into the week like a Guinness and red wine hangover. On Monday I sent Sharon a text to see if she had any other cases that I could help with but got no reply.

On Tuesday Karen's folks came and cleared out her room while we were at work. They didn't leave any information about the funeral. It just felt weird. I know they must have been grieving and I don't know what I'd have said to them, but I'd have liked to say something.

I talked it over with Greg and Chloe and we all felt they didn't want us there. I couldn't really afford to get to Chesterfield, but we'd have gone if they'd asked us. Greg had talked to Mr. Patel too and, just as I'd expected, he wasn't going to let us out of the tenancy agreement without coughing up two month's rent—bastard.

I didn't cheer up until Sharon phoned on Wednesday afternoon.

"You got an hour, Charlie?"

Damn right I had, and fortunately Prof was occupied with a visiting industrial supervisor. "Another trip to the mortuary?"

"'Fraid so."

"You take me to all the best places."

"Pick you up at the same place in ten minutes."

I remembered to bring a sweatshirt this time and got up to the library before she did. She was in jeans and sweatshirt again and had her hair up and was driving the Astra again.

The same middle-aged technician was on duty. He smiled at Sharon as he unlocked the doors to the mortuary.

"You should wear your hair down," he said in a thick Indian accent. "You look much prettier."

"Thank you, Sanjay," she said. "Always appreciated."

"But you're looking too pale. You need to get outside in the sun more."

She laughed. "Yeah, Sanjay. I'll keep that it mind."

Sanjay consulted his ledger then opened one of the refrigerated cabinets and slid out the shelf. He unwrapped the body and the smell nearly knocked me over. Holding my breath, I stepped forward and cautiously touched the body trying to keep a little of my focus in the room. It was slimy and felt like jelly under my hand. I closed my eyes and concentrated but got nothing.

After a few moments I pulled back, turned to Sharon and shook my head.

"Nothing at all."

She shrugged. "Not really surprising. Coastguard fished him out of the Solent this morning. Looks like he's been in there a while. Okay Sanjay, put him back in."

I went to wash my hands as Sanjay rewrapped the corpse and slid the drawer back.

"You alright, Charlie?" asked Sharon quietly.

"Yeah. No worries," I said as I dried my hands. "He's just been dead too long."

"It thought it was worth a try. I owe you. I'd buy you coffee, but I've got a load of stuff to get on with."

"Another time," I said, trying to mask my disappointment. I'd have liked nothing better than to sit and chat to her for an hour or so. "You know I'm happy to help. How about later this week?"

"Sorry, Charlie. It's mad busy at the moment. I've barely got time to sleep."

The pissed-off feeling returned instantly.

As to underline her point as we walked back to the car she got a call on her mobile. From what I heard of the conversation she was supposed to be somewhere else.

"I'm on my way," she said and closed her phone. "That was the boss. We gotta fly, Charlie."

"You get going. You can't keep the boss waiting. I'll get the Unilink."

"You're a star, Charlie. I owe you again." She reached up and kissed me, so quickly that I didn't have time to pick up the usual river of information, and then she was off running towards her car.

I spent the next few days waiting for phone calls that didn't come. Sharon sent me a text apologising for having to rush off and saying she'd make it up to me, but that was all. I was more disappointed at not hearing from mother. I thought maybe she'd changed her mind about talking to my father, but then on further reflection realised I had no idea of how easy it was to contact him, whether he always turned up when called. Plus she had a job to hold down.

I was still half asleep when Sharon phoned on Sunday morning.

"I promise this one is worthwhile," she said. "I'll buy you lunch."

I'd have said yes without the offer of lunch.

She picked me up twenty minutes later in the Astra looking a little rough; there were dark rings under her eyes and a couple of small spots beside her mouth.

She must have read my mind. "I know I look like shit," she said. "Only went to bed at three last night and got the call on this one at seven. Early morning dog walker found the body about six thirty."

I felt a sudden pang of jealousy wondering what she had been doing until three o'clock.

It took less than ten minutes to get to the General. Sanjay was again on duty; I was tempted to ask Sharon if he lived there.

"Good morning, Sergeant," he said. "You're looking particularly lovely today."

"Give it a rest, Sanjay. I'm not in the mood today."

"Suit yourself Sergeant. Got your period today, have you?"

I wouldn't have been surprised if she slapped him, she just

gave him a hard look.

"Just show us today's body, Sanjay," she said. "And cut out the talk."

Sanjay opened his ledger, and ran his finger down the page.

"Female. Brought in at seven fifty," he said. He walked over to the wall of cabinets, opened a door on the bottom row and pulled out the body.

I knelt beside the drawer and tried to prepare myself for the rush of information. I wondered what terrors awaited me and whether I could keep myself from being drawn in as I had been by Alan Wilson's memories.

"You okay, Charlie?" asked Sharon.

I nodded; if I was going to keep my promise about doing this then I had to learn to cope. I took a deep breath and laid my right hand, palm down, on the shoulder of the corpse. The flesh was firm and only cool; the rush of fear strong and immediate.

An acrid choking smell filled my nose, an ugly inhuman face leapt out at me. I gagged and lifted my hand, breaking the contact.

"What is it, Charlie?" asked Sharon.

I didn't answer but took another deep breath and laid my hand back down, searching for more detail. The hideous face came screaming at me again, pursuing me through dark woods. I stumbled and tripped then the pain began.

"Charlie? You still with us?" Sharon's voice reached me and I could hear her concern. I lifted my hand and the river of memories ceased.

I turned and looked up at Sharon and Sanjay, who was staring at me, wide-eyed. I shook my head to try and lose the image of that evil face.

"OK. I'm back," I said, my voice croaky from the second-hand memory of the stench.

"You able to get anything?" asked Sharon.

"Oh yeah. Plenty." I stood up and nodded to Sanjay. "I'm finished now."

Sanjay set about rewrapping the body as Sharon and I walked out to his office. I sat on the cheap plastic chair and looked around the room, fearing that somehow the hideous creature would appear out of a corner. Sharon perched on the corner of the desk and pulled out her notebook.

"Whatcha got then?"

I paused for a moment to put my thoughts in order. "Her name was Julie Maynard. She was thirty eight and lived in Totton, one daughter, Michelle." A pretty face surrounded by dark curls flowered in my mind; beautiful and a half-breed like me. I had to find a way to meet her. "She went into the forest to meet a lover yesterday evening. She met him and they made love. She was attacked after leaving him."

Sharon scribbled furiously. "Did she see who attacked her?"

I saw again through her eyes what had leapt out of the undergrowth swinging a club in the twilight.

"Yes." The evil face flared again in my mind and I wondered how tell her.

"Who was it? Someone she knew?"

"No." I struggled to find the words.

"Can you describe them?"

"It wasn't a person, it was a…thing, a creature."

Sharon put down her pen and stared at me.

"What was it then?"

"I don't know. It was around her height, two-legged and hairy. I mean completely covered in thick dark hair, like a dog." Her memory supplied the harsh feel of its coat and its foul smell as she grappled with it.

"Could it have been a big dog?"

"It hit her with a club." Sharon was no longer writing down my words. "She wrestled with it. It didn't bite her; it caught hold of her with a hand, a clawed hand, and held her down." I relived the bite of the claws.

"Someone wearing a fur coat?"

"The face didn't look human, more like a monkey."

"Could it have been some kind of hallucination?"

I ran through the memory again, trying to keep a distance from it so that the confusion and pain she had felt didn't engulf me.

"I don't think so. Her memory is continuous and coherent.

Just like Alan Wilson's."

Sharon scowled; this was clearly not what she wanted to hear.

"What about the guy she was meeting?"

I paused; she wasn't going to like this either. "He's not human either, he's from somewhere else."

She looked at me blankly for a moment. "What the fuck do you mean?"

I was about to answer when Sanjay came into the office. Sharon glared at him and slid off the desk.

"OK Charlie," she said. "Let's get out of here."

Once we were out in the open she lit up a cigarette. After a deep drag she perched on a bollard and looked at me, squinting a bit in the sun.

"OK. Tell me about the guy she was meeting. What did you mean when you said he's from somewhere else?"

"He's one of the Otherfolk."

Her blank look told me she didn't get it before she said. "What?"

"He comes from another world that is linked to here."

"What? Like Narnia?"

"Well yeah. I don't understand how it works, but people can travel between here and there. I'm sure they're responsible for some of the old stories about Faeries. Not the pretty little things with gauzy wings, those are a Victorian invention."

"Sounds like you know a lot about them."

"Yeah, I do." I thought briefly about what to say next because I've never told anyone before, but from the way she had handled learning about my Gift, I thought she could handle this. "My father is from over there. That's where I get this touching thing from."

She took another long drag of her cigarette, then dropped it and ground it under her foot. "Fuck me, Charlie. This is just too weird to deal with right now. I need something to eat. Let's get some lunch."

She took me to The Cowherds on the edge of the common where they do a good Sunday roast. We sat outside so that she could smoke.

"I'll have the roast beef, get me lager and whatever you

want," she said holding out three tenners. "This was supposed to be my weekend off."

I got a pint of Fortyniner and a Foster's for Sharon. She was on her mobile when I got back to the table and finished the call as I put the drinks down.

"Looks like you're right about Julie Maynard. Her daughter reported her missing this morning."

I nodded and sat down.

"This is seriously fucking hard to believe, Charlie?"

"Has anything I've told you so far been bollocks?"

I waited while she thought about it for about twenty seconds. "No. But we'll see if it's like you say. The PM will show any blunt trauma injuries, and I'll make sure they look at any animal hair on her clothes." She picked up her pint and took a long drink.

"So what do you reckon it was?" she said after more thought.

"I don't really know. I've read some of the old stories, but I've never heard of anything quite like this. I need to have a serious trawl in the library."

She looked at me sideways as trying to decide whether I was taking the piss. "And what's the connection between the lover and the...hairy thing?"

"No idea. But there must be one."

"So what am I going to tell my boss if you're right? That we're looking for a hairy ape-like creature? I don't think so."

A waitress delivered the roast dinners, stopping the conversation. Sharon certainly had a good appetite; she had finished when I was still half way through mine. She drank the last of her lager and looked at me; her head cocked to one side.

"Julie Maynard had a lover from this other world. Your mother did too. So all across the country woman are slipping out into the woods for a crafty shag with someone, or something, from somewhere else," she said. "How come I've never heard of it before?"

I thought about it for a moment. "Julie Maynard was a country girl, brought up in the forest; moved to Totton as an adult. She learned about it from an older cousin. You're a town girl, and I bet you haven't got any cousins in the country."

"No, you're right about that. So why hasn't this been in the News of the World?"

"Who'd believe it?"

"The News of the World has printed less believable stuff."

"True. Maybe there's just not that many women doing it."

"Whatever." She shrugged. "We're still up shit creek without a paddle. Is there any way we can get to talk to this lover of hers?"

"Maybe." I'd like to know that myself. "Her daughter might know. She's met him."

"OK. We'll be talking to her anyway."

"Can I call in a favour?" My stomach tightened with tension. "I want to meet the daughter."

"Why?"

"She's half-breed like me. I've never met anyone else who is."

She thought for a moment and I tried to conceal my anxiety. "How old is she?"

"Twenty."

"Can she do weird stuff like you?"

I shook my head. "If she can, her mother didn't know about it."

"Have to see how she handles the news. It could be months before she's in any state to meet people. Thank God I don't get the job of telling her. I hate doing it, and I always get lumbered with it. Just because I'm a woman, they think it comes better from us. It's pretty likely that I'll be talking to her in the next day or so, and I'll see if she wants to meet you. OK, drink up. Time to get out of here."

I stood up feeling relieved; the answer wasn't no, and, in all honesty, was about the best I could have expected.

"Any chance of seeing you this week?" I had to ask.

"I dunno, Charlie." She gave me a tired smile. "I'll give you a call when I've caught up on my sleep."

After Sharon dropped me off I got a text message from mother: "come next Sunday meet father." A small explosion of joy went off in my stomach, then I thought about Julie Maynard. I tried to call her immediately, but all I got was her answer machine. I wanted to tell her what had happened, to warn her of the danger of a club-wielding hairy beast ambushing her in the forest. I think she would have laughed at me and then told me she could look after herself. But I wanted to tell her anyway; it seemed most unlikely that Julie Maynard's death was the result of some random attack.

Instead of going home I went to the University Library; not to the Chemistry section that I usually used, but to the English folklore section of Anthropology. I started with my old favourite: KM Briggs' Dictionary of Fairies. My copy that mother gave me for my fourteenth birthday was still in her bookshelf. I dug around the shelves for a couple hours trying to identify the thing that had killed Julie Maynard, but came away more confused than informed. There was simply too much contradictory information and the list of possible creatures too long.

As I walked back home I also thought about Michelle Maynard, about what I would say to her if we met. "I'm Charlie, and I'm half Otherkin just like you. Sorry about your mother. Will you be my friend" seemed to cover it, but yet lacked a certain something. I reckoned I had some time to work on it.

CHAPTER 4

I wasn't able to talk to mother until Tuesday. I figured it was too late to tell her about Julie Maynard as she had recently survived going into the forest to meet one of the Otherfolk and I couldn't answer the obvious question of how I knew what had happened. I wanted to pick my time to tell her about working with the police, and now wasn't it.

I said Sunday was fine for me, that I'd come out on the bus again and asked if I needed to bring anything.

"Bring chocolate," she said and laughed. "He likes our chocolate."

That made me laugh too, and made me wonder about how different wherever he lived was.

"How was he about seeing me?"

"Mildly interested, I suppose. He doesn't get excited about things in the future." She paused. "He's just different. He's very much a now person. It's difficult to describe. You'll understand when you meet him."

I was pissed-off and confused that he wasn't keener to see me; his long-lost son, but then I guess he has a lot of sons if half the folklore books I'd read are accurate. I probably have a whole army of half-brothers and sisters scattered across the years. Still, I felt a little shiver of excitement at the prospect of finally meeting him when I finished the phone call.

The fizz of excitement and nervousness grew as the week went by. By turns I was buzzing with the idea of meeting him, then scared in case he turned out to be the bastard I'd grown up believing he was. I took to writing down the things I wanted to ask him about as I thought of them until Prof gave me a bollocking for not paying attention in a seminar. It wasn't too bad a bollocking though because I'd just managed to find a way around something that had been hanging my synthesis up for a month, and he thought there might be a paper in it.

Sharon phoned late on Thursday evening and asked me if I fancied a drink. She sounded a bit fed up and I'd been thinking of calling her all week, so it was easy to say yes. We went to a little backstreet pub in Shirley I'd never been to before. I made sure that I bought the first drink this time and we sat out in the little back garden so that Sharon could smoke.

"Looks like you were right, Charlie. The PM found blunt trauma injuries and there were unidentified animal hairs all over her and the murder scene. So now my DI is looking for a nutter with a dog and a hammer." She took a drag of her cigarette and blew smoke out of her pretty nose.

"What do you think? Have they looked closely at the hairs they found? Have they said they're from a dog?"

"Not yet. They've been sent off for analysis." She took another drag of her cigarette. "They won't be dog though will they? I don't know what I think. Keep an open mind, let the evidence lead you. They said it all the time on the training courses I did." She shook her head. "It's just the evidence is leading me into the fucking twilight zone." She took a swallow of her pint of Fosters.

I figured she wasn't expecting an answer to that. "Have you talked to her daughter?"

"She says she doesn't know who her mother was meeting."

"Well she can hardly say she was meeting someone from a parallel world. I can't imagine your boss taking that well."

"Right. That'd go down like a bag of spanners. But the boss knows she's lying, and it's got him all wound up. She's putting herself in the frame. I can't say anything, of course, because how would I know any different? The boss is careering off down the wrong track, and all I get is grief when I try to steer him away." She took another mouthful of Fosters. "Dunno what to do."

Nor did I, but it made me feel sorry for Michelle Maynard; someone that I hadn't met but felt a strong connection with.

"How's she handling it?"

"Well, considering the pressure the boss is putting on her. And that makes her look more suspicious. I can see the boss's point. In any normal case the prime suspect would be Julie's lover, and if Michelle was lying about him then she'd be in on it. We've all seen 'em. But this time it isn't. She's got a solid alibi for Saturday evening, but I've still got to go through every number she's called on her mobile since she's had it and read every e-mail she's ever sent. It's a waste of my fucking time."

"Is there anything we can do to help her?"

"Not at the moment. Just keep our heads down." She ground out her cigarette in the sand box.

"I'm smoking too much," she said as she lit another.

"You got anything else I can help with?"

"Maybe. I'm working on something, but we need to be careful. Can't use you too much, or I'll start getting asked questions I don't want to answer."

"By DI Brown?"

"No. He won't care so long as the arrest's good. It's higher up I have to watch out for. Some of them have forgotten what we're here for."

"OK. Whenever you're ready give me a shout."

"Thanks Charlie. I appreciate it." She exhaled smoke and looked at me like she was imagining me naked. "Have you sorted that touching thing yet?"

"No." I said, embarrassed to admit it. "I'm meeting my father this weekend. I'm hoping he'll be able to help."

"Shame," she said. "Want another drink?"

I took the earliest bus on Sunday morning that I could, which only got me to mother's by 10:00. Sitting at the back of the bus I read through my list of things to ask my father with my stomach full of butterflies. For years I'd been angry with him, but that anger had melted away and I really hoped that the picture I'd painted of him was wrong. If he truly was the bastard I'd accused him of being then I was screwed. That he'd continued to express interest in me, despite mother keeping me away from him, gave me some hope that he wasn't a scumbag who collects girls, impregnates them and then moves on.

It felt as bad as facing my finals again; I'd been awake half the night, hadn't felt like eating any breakfast and now the nerves were making me feel slightly sick. That really would be too embarrassing; to get sick the moment I first met him.

When I got to mother's she sat me down and fed me bacon and eggs and sweet tea even though I told her I wasn't hungry. As I ate I discovered I was, in fact, very hungry and she was right again.

"What time did you arrange to meet him?" I asked as I reached for another slice of toast.

"I didn't." She laughed. "Time doesn't mean very much to him. When you're ready we'll go out and I'll call him. If he doesn't come, we'll come back and try again later."

"You mean there's a chance he might not turn up at all?" I suddenly felt as if someone had turned a light off.

"There's always a chance he won't turn up. He's Otherkin. They're less reliable than plumbers."

That made me laugh, but the fear that he might not show up hung around me like t-Butylthiol—the stuff they put in the gas supply to give it a smell.

"Are you ready?" asked mother. "We might as well go when you've washed your hands. Make sure you've nothing on you that's made of iron."

I'd deliberately worn trainers and a pair of tracksuit bottoms that had no metal parts at all. I left the change out of my pockets on the shelf by the door with my mobile phone.

"Take your watch off too."

I put my watch beside my phone, and stepped outside. Mother pulled on a black cotton jacket over her Guns N' Roses t-shirt, locked the door, put the key under a potted geranium beside the porch and we set off down the lane. After a hundred yards or so, the tarmac turned first to gravel, and then rutted half-dried mud. We followed the lane until it met the Darkwater River and left it to follow the riverbank upstream. This was an area I knew well from my childhood, though I hadn't been here for probably ten years. I used to have several dens around here and I wondered if we were heading for one.

The river took a wide bend, creating a tiny beach of white sand and pebbles with a little sloping lawn that caught the afternoon sun. With a screen of oak trees, scrubby bushes at their feet, to shelter it from prying eyes, this had been one of my favourite places; it was no surprise when mother sat down on the grass and announced "We're here."

Was this where I was conceived? I wondered.

She took off her trainers and sat on the bank in a patch of sunlight, dabbling her feet in the water.

"Sit down and make yourself comfortable. I'll call him."

I sat down cross-legged beside her and she started to sing softly. I was surprised; I'd never really heard her sing before. She wasn't one for singing along to the radio or anything like that. It was curious melody with several verses and a lilting chorus; I tried to follow the song but couldn't pick out the words. She finished, looked at me for a moment and began again, louder this time. I sat there; fists clenched tight, waiting for something to happen. A cold certainty in my stomach that he wouldn't show.

There was a rustle in the bushes from behind us. Mother turned to look with a broad smile on her face. A slim figure clad in greens and browns appeared as if he had stepped directly out of the bole of the oak behind him. Mother leapt up, threw her arms around him and kissed him enthusiastically, her hair swirling loose. I watched them for what felt like a long time, feeling uncomfortable; I'd never seen her like this. They finished their kiss, Mother turned to me, her arm around his waist.

"This is our son."

He stepped forward into the sunlight and I looked at my father for the first time. He was a little shorter than me, maybe five foot nine, with shoulder-length dark curly hair and smooth tanned complexion. He looked absurdly young; like one of those Greek or Italian teenagers who hang around the beach and flirt with all the tourist girls.

He stared with dark eyes, his head cocked slightly to one side. His nose and eyeline looked very familiar from the mirror; he was just five times better looking than me.

"Yes. He is mine," he said, his voice soft and lilting. He could almost have been Welsh. He reached out a brown hand to me. "Charlie."

I released the breath I don't know I'd been holding and took his hand bracing myself for the torrent. Nothing happened. Relief and surprise. His hand was warm and smooth yet strong like old polished oak; he smiled at me showing even white teeth.

"Aye. The grym hud is strong in you. Your mother was right."

I wondered what he was reading from my touch; could he read minds like me, or something similar?

He turned to mother. "You should have brought him to me sooner."

"And you know why I didn't." There was an edge in mother's reply.

"And now he has to learn what he should have learned ten years ago."

This sounded like the restart of an old argument. "What do I have to learn? Can you teach me to control it?"

"It would have been better done when it first showed," he said. "I can teach you, but it will take time." He squeezed my hand gently in reassurance and sat down on the grass between us. "But first I want to know about my son."

So we sat in the sun and I told him about my life as he ate the chocolate I had brought. He appeared fascinated by my account of the research project, though I did wonder how much he really understood.

"And what will you do with all this learning?" he asked.

"If I stay with chemistry then the pharmaceutical industry is the obvious place to go. I could try to stay in the university system, but I don't really think I'm good enough."

"Not good enough. Why is that?"

"There's a limit to my knowledge of what I'm dealing with, and some people just have a better intrinsic understanding of it. They can just see how things work better than me."

"I understand. It is good that you accept this."

"You've worked hard to get where you are, haven't you Charlie?" said mother.

"Yes. And I'm proud to have gotten as far as I have, but there's a limit to where hard work can get you."

"You'll do well when you've finished whatever you choose, Charlie," said mother. "I'm proud of what you've done."

"And you have the grym hud," said my father. "That is not a gift to be undervalued. Once you have mastered its use, it will define your road."

I thought about that for a moment. I had spent years running away from it, and in the few weeks since I had started to use it; it had turned my life around. "I think it's already started to. I need to know how to control it."

"You have just started to use it?" He asked, dark eyes fixed on me.

I nodded.

"There's the problem. If I had had you when it first showed, when it was weak, I would have had you use it every day. Now it is strong. You have a lot of catching up to do."

"You mean I just need to use it more? That's like trying to learn to swim in a whirlpool."

"But swim you must. By small strokes at first." He took my hand again. "When you use it, try to focus on one scrap of information, one tiny thought or memory. Let everything else pass you by as you concentrate."

I thought about the flood of thoughts and emotions I had received from Sharon when we kissed, and wondered how I could possibly concentrate under similar circumstances. That probably represented the greatest challenge I could think of.

"Every day," he continued. "You must practice this. Take someone's hand and focus on something small. What they ate for breakfast perhaps. In time it will grow easier to ignore the other thoughts. Show me now." He turned to mother. "Give him your hand."

She hesitated a moment then stretched out her hand. I hesitated too; I was pretty sure I didn't want to find out how she felt around him.

"Breakfast," he said.

I reached out and took her hand. Instantly there was the expected deluge: pride and concern for me, annoyance with my father and lust for him.

"Breakfast." His voice softly in my ear.

Maybe mother made it easy for me, but the memory of toast and fresh coffee presented itself from the flood. I seized it; concentrating on the smell of the coffee, the sharpness of the marmalade. The other thoughts and emotions faded out of focus. So long as I concentrated, I could look her in the eye and keep the contact.

"Good. Well done," said my father. "Do that every day and you will learn to control it." He looked up at the sky, squinting as he examined the position of the sun. "And now I must go."

"Wait," I said, feeling as if the sun had suddenly gone behind a cloud. "When am I going to see you again?"

"When next you call me, I suppose." he said and skipped to his feet.

"But I don't know how to."

"Didn't you teach him that?" He said to mother.

"No." She paused. "I didn't know if you would want me to."

"You can teach him. Now I must go." He bowed theatrically then ran lightly into the trees. I leapt to my feet to go after him, but he disappeared behind a tree and I lost sight of him before I'd taken a dozen steps.

"There's no point trying to see where he went," said mother. "I never managed it. He's gone back to wherever it is he comes from."

I came back a little sheepishly and helped her to her feet, carefully avoiding skin contact.

"So that's your father then," she said. "What do you think? Was he what you expected?"

"I don't know what I expected. He's just..." I let it hang, struggling for words.

"Fascinating. Annoying. Unlike anyone you've ever met. Yeah, that's him."

She turned towards the narrow path we had followed to get here and I fell in behind her.

"So you going to teach me how to call him?"

"Yes. I'll do that when we get home," she said over her shoulder.

"Do I have to come here to call him, or can I do it anywhere?"

"I don't know. I think you'd have to be outside somewhere.

He doesn't like our buildings. He says the iron makes him feel sick and weak." She pulled aside the branches of a bush and held them for me to go through. I walked a few yards on up the path and caught a faint whiff of something burnt on the evening breeze.

I turned to look at her and a movement behind her caught my eye.

"Look out!" I yelled as a hairy figure pushed through the bushes behind her.

I recognised it instantly from Julie Maynard's memories. Mother turned. The creature raised its club up over its right shoulder and advanced on her. A moment's hesitation then mother ran towards me. The creature sprang after her; God it was fast, and the path so narrow that I could do nothing until she was past me. It tripped her as she reached me. She went down and I launched myself at it as it swung the club.

It caught me on the left shoulder. My arm went numb, but I hit the creature solidly in the chest with my full weight. It fell backwards, dropped the club and rolled on top of me, scrabbling for my throat with sharp claws. I grabbed one claw with my good hand and tried to pull it away. The acrid burnt-tyre stink of it filled my nose. I pulled my head back and butted it as hard as I could in its ugly monkey face. It shrieked, but the grip on my throat did not loosen. Blood pounded in my head and the edges of my vision started to go dark.

There was a thump. It shrieked and released my throat. I sat up holding my neck, my heart beating wildly. Mother dropped the club and knelt beside me. There was no sign of the ape-like creature. I took my hand away from my neck and looked down; my fingers were covered in blood.

"Are you alright?" she asked. "What the fuck was that?"

I flexed the fingers of my left hand experimentally; they moved, but my shoulder ached like hell.

"No idea. Not something that belongs here. Must have come from somewhere else." I nearly mentioned what happened to Julie Maynard, but enough of my brain was still functioning that I stopped myself.

She gently moved my right hand aside to look at the wounds

on my neck. As her fingers touched me my mind filled with a deluge of concern and fear and a dull pain from her knee where she'd hit the path. I closed my eyes and tried to concentrate on the sharp taste of marmalade. When that failed I steered her hand away with mine.

"Sorry," she said. "Those are some deep scratches. They'll need cleaning and maybe stitches. Better get you to A and E."

I probed at my neck with my right hand; the wounded area was starting to burn.

"We're going to need a good story to tell them," I said.

CHAPTER 5

"What the hell happened to you?" asked Sharon. She reached out to touch the stitched wounds on my neck, but then drew back her hand as I pulled away.

"I met a hairy ape thing. Same one as killed Julie Maynard."

It was Monday evening and I was sitting in her Mini. I'd sent her a text saying I knew more about Julie Maynard's killer and she'd responded readily. My left shoulder ached like hell and my arm was purple to the wrist, but I wasn't going to pass up the opportunity to see her.

"Fuck! You sure?"

"How many killer beasts do you think are out there?" I answered instantly and regretted almost as quickly. She looked rough with dark circles under her eyes, and didn't deserve a snappy answer.

"Fair enough," she said. "What did it look like close up?"

"Ugly. Bit shorter than me, maybe five eight, but really strong with big claws. Tried to strangle me and did this." I ran a finger over the stitched wounds. "The hair is coarse, like horse hair. Stinks too."

"Not a bloke in a gorilla suit?"

"No. Way too fast."

"How did you get away from it?"

"Mum. She smacked it with its own club."

"Where was this?" She reached into her bag and took her notebook out.

"Out in the forest at the back of West Common, about half a mile from mother's house."

"Did you report it?"

"No," I said with a degree of embarrassment.

She looked at me with a frown. "It'll help if you do. Give my boss something else to chew on."

I thought about it for a moment before I answered. "So I go into Southampton Central nick and report I've been attacked in the woods. What are they going say? Did you see your attacker, sir? Yes, it was a hairy ape-thing with a club. They'll think I'm taking the piss. I'll get chucked out, if they don't nick me for wasting police time."

"Don't say it was an ape-thing."

"OK. It was about five eight tall, hairy all over and with a face like a monkey. Is that any better? It isn't is it?"

"Not much."

"That's why I didn't report it."

"What did you tell them at the hospital?"

"That I was teasing our dog and it jumped me."

"They believed that? I wouldn't have." She shook her head. "So did you get to meet your father?"

"Yeah. We'd just come from seeing him when we were attacked."

She scribbled something in her notebook. "How did it go with him?"

"It was…interesting." I'd thought about it a lot since in the last twenty four hours; when I wasn't thinking about a hairy ape-thing or attempting skin-to-skin contact with Sharon.

"Yeah? What did you think of him?"

I thought for a moment, remembering him eating the chocolate, sitting there holding mother's hand. "He's an odd mixture. Like a kid one minute, grandfather the next."

"Well I suppose he is incredibly old."

"I think time just works differently where he's from. Everything I've read says it does, but no one agrees on how. I must ask him about it."

"You're seeing him again?"

"Oh yeah. Mum taught me the little song to call him." I was tempted to sing it for her, but thought better of it.

"Did he say anything about handling your gift?"

"Yes. We talked about it, and he told me what I need to learn to handle it." It seemed as good a time as any to try the exercise. "Give me your hand."

She held up one hand with chipped scarlet nail varnish. After a deep breath, I took it and tried to find her memory of breakfast this morning, a single leaf in a pile picked up by an autumn squall. For a moment I held the taste of black coffee and a cigarette before the image of Detective Inspector Brown standing at a whiteboard swept it away in a wash of anger and frustration. I released her hand.

"So how was that?" She asked with a tilt of her head.

"Easier."

"Good." She leaned over and kissed me.

I tried to pick one thought from the multitude and hold on to it; her anticipation of sex with me seemed like a good one. Not too hard to find with the urgency of her desire and a beautiful thought to wallow in like a hot spa bath. I gave myself up to the pleasure and inevitably lost focus. Quickly her memories of sex with her first boyfriend Tom piled in. I pulled gently away from her. For a moment she pushed forward and then drew back.

"Getting closer, Charlie," she whispered.

"I'm going to need more practice." I wanted to reach for her again, but my shoulder twinged and the moment was lost.

"Not tonight," she said. "I'm in court tomorrow and I need my beauty sleep if I'm going to be any use."

I felt a bit disappointed, but pleased that I'd managed to kiss her and it enjoy for more than a couple of seconds.

She reached forward to start the car.

"Hah. I know what I was going to say," she said. "I might have something for you soon. Could be next week. I've been working on this a while. You gonna be fit for it?"

"Don't see why not. Won't need to do anything strenuous will I?"

"Shouldn't do."

"Cool then." I opened the car door. "Give me a call whenever."

"Sure," she said.

As I watched the tail lights of the Mini vanish down the road I felt I'd passed some kind of milestone. The way was there for us to develop our relationship, all I had to do was follow.

My arm improved as the week went on; the swelling subsided and the dark purple shades faded to a dirty yellow. I struggled a bit to do the lab work with my bruised arm, but one look from Prof when I came in on the Monday morning made it clear that it wasn't worth discussing.

I arranged to go and see mother again on Sunday, and together we would try to see my father. We agreed that we needed to tell him about the attack and I wanted more time with him anyway. I spent more hours in the library trawling through the folklore books, but still drew a blank on references to hairy murderous apes.

Sharon called on Thursday afternoon.

"You on for something Saturday evening?" she asked.

"Yeah. For sure. What are we doing?"

"You'll see." She ended the call before I could ask her if there was any chance of seeing her before then.

By the time Sharon phoned at around nine Greg and Chloe had breezed in, eaten the Spaghetti Bolognese I'd cooked and gone out to the pub. They tried to drag me with them, but I swore I was waiting in for a call. I had just about resigned myself to being stood up when she called.

"You ready to go?" she asked.

"Yeah."

"Where are you?"

"Arnold Road."

"I'll be there in ten minutes."

I put my jacket on and wrapped a scarf around my neck to hide the stitches and went outside to wait. She arrived in the Astra spot on ten minutes later.

I felt a little surge of excitement as I got in the car. "Where are we going then?"

"We're going to see a guy called Tommy Rowe. About a quarter of the cocaine that comes into Southampton comes through him. Word is he's got a big shipment due. You're going to shake his hand. Okay?"

My stomach tightened for a moment. "Yeah. Provided

you're going to get me out afterwards."

"Don't you worry, I know Tommy." She grinned at me. "He's a vain bastard, big shot in his own mind. I'll tell him you're a journalist, he'll go for that." She accelerated through an amber traffic light onto Portswood Road.

"What information do you want?" I asked, feeling only slightly reassured.

"Anything you can get me on the shipment would be good. The number of his latest mobile would be even better."

"Alright. I'll do what I can." The mobile number would be tricky, but details of the incoming shipment should be easy enough.

We parked in a side street of red-brick terraced houses in Freemantle. Sharon locked the car and we walked down the road to the pub on the corner.

"This is Tommy's local. He owns it. Plays snooker in here every Saturday night."

Fear tightened around my stomach. I remembered my promise to the ghosts of Karen and Alan Wilson; if I was going to keep it then I'd better get used to doing stuff like this.

Sharon opened the door and walked into the bar. It was as crowded as you would expect on a Saturday night. Sharon pushed her way through the throng to a door at the back of the bar. The sign on it read Snooker Room, below it a taped-on paper notice said 'Private Party'. She pushed the door open wide and I followed her through. The room was dominated by a brightly lit full-size snooker table. A man was bent over it taking a shot, a dozen or so people watched from tables round the edge of the room.

"What the fuck?" said a voice in the shadows to our right. "This is a private party mate." A couple of big guys got up from their seats by the door.

Sharon turned and looked at them. "Evening Billy, Deano."

They sat down again and I remembered to breathe. Sharon took a couple of steps into the room.

The guy bent over the table stood up and turned to face us. Mid-thirties, much shorter than me, maybe five foot six but with the deep chest and thick neck of a man who had devoted a lot of his time to moving large lumps of metal around a gym. "Good evening, Sergeant." He was better spoken than I expected. "What brings you here on a Saturday night? Nowhere better to go?"

"Brought someone to see you, Tommy." He turned to me. "This is Charlie. He's a journalist. He's writing an article on scumbags so I thought of you."

Tommy grinned at me, displaying a gold tooth, and stuck out a hand the size of a shovel. "Alright Charlie? Who's the article for?"

"Telegraph Magazine if I'm lucky," I said as I reached forward, trying to prepare myself for the rush of information.

"Good one," he said and grasped my hand, just short of crushing it. His thoughts rushed in borne on a wave of confidence and amusement.

"You alright mate?"

He released my hand and the flood ceased instantly. I must have zoned out for a moment too long, concentrating on picking through his mind.

"Yeah, sure. It's just hot in here." It wasn't, but I couldn't think of anything else to say.

"He's overcome by your charisma, Tommy," said Sharon. "Or maybe it's your aftershave."

Tommy grinned, showing the gold tooth again. "Getting better, Sergeant. I'm putting some stand-up on here. You want a slot?"

"No thanks, Tommy. There's only one thing I want." She turned towards the door. "Seen enough Charlie?"

I looked at Tommy wondering what to say. "How about an interview?" I was supposed to be a journalist after all.

"Yeah, why not. Gimme your number. End of next week all right?" I pulled out a post-it pad swiped from the lab, scribbled my number, transposing a couple of digits, on the top leaf and passed it over.

"See you next week then, Charlie," said Tommy. "Good to meet you." He turned back to the snooker table. Deano got up and opened the door for us, watching us with hard eyes as we passed him.

We walked away in silence, my heart thumping way too

fast; I felt quite shaky by the time we reached the car.

"What did you get?" asked Sharon once we were in the car. She took notepad and pen out of her bag.

"Plenty," I said mentally arranging what I had picked out of Tommy's mind. "The shipment is on Monday. Quarter of a million's worth of gear. He's hiring a Merc from some place in West Quay, taking two guys with him, Deano and Fizz. They're picking up at the southbound side of Fleet services. They've got to be there by eleven, then wait for a phone call."

"Who's he buying from?"

"Some guy called The Spaniard. He has met him, but I didn't get a lot more."

"Okay." She wrote in the notebook for minute or so. "Anything else?"

I thought for a moment about how to phrase what I'd picked up from Tommy Rowe and decided there was not a comfortable way of saying it. "He has no respect for you. He's laughing at you. He thinks you're a joke."

"Yeah. I got that already." She started the engine. "Just make it sweeter when I nail him."

She revved the engine and pulled away. "Anything else?"

"Yeah. There's some hassle with another dealer in town, Mikey Thornton, but I only caught the edges of it. I didn't get long. I thought he was on to me as it was."

"Nah. He thinks you're a journalist just like I told him. It won't occur to him that you're anything else. In his mind he's already a celebrity, so why wouldn't a journalist want to meet him?"

That made me feel rather better; a glow of satisfaction started to build within me.

"Have you got enough to nail him?"

"Yeah. If we catch him with that much gear then he's going down for a long time. We'll have all his assets off him too, including that pub." She changed gear aggressively and looked over at me. "We'll have a good night to celebrate if we nick him, I promise."

"Happy to do what I can. Fancy a drink?"

I was hoping for some immediate form of thanks; a quiet

drink somewhere and a chance to practice my focus.

There was a pause before she answered. "Yeah, just one though."

She took me back to the backstreet pub in Shirley. She bought the drinks and we went out into the back garden. It wasn't busy despite it being Saturday night.

"Thanks for helping tonight, Charlie. It makes me feel I'm doing something worthwhile, and right now I need that reassurance." She lit a cigarette and took a long drag. "I've spent the last two days watching my boss tear into Michelle Maynard and it's getting to me."

A memory surfaced stolen from Julie Maynard's dead mind; her pride in her daughter. A pretty face framed in dark curly hair.

"How come?"

"He's pissed off at getting nowhere. All he could think of doing was pulling her in and squeezing her about who her mother was meeting. He thinks she's protecting the killer. She finally told him about her father; that he's from some parallel world and that just pissed him off more. He's had to let her go, but he's chewing the carpet and isn't looking for anything that doesn't point to her."

"She got a lawyer?"

"Yeah, but he's no help. He doesn't believe her any more than the boss does." She took another drag of her cigarette.

"Nor would you though."

"I don't know. Who's going come up with a story that crazy to cover for something else? It's so nuts it has to be true, but the boss doesn't see it like that."

"How's she handling it?"

"Better than I expected, but she shouldn't have to, you know." She paused. "I just want to do something that will get the boss off her back."

"Got any thoughts?" I had an idea what she was going to come up with and it didn't fill me with joy.

"If you were to make a statement about the attack, it would help."

Yep; no joy at all. "If he doesn't believe her why would he

believe me?"

"He won't, but a second report makes it easier for me to build the case. You still got the clothes you were wearing?"

"Yeah."

"Haven't washed them have you?"

"No." I'd been meaning to get round to it, but I generally only did my laundry when I'd run out of stuff to wear.

"Good! Don't. We might get some forensics off them."

"Would that convince him?

"Might do. It's the best we've got." She took a final drag of her cigarette then stubbed it out. "Finish up and I'll drop you back. I need to get back to the office and set up Monday's operation."

As she drove me back I thought about what she'd said. She was right about trying to do something to help Michelle Maynard. Even though we'd never met, I felt a connection to her through her mother's stolen thoughts. Maybe making a statement about the attack might eventually help, but I doubted it, and it wouldn't do anything for her in the short term. Meeting someone who believed her and could tell her what happened might though; someone who was half-Otherkin like her. And I thought she should know about her mother's last moments. It would be easy to do; I knew where she lived from her mother's memories and it was only a short walk from the bus route.

On the other hand, how would she take a complete stranger turning up on her doorstep talking about her mother's murder? Sharon had said she was handling it better than she expected, but still this could go down like a bag of spanners. I imagined what my first words to her would be: "Hi. I'm Charlie, and I know what killed your mother" and how she would react. All scenarios seemed equally possible, including a slap in the mouth and the door slammed in my face.

I needed to think about this a bit more.

CHAPTER 6

"Right, let's go and see if he's to be found."

We were standing outside in the back garden enjoying the sun after a full cooked breakfast. Mother finished her tea and threw the dregs into the vegetable plot. "Just remember not to push him if he doesn't react much when we tell him about the attack. He doesn't like to talk about anything to do with the other side."

Back in the kitchen she set the dishwasher running then went to the cupboard under the stairs and drew out two pieces of wood about four feet long. I recognised them as pick-axe handles. She passed one to me, keeping the other for herself.

"Just in case we meet any hairy beasties," she said with a tight smile.

"Nothing iron on you?" She asked as she locked the front door behind us.

"No." I patted my pockets as she put the key under the geranium, then we headed off down the lane arm-in-arm, pickhandles over our shoulders.

"What should I call him?" It had been nagging at me for a while. "It feels uncomfortable calling him Dad or father, and everything I've read in the folklore books says how important names are."

"I call him Jack, from the Jethro Tull song Jack in the Green, but you should ask him. I'm sure he'll tell you."

When we came to the site of the ambush I turned aside and probed through the undergrowth with my pickhandle; didn't find anything more than an angry blackbird.

We reached the little beach and lawn, sat down and Mother

began the calling song. I listened to its strange lilt feeling oddly tense as if I feared what it might bring. I rested my right hand on my pickhandle, gripping it lightly.

She reached the end of the song and nothing much happened.

She smiled at me and began again.

She was on the fifth rendition when he appeared. I'd been on high alert for him, but still heard nothing until he stepped out of the bushes right beside us. Mother leapt up and embraced him. I stood around feeling like a spare part until they had finished greeting each other and he noticed me.

"You've taken hurt." He reached out and touched my neck.

"We were ambushed by something right after you left us last time," mother said. "It was waiting for us. Charlie fought with it."

He moved closer and looked intently at my neck. "These wounds were made by claws."

"Yes," I said. "We think it was something from your side."

His head jerked up and he stared at me, dark eyes intense. "What manner of creature was it?"

"About the same height as me," said mother. "Thick dark hair all over. Face like a monkey. Attacked me with a wooden club."

He said nothing but his eyes narrowed, no longer staring at me.

"How did you escape it?" he asked after a long pause.

"I hit it with its own club while Charlie was wrestling with it," said mother.

"It was really strong, fast too," I said.

"If either of us had been alone we'd be dead," said mother.

"Is it possible that this is something that followed you from your side?" I asked.

Again he said nothing, but his eyes lost focus as if he was looking at something far far away. He nodded, more to himself than in answer to me. "Yes. Very much possible. I hadn't realised it had come to this."

He lapsed back into silence with that faraway look again. Mother caught my eye then and shook her head. I swallowed the question that had been forming on my lips and waited.

After what felt like a long time his focus returned to me. "Are you practicising focusing your Sight?" he asked.

"Yes." I said. "It helps."

"Have you been with the girl?"

"Yes. How did you know about her?" I knew I hadn't mentioned Sharon to him.

He just smiled. "For you there will be lots of girls, I think. When you learn how to focus."

Mother laughed. "A true son of his father then."

She produced a bar of Fruit and Nut chocolate from a jacket pocket, unwrapped it, broke off a chunk and fed it to him. I watched the interaction, the way mother looked at him, and wondered if I should leave them alone for a while. The thought of another ambush stopped me.

He finished the chocolate and looked at me. "Tell us about this girl then."

We all sat down on the sun-warmed grass and I told him about Sharon, leaving out the bit about her being in the police.

"A girl with spirit," he said. "I like the sound of her."

"You like the sound of most girls," said mother and pinched him on the backside.

"Oh! That is most unfair."

He rolled her over onto her back and the two of them wrestled like children. Mother squealed as she was tickled; I'd never seen her like this. *He'll have her clothes off in a moment.* I thought. I so did not want to see that

"Hey guys. Just get a room right."

They remembered I was there and sat up panting, cheeks flushed, grass and leaves in their hair. I didn't know what to say so I just looked at them.

They looked at each other somewhat shamefaced and burst out laughing, after a moment I laughed too.

Jack stood up and pulled mother to her feet.

"It is time for me to go," he said. "I will take you to within sight of your dwelling."

We gathered up our pickhandles and followed him along the narrow path towards home, moving warily and stopping to listen every few yards. He took us as far as the tarmac road and turned back only when a pair of dog walkers came into view. The dogs started barking like mad and when I turned round he was gone.

I knew better than to try to see where he had gone so we carried on up the lane to the cottage. We stashed the pickhandles back in the cupboard under the stairs. I put the kettle on while mother went to brush her hair.

I caught an earlier bus than usual back to town to give myself time to stop in Totton, though I hadn't decided if I was definitely going to see Michelle Maynard. I sat at the back tossing up what I was going to do, the rhythm of the summoning song that mother had taught me running through my head. What finally tipped the balance was my father's near confirmation that the killer was something that had followed him from Faerie. If Michelle attempted to meet her father she could be putting herself in danger; she needed to know that. I made up my mind as the bus passed through Marchwood and, ten minutes later, got off on Totton High Street.

Michelle had a flat over the hairdresser where Julie Maynard worked and this was where I headed for; if she had moved out then finding her was going to be a lot more difficult. She did have a boyfriend, who Julie hadn't thought much of; it was possible she might have gone to him.

The thought that the boyfriend might be there with her stopped me in my tracks as I reached the parade of shops containing the hairdresser. Bad enough I risked upsetting her by talking about her mother, upsetting her boyfriend could get me beaten up if Julie Maynard's memories were accurate. My shoulder twinged at the thought.

After a moment I pushed myself forward. I had to give her the information and I had to get it right. I didn't want to lose the chance of getting to know the only other half-Otherkin person I'd ever heard of by coming over as some gibbering nutter.

I marched up to the door and again my resolve failed. I looked at my watch, heart thumping, wondering how long I had until the next bus; plenty of time left.

"Hullo. Are you looking for something?"

I turned. A girl in a long shapeless black coat, dark hair falling past her shoulders. Caught up in my indecision I hadn't noticed her approach.

"Michelle." I recognised her immediately from her mother's memories. "Michelle Maynard?"

"Yes," she said in a guarded tone.

"I'm Charlie Somes. DS Wickens said I should talk to you." Not true, but a reasonable lie. I didn't offer her my hand.

"Are you Police?" More guarded.

"No. I'm..." I paused not sure what to say. "I want to help you. I know what killed your mother." There, I'd said it.

"You said what, not who. What do you mean?"

I'd spent plenty of time rehearsing what I was going to say, but it still sounded crazy when I said it. "It was a creature that followed your father from the other side."

Her dark eyes widened and she looked intently at me while she processed what I'd said. Then she reached a decision.

"You'd better come in." I silently let out the breath I'd been holding.

She dug in her bag for the key and then opened the door. I followed her up the stairs relieved that it had gone well so far. The flat she led me into was small but tidy. Michelle waved me to an armchair, put down her bag and took off her jacket then sat down opposite me on the two-seater sofa in front of a bookcase overflowing with books. I recognised some of the titles from Chloe's collection: George RR Martin, Robert Jordan and Juliet McKenna.

"Okay. Tell me about it," she said with just a touch of a Hampshire accent. "What killed my mum?"

"Like I said, it was a creature from the other place. She met your father in the forest. This thing ambushed her as she was coming away, chased her, hit her with a club. Then it went back to where it came from."

She said nothing. I watched her face, noting what lovely eyes she had.

"Where did you get this from?" she said eventually; considering what I'd said she was very calm and reasoned.

"It attacked me and my mother. We were coming back from

meeting my father in the forest. I'm half Otherkin too. My father says it followed him from over there." The words tumbled out of me. She brought her hand to her mouth and started to cry. I felt an overwhelming urge to reach forward and comfort her but resisted.

After a minute or so she composed herself.

"You don't know what it means to find someone who believes me," she said softly. Then, "How did you know about my father?" louder.

"Sharon Wickens told me. She believes you."

"She's got a strange way of showing it."

"Can't do anything in front of her boss, can she?"

She pouted a little, looked down at her hands for a moment then raised her eyes. "This thing that killed mum. How big was it?"

"A bit shorter than me, but really fast and strong." I lifted my head to show her the wounds on my neck. "It did this with its claws."

She turned away rather than look. "She didn't really have a chance, did she?"

"I only got away because my mother hit it with its own club."

"But why? Why would anyone want to kill her? She never hurt anyone her entire life."

She welled up again and I waited until she had finished wiping her eyes.

"I can't answer that. I don't know if it was something that just followed my father, or if someone sent it."

"Sent? What makes you say that?"

I thought about it for a moment. "Two similar attacks within a short time. And it didn't seem intelligent. It attacked the two of us just the same as if there'd only been one." I couldn't say 'the same way it attacked your mother', not yet.

"If someone sent it then I want to know who. I'll ask my father. If it came from over there then it is something he would know about."

"Have you seen your father since it happened?"

"No. I tried once, but he didn't come when I called him. I wanted to tell him about mum, and just talk to him. He's always been really good when I needed someone to talk to."

I just about succeeded in suppressing the envy that threatened to choke me.

"That might've been a good thing. If the creature is hunting humans meeting with Otherkin then it could've targeted you. My mother bought a couple of pickhandles for us to carry when we meet my father. Even with one I wouldn't fancy my chances on my own."

I remembered the terrible power of its grip on my throat and shuddered. There wasn't much of her and she'd have no chance.

She looked at me with red-rimmed eyes, but whatever she was going to say never got said because the doorbell rang. She jumped up, an anxious look on her face.

"That'll be Dave, my boyfriend. You'd better go now."

"OK." I stood up. There was a pen and pad beside the phone. I quickly scribbled my name, e-mail address and mobile number on it while she went down to answer the door.

Dave lumbered up the stairs after her and looked at me radiating hostility like bad aftershave.

"Who are you then?" There was a lot of him and most of it seemed to be tattooed.

"Charlie Somes," I said looking him in the eye. "I'm a bereavement counsellor."

"Uh right," he grunted and lost interest in me. I turned away and walked down the stairs. Michelle followed me down.

"This is my e-mail and private number. Call me any time you want to talk." I held out the sheet of paper.

"Thank you, Charlie. You've helped." She smiled at me and reached out. Her fingertips touched mine as she took the paper and I felt…nothing. Then she closed the door.

I looked at my watch; ten minutes until the Southampton bus was due. I hurried back to the High Street thinking that things had gone better than I could have reasonably expected. She hadn't shut the door in my face; in fact she'd been pretty friendly given the circumstances. I'd possibly saved her life by stopping her trotting off to see her dad all alone, but we'd made no progress in getting DI Brown's considerable weight off her back. Now that I'd met her I was certainly going to do whatever I could to help. That last touch where I felt nothing intrigued me; maybe the half-Otherkin heritage prevented my talent working with her. Just what I'd been looking for; a girl I fancied and could touch without getting the entire contents of her mind. Shame about the tattooed troll.

I spent most of Monday morning alternately thinking about Michelle Maynard and wondering what was happening at Fleet Services until I got a text from Sharon about two o'clock. "Got Em All. I Owe You." A warm glow of satisfaction filled me at the thought that I'd done something really useful. I wondered what she might have in mind for the celebration. I sent her a big smiley in reply, and then a second text to tell her I was coming in to make a statement later on but got no reply.

I left the lab about six and caught the bus down to the city centre. I sent another text to Sharon, still no reply. I sat on the bus thinking this a waste of my time, but I'd promised I would make a statement and I keep my promises.

The reception area of the Civic Centre Police Station was empty and could do with repainting. I rang the bell on the front desk and a middle-aged PCSO came out from the back carrying a mug of tea.

"Is DS Wickens available?" I asked. He buzzed her extension but, as I expected, there was no reply.

"Sorry sir. Can I help at all?" he said.

"I want to make a statement. DS Wickens asked me to come in. It's related to the Julie Maynard murder."

"I'll see who's available to help you. Please take a seat."

I sat for about ten minutes on an uncomfortable bench in the reception area reading the banal crime prevention posters before a plump dark-haired woman of about thirty came out from the back carrying a statement pad.

"I'm DC Ball," she said with the hint of a Scots accent. "You wanted to make a statement?"

She took me into an interview room with a bare table and two plastic chairs. I sat down across the table from her.

"You said this relates to the Maynard murder?"

"That's right," I said. "I've already talked to DS Wickens about it."

"Right. Let's have your name first."

"Charlie Somes." I spelled it out for her.

DC Ball started writing and I carefully told her the version of events I'd worked out. When I reached the description of my attacker she stopped.

"Are you sure you want me to write this down?" she asked. She didn't need to say she didn't believe me, her expression said it for her.

"Quite certain, thank you," I said.

She resumed writing with a tight-lipped frown. It took her ten minutes to fill three pages of text.

"Anything you want to add?" she asked, passing the pad over.

I read it through and pointed out a couple of things to add about the creature. DC Ball added them.

"Looks pretty well right to me," I said.

DC Ball looked at me, her expression a mixture of pity and contempt.

"Sign and date the bottom of each page please."

I signed and held the pages out to DC Ball.

"Can you make sure this gets to DS Wickens," I said.

"Of course," DC Ball said without looking at me. "And I'll send a copy to the head of the murder squad."

That would be DI Brown. I didn't think he'd be too impressed with it, but I'd done what Sharon had urged us to.

DC Ball held the door open for me with the invitation to clear off as fast as possible written across her face. I thanked her for her time and walked briskly away.

Sharon called me as I was walking back from the lab the next evening. "Sorry I missed you last night, but it looks like your murderous hairy thing has been busy again. I'll tell you more about it when I see you. You want to meet up tomorrow night?"

I felt a brief surge of fear at the mention of the creature and my arm twinged. "Yeah sure. Love to," I said when it had passed.

"Okay. I'll call you tomorrow. Should be able to make it unless something big turns up. I've put in enough overtime the last couple of days so they owe me."

She ended the call leaving me with a warm glow of anticipation. There was the celebration to look forward to. Time to practice focusing my talent again. I slipped the phone into the inside pocket of my jacket and carried on walking down Welbeck Avenue. I had just reached the corner of Grosvenor Avenue when it rang again. I looked at the number—unrecognised. Curiosity piqued I answered.

"Charlie Somes?" A girl with a soft Hampshire accent.

"Yeah."

"It's Michelle Maynard. Are you OK to talk?"

"Yeah sure." Sounded interesting.

"Look, I wanted to thank you for coming by on Sunday. It really helped and I...wanted to ask you a favour."

"OK. Ask away." Really interesting.

"I really want to talk to my father, and after what you told me I need someone to come with me. I was hoping you might do it."

"What about your boyfriend?" Dave the troll would surely make a better bodyguard than me.

"No. I haven't told him about my father. I don't want him to know." There was a whole week's discussion in that alone.

"OK. When do you want to do it?"

"When could you come?"

Not tomorrow obviously. "Thursday?"

"Yeah. Thursday's good. What time?"

I did a quick calculation of what time I could get out of the lab and down to Totton by bus; I didn't much like the answer.

"Seven thirty?" It didn't give us much daylight and I didn't fancy playing tag in the twilight with the hairy thing.

"Can't you get here any earlier?" I could hear the disappointment in her voice and wondered how much I dared risk Prof's displeasure. It would be worth it to get to know someone else who knew what it was to be half-fae.

"OK. Six thirty." Maybe I could get there quicker by train, I'd have to look that up.

"Six thirty. See you then…and thanks."

I put my phone back in my jacket my mind filled with intriguing possibilities, this certainly beat worrying about a reaction that was going much slower than expected.

My reaction had gone to completion by next morning, which was a relief and an object lesson in patience, for all that the reference I was working from said it took two hours. I set about passing the reaction mixture through a short silica column to purify it for the next step keeping my mobile close by to make sure I didn't miss Sharon's call.

I went in to talk to Prof at eleven thirty and twitched like mad imagining her calling while we were going through the last week's work; she didn't, of course. I carried my phone around in my hand at lunchtime like some pathetic first year but still nothing, and when my service provider sent me a text about its newest special rates at three thirty, I nearly threw the thing across the lab.

Sharon called just before seven, when I was certain something had come up and she wouldn't be able to make it.

"Pick you up in an hour, okay? Thought we might go to that Italian again, unless you want to go somewhere else."

"Yeah great." My heart soared. I shelved the idea of cooking a pot of Chicken Jalfrezi and hurried upstairs to change.

Greg arrived back just as I was coming downstairs.

"Hot date, Charlie?" He had a dirty great grin on his face. "Your lady copper?"

"Yeah." My grin matched his.

A car horn blew in the road outside once, twice.

"That'll be her. See you later. Maybe." I hurried out, blood singing with excitement.

I climbed into the passenger seat of the Mini hoping for another opportunity to put my focus to the test, but she put the Mini into gear and pulled away.

"How've you been then?" I asked. The dark trousers and white blouse suggested she had come straight from work and she wore only the merest trace of lipstick.

"Tough week so far, Charlie. Monday was good, but there's been another murder."

"Yeah. You said. I'd been half-expecting another trip to the mortuary."

"Not this time. Someone else's patch, someone else's case. Body was found in woods near Redlynch. Just inside Wiltshire so it's their show. Looks like our boy and his club though."

My arm ached at the memory. "Did they find any of the same hairs as on Julie Maynard?"

"Don't know. I told them to look though." We slowed for the traffic lights on Portswood Road. "Thanks for doing the statement." She turned to look at me. "I don't think it's going to be as useful as I hoped. If it was just my boss then maybe I could do something but he's not in charge anymore."

"No? How come?"

"Two linked murders. That makes it a much bigger deal. They've put a Chief Superintendent in charge and the first thing he's going to do is go over everything we've done."

"And Chief Superintendents don't believe in parallel worlds."

"Even less than Inspectors." The lights changed and she accelerated away. "I expect they'll pull Michelle Maynard in again. Poor girl."

"I went to see her on Sunday. To tell her what happened to me. Thought it might help her to know she's not alone." I wasn't sure how she would react, that maybe I had done something that would mess up the investigation.

"Thought you might do that. How did it go?"

"Okay. I think it helped. She seemed pleased I'd come, until her boyfriend showed up. I don't know. At least I didn't make too much of a fool of myself."

"Doesn't sound like you did, Charlie. That was good of you; she's going to need all the support she can get. I'm not going to be able to do anything to help her; it'll be someone new who re-interviews her." She smiled a tight smile and shook her head. "At least we might get some priority at the forensics lab with the Chief Super running the show."

"I've still got the sweatshirt I was wearing when the thing attacked me. That should go to the lab shouldn't it?"

"Should but probably won't. They haven't analysed the hair

samples from Julie Maynard's murder scene. If no-one takes your statement seriously it ain't gonna happen. Don't wash it though." The Stag Gates lights changed just as we approached and she had to stop with a muttered, "Bollocks."

Instead of heading straight for Shirley High Street, we turned off and parked outside Sharon's flat.

"We'll walk from here. Reckon I might want more than one glass of wine tonight," she said as she picked up her handbag from the back seat. "We're celebrating."

"Tommy Rowe?" I asked.

"Damn right," she said. "We got them all. At Fleet services just like you said. Tommy and his team bagged red-handed, and the London couriers too. My DCI is very happy and that makes me happy."

She didn't look or sound happy though.

Roberto's was pretty crowded for a Wednesday night - sign of a good place I suppose—and if we had wanted a bigger table we'd have been out of luck, but they found one for us in a corner. Sharon ordered a bottle of Chianti Classico and her first glass was finished before we had even ordered food. She poured another and we talked, or rather she talked and I listened.

The bottle was empty by the time we'd finished the starters and she ordered another. I was halfway down my second glass. The main courses showed up, we ate them, and I carried on listening to her frustration and fears that the new team was repeating all her boss's mistakes and making her look bad. It didn't feel too much like a celebration.

"Bastards are going to be crawling all over everything I've done looking for a mistake. Anything they can use to screw me over." She took a final forkful of wild mushroom risotto. "It's worse than being a fucking probationer."

"But I thought it was all about re-examining the details of the case."

"That too, but mostly it's a golden chance to piss on your colleagues." She drained her glass and refilled it. "I hate it. Might need you to do me another favour. Look good if I could wrap up another case while they're picking over my files."

"Sure. Happy to." I meant it too. I looked at her across the table; the soft lighting failed to disguise the dark circles under her eyes.

"I'll have a look at what we've got. Should be a few contenders." She mopped her plate with a piece of bread, wiped her mouth with her napkin then topped up my glass, emptying the bottle.

She paid the bill and we walked back towards her flat. She slipped her arm around me and I anticipated an extended opportunity to test my focus when we got to her flat; I was glad I'd limited my wine intake. We came to the junction with Atherley Road, she turned towards me and raised her face to me to kiss.

I knew as soon as our lips met. It was right there at the front of her mind carried along on a wave of lust. She'd fucked her ex-boss on Monday night.

I pulled back instantly, my stomach filled with deep frozen shit. For a moment she pulled me back towards her, then released me.

"Charlie?" My horror must have been written on my face.

"Mike Scott." I croaked through a paralysed throat. "Monday night."

Her face hardened. "I'm not your girlfriend, Charlie. It's none of your business who else I see."

I stood there, not wanting to hear any more, trying not to cry in front of her.

"It's supposed to be just a bit of fun," she said.

I stared at her, images from Monday night superimposed on her face.

"I'm sorry, Charlie. I didn't mean to hurt you."

I turned away from her and started walking, not caring where I was going.

"Charlie!" I kept walking.

Up ahead of me a man hurried out of a house carrying a Nike sportsbag and walked towards me. Sharon caught up with me and put a hand on my shoulder.

"Charlie, back me up," she whispered then strode past me.

"Hullo Ryan," she said as she reached the bag carrier. "Want to show me what you've got in the bag?"

Ryan didn't. He gaped at her for half a second then ran for

it up Atherley Road. Sharon pelted after him and with less than quarter of a second's thought I followed right behind.

We caught him in about three seconds. I'm faster any day of the week than a scrawny junkie carrying a bag of nicked gear. So is Sharon; she was pretty swift considering how much red wine she had drunk. She caught up with him ahead of me. He swung his bag at her, lost his balance and fell arse over tip into the road. I grabbed him by the wrist. He pulled me onto him and butted me as his anger and fear flowed into my mind. I twisted my head aside to save my nose, but he caught my cheek. Pain flared on the impact. My anger surged blotting out his and, for a moment, I wanted to pound his face into the tarmac. He stopped struggling suddenly, falling limply back.

"Oh fuck! Make it stop," he gasped.

I kept hold of him, and as the pain and anger subsided took a swim in the dirty canal of his mind while Sharon examined his bag.

"You want to tell me where you got this lot, Ryan?" she said. "Or shall I just nick you?"

"I was helping a mate move flat," he said, his voice a mere whisper. "I wasn't doing nothing."

"Yeah sure you were, Ryan." She extracted her mobile from her bag. "Tell that to the boys down the nick. I'm arresting you for burglary and possession of stolen property. Weren't going anywhere tonight were you?"

"I'll have you for brutality," he whined. "I think you've broken my arm."

"Yeah sure you will. Got any witnesses?"

I kept hold of him as she called for backup. He sat resignedly in the gutter and I didn't feel the least bit sorry for him; his arm did hurt, but it was his own fault. I knew exactly which houses he'd been in a few minutes ago.

The police van took about five minutes to show up. Two chunky uniform guys bundled Ryan into the back, took his bag and sped off into the night.

Sharon lit a cigarette and watched the blue lights diminish into the distance. "Did you read him, Charlie?"

"Oh yeah. I know which houses he was in. Where he stashes

the take. Who he sells it too, and who his dealers are. Did I miss anything?"

She took out a pad of paper, not her police notebook, and started to write. I told her everything I had lifted from Ryan. She asked the occasional question to clarify the information but otherwise wrote solidly, eyes down on the paper.

"Spot on, Charlie," she said, putting away the pad in her bag. She looked at her watch. "Gonna have to be an early start tomorrow. You want me to call you a cab?"

I looked at my own watch. Eleven thirty; late enough that I didn't fancy walking. "Please."

She took out her phone again and keyed in a number. I sat down on someone's garden wall feeling suddenly tired as the adrenaline drained out of my system.

"Cab'll be a couple of minutes," she said. She put her phone away and sat down next to me. "We can still be friends, can't we?"

"Don't know," I said after a moment. I felt cold and empty and didn't know what I wanted.

I barely slept that night, turning things over and over in my mind. I reached the uncomfortable conclusion that it was mostly my fault that I'd gotten hurt. I'd made unjustified assumptions about Sharon and our relationship, and generally made a prat of myself. If I wanted to carry on using my talent and to help Michelle Maynard then I needed Sharon, even if she was using me. I had to deal with our relationship as it was rather than as I wanted it to be.

I got into the lab early, mainly to avoid Chloe's questions over breakfast about how my date had gone, but also to try and keep my lab hours up. I didn't feel like eating much come lunch-time so I worked through. There was a visiting speaker in the afternoon which took me out of the lab for an hour and a half and made it easy to slip away before six.

It took me about one minute on the Net to establish that it was much quicker to get out to Totton by train than take the bus. I also looked at the weather forecast; several hours of rain were expected for the evening. I wondered if Michelle would go ahead with trying to contact her father. The prospect of seeing her seemed the only bright spot in my day and I more than half expected her to call it off.

My phone was on, but she didn't call. If the police did come to take her in for a further grilling I presumed she wouldn't have a chance to and I could be in for a wasted journey.

It was already raining as I jogged down the hill towards Swaythling station carrying my cricket bat; sadly underused since I'd started my PhD. I wasn't sure if it would be much use if I met the creature again, but it was better than nothing and not too conspicuous to carry on the train.

The trains ran on time and Michelle didn't call so, at half past six I was soaked and hungry and ringing Michelle's door-bell fully expecting to get no answer.

A few seconds later I heard footsteps and a figure appeared distorted by the frosted glass. To my relief it looked too small to be Dave the troll.

Michelle opened the door. "You made it. I'm so glad." She smiled. "I thought you might decide to cancel with the rain."

I instantly felt warmer at her smile and remembered why I had thought it important to do this.

She took her big black coat from the pegs just inside the door, piled her hair up and pulled a blue beret over it and stepped out to join me in the heavy drizzle.

"I've got mum's car, so we don't have to walk." She waved a bunch of keys at me.

Just as well, I thought. It would be a long walk to find the appropriate rural solitude away from the dreary sprawl of Totton.

She drove us out along the Ringwood road in her mother's little diesel Polo. We didn't talk. It seemed she needed all her concentration for driving; even so her gear changes were hesitant and jerky. After Netley Marsh we turned off left down a country lane, went past fields and copses until we reached a gravel track sign-posted car park and picnic area that led into woodland. We parked up; Michelle locked the car and led me down a grassy path between the dripping oak trees.

"This isn't where I usually come but I've used it before," she said over her shoulder. "I couldn't go to Mum's place."

That would be where she was killed. "I understand."

"Do you have your own place where you meet your father?"

"No. I've only met him a couple of times." I felt embarrassed to say it.

The path dipped downwards into a little valley, the overhanging trees creating the impression of a tunnel. Michelle stopped and gave me her handbag. "You wait here. I'm going just up there to call him. He won't come if I have someone with me he doesn't know."

She walked down the slope, stopped about fifty yards away and knelt down facing a large oak. I chose a relatively dry spot under an overhanging tree and sat down to wait.

It was quiet there under the trees but I was too far away to hear her song. I watched her for a while, fiddling with the grip of my bat, then looked away to survey the forest. When I looked back I couldn't see her, the foot of the oak tree was lost in deep shadow. *He's here.* I wondered if Jack cast a shadow like that around us when we met. It had never occurred to me that he might, but it would account for why we had not been disturbed. *That's a useful trick. Could I learn to do that? I'll have to ask him.*

My legs were going to sleep so I stood up and walked slowly around, listening intently for anything that might be my first warning of the hairy horror. The rain fell steadily, pattering through the new leaves, dripping off the trees and deadening any other sound. I tried to not think about how hungry I was, and failed. I should have brought something with me, or bought something at Southampton Central, but I'd been focused on getting to Totton on time.

It was too dark to read my watch when Michelle emerged out of the shadows. She didn't say anything as I gave her her handbag. I wanted to ask her what her father had said, whether he had offered up any clue about the killer creature, but her silence and the slump of her shoulders suggested it wasn't a good idea to ask how it had gone.

We were halfway back to the car, in the tunnel of trees, when I caught a whiff of burnt tyres. I almost retched at the stench.

"It's here. I can smell it."

"What?" she said.

"The thing that killed your mother." I raised my bat looking around into the shadows for a clue to where it was.

"Shit. What do we do?"

Good question. "Run for the car." There was still enough light to see the path between the trees. "Can't be more than a couple of hundred yards."

Another look around. Nothing, but I caught the smell again. "Come on."

Michelle started to run and I followed; not flat out but pretty fast.

Branches snapped loudly away to our right. A dark figure bounded onto path ahead of us, club in hand, blocking our route to the car. Michelle cried out and slid to a halt. I carried on until I stood between her and the stinking menace, bat raised.

"Spread out," I said. "It can't deal with two targets."

She moved away to my left and I moved right. The beast advanced club raised; snarling and moving its gaze between us as if trying to decide where to strike first. I watched intently, trying to pick the first sign of an attack, remembering how fast it had been last time. The smell of it almost had me gagging.

Time slowed as I watched it gather to swing. I had time to wonder if I could do enough to block it. There was a sudden flash of white light off to my left. The beast's head jerked round and I grabbed the chance to swing my bat. I caught it squarely on the side of its ugly monkey face with as much strength as I could put into it. It felt like hitting a tree.

The beast screamed at me; displaying a mouthful of sharp-looking teeth and swung its club. I hopped backwards just in time and felt the wind of it rush past my face.

There was another white flash. The beast screamed again and then ran, crashing its way through the undergrowth away from us. I lowered my bat and turned to Michelle.

She held up her camera-phone. "I got two pictures of it," she said in a breathy little whisper. "Maybe they'll believe me now."

She pressed a key on the phone and held it out to me. "See."

I looked at the bright window as she scrolled between the two pictures; she'd caught it nicely, and in focus too.

"That was really brave of you," she said quietly. "No-one's ever done anything like that for me."

I didn't feel brave at that moment. I was cold, shivery and trying to not throw up. I managed a weak smile. "Let's get out of here. It might come back."

She slipped the camera into her handbag and we hurried up the path towards the car and moments later I was sitting in the dryness, reassured by the amount of iron around us.

Michelle took off her beret, tossed it onto the back seat and shook out her hair. She looked at me for a moment, dark eyes wide.

"So that's what killed my mum?" Ice and acid in her voice.

"That, or something very like it."

"How do I catch it? How do I kill it?" Her voice cracked.

"Shotgun? Crossbow? You don't want to get close to it, it's really strong." I looked at her a moment. It was too dark to see whether she was crying. "Your father would know."

"He won't tell me. He won't tell me anything about it. He talked a lot about mum, but he wouldn't explain what happened."

I remembered my father's reluctance to discuss it. She turned the key in the ignition and revved the engine. The clock on the dashboard lit up and told me it was half past nine; my stomach reminded me I hadn't eaten anything for over twelve hours.

"You hungry?" asked Michelle, making me suddenly believe in telepathy.

"Yes." Bloody starving more like.

She put on the headlights and accelerated sharply across the carpark.

"I'll fix you something. It's the least I can do. You got time?"

"My last train is just before midnight."

"OK. I'm not a great cook mind."

"I'll eat pretty much anything."

"Good."

We turned onto the main road and there was enough traffic to demand her concentration then until we reached the road to her flat. I expected her to pull up, but she kept driving past it.

"Sorry," she said. "That's Dave's van. I didn't think he'd be around tonight."

And I didn't think he'd be pleased to see me one little bit. Typical of trolls; always turning up when you don't want them.

"There's a chippy by the station. You can get something there. Sorry." she said with a sad lilt. I didn't think Dave was going to be getting a good night tonight.

A couple of minutes later we pulled up under a streetlight across the road from the chippy. I undid my seatbelt and prepared to face the rain, wondering what I should say to her. She undid her seatbelt too and turned to face me.

"You know that copper, DS Wickens don't you?"

"Yeah." Though not as well as I thought.

"If I send you the pictures, will you show them to her? They won't believe them if they come from me."

"Yeah. Sure." Which made me contact Sharon again.

"Thanks. It's good to have someone on my side," she said quietly. "I meant what I said back there. You were really brave. I owe you."

I didn't know what to say; mostly because I was looking into her dark eyes and drowning. Very slowly she leaned forward and kissed me.

Nothing happened. At least, no great rush of thoughts and emotions flooded into my mind. A very pretty girl kissed me and I savoured every moment.

She pulled back after a minute or two. I waited for her to say something but she didn't—just looked at me with a half-amused expression on her face and then started the car.

"Come and see me again soon," she said. "I'll cook you something next time, I promise."

"Sure. Whenever. Give me a call. And send me those pictures."

I got out of the car a little reluctantly, and she drove off. The smell of hot cooking oil reminded me how hungry I was. I hurried into the chippy out of the rain, still carrying my bat. I bought their last piece of cod, chips and a can of Coke, and two minutes later was hurrying for the station.

The train arrived within five minutes. I took a seat in an

almost empty carriage and settled down to eat my delayed supper. By the time we got to Swaythling I was down to the last few crispy bits at the bottom of the bag, no longer hungry and trying to get my head around what had happened. The memory of Michelle's kisses left me with an inner glow; how had that come about? Technically, I suppose, I had saved her from the creature, but then she had saved me too with her camera flash. So we were even.

She had a boyfriend, her mother had been murdered very recently and the police were all over her, so what was going on? Everything in her life must have turned upside down. I had no idea what she could be thinking so the only thing I could do, was do what I promised and make no assumptions. She was really nice, and I didn't want to get it wrong again.

CHAPTER 7

When I logged on in the lab next morning, there was an e-mail from Michelle with the pictures attached. "You were a hero today" was all she said. I opened up the pictures and came out a cold sweat looking at them. The beast caught sharply in focus, mouth open, club raised. The memory of its stink closed my throat. Looking closely at the second picture I noticed its teeth, the incisors much longer than human. No way could that be someone in a costume, not that I'd ever seriously thought it was.

I replied to Michelle then printed off a few copies of the pictures on the colour printers that we used for the 2D-NMR spectra, making sure that no one saw them. I wanted to show them to Sharon and my dad; maybe if he saw them he might open up a bit about what was going on.

I didn't have an e-mail address for Sharon so I sent her a text "Got pictures 2 show you" and got down to work, though my mind was far from the modified Wittig I was cleaning up. I spent the whole morning with my mobile within reach waiting for a call that didn't come and checking my e-mail every five minutes.

I barely touched my lunch, and nearly wrote off a reaction in the afternoon by adding methanol instead of tetrahydrofuran but just stopped in time. I quit the lab early before I really did some damage and retreated to the library, but couldn't settle even there so I went to the gym.

Sharon called about half past six as I was walking back to the lab from the gym figuring to get another couple of hours work done.

"Charlie. How you doing?" She sounded happy.

"I've got a couple of pictures I want to show you."

"Oh yeah. I've heard about those. I'd like to see them." Her tone had me wondering how she knew so much about them as she continued. "I've got another hour's work here. How about after? We'll go for a drink."

"Okay."

I went home happier, but it bothered me that Michelle hadn't gotten in touch.

The warm grill pan and smell of garlic in the kitchen told me that Greg and Chloe had been and gone; not surprising, it was Friday night. I felt a surge of nostalgia for the uncomplicated Friday nights of pub and takeaway curry of only a few weeks ago. There was a note stuck to the side of the fridge with a magnet in the shape of a dolphin. I don't know how I didn't see it before. It said: *Charlie, your turn to buy toilet roll.* Karen's handwriting. We still needed some.

I'd just about given up on Sharon when she turned up just before nine. She looked like she'd come straight from work.

"Evening, Charlie." She looked and sounded happy. I got into the Mini and she headed back into town. "Sorry I'm late. I've had a busy couple of days. I've been cleaning up Ryan's dodgy pals. Ryan was up in court this afternoon and got bail, his main dealer is on remand in Winchester and his fence is in court on Tuesday."

"Result then." Something good had come out of that evening.

"Oh yes. My boss is happy with me. And it takes a lot to make him happy at the moment. And there's one loose end I want to talk to you about."

"Things still tricky with the new team?"

"Yeah. They went all through what we did and they're no better off, so they've got your pal Michelle in for another interview."

My stomach suddenly felt cold. No wonder I hadn't heard from her. "But that's not going to help. She won't change her story 'cos she's telling the truth."

"They don't think so."

"Did she show them the pictures?"

"Yeah; and they laughed at her. Didn't convince anyone."

"I was there when they were taken. They're real."

"Did you bring copies? I haven't seen them."

"Yes." I pulled them out of the inside pocket of my jacket.

"I'll look at them when we get to the pub."

We went to the backstreet pub in Shirley she'd taken me to before. Despite it being Friday night it was half empty and we had no trouble getting a table.

I gave her the pictures and went to the bar to get the drinks.

"Did you notice the teeth," I said, passing her a small diet Coke.

She looked at the photos again. I sampled my pint of HSB and waited for her reply.

"Stage fakes, vampires' fangs from a costume shop, or they could have been Photoshopped."

"But they weren't. That's what killed Julie Maynard."

She frowned in thought a moment. "Where were these taken?"

"Out in the forest past Netley Marsh, last night."

"What were you doing out there?"

"Michelle wanted to talk to her father, to tell him about her mother. She asked me to go along to watch her back."

"And not her boyfriend?"

"She hasn't told him about her father, and didn't want to get into it now."

She pursed her lips and swallowed a mouthful of Coke. "How did you get away from it? You got scratched up pretty badly last time."

"Camera flash scared it off." I shivered at the memory. "Don't think I'd have been able to fight it off without it."

"How big is this thing?"

"About your height; really strong and so fast. You know how chimps are way stronger than people. It's strong like that. Stinks too." I took a mouthful of HSB to try to wash away the memory of its stench and failed.

"Was it the same one as attacked you when you were with your mother?"

I stopped to think. I'd had time to look at it yesterday, but it had been pretty dark and my focus had been on what it was going to do.

"I couldn't say. Maybe."

"You see what I'm getting at? If there's more than one, then it's a very different problem."

"It's a very different case anyway."

"Well that's true…if you're right." She took another mouthful of Coke.

"What would it take to convince you?"

She pursed her lips in thought for a moment. "Solid evidence. A murder weapon, a killer, preferably alive."

"That's a pretty tall order."

"It's a pretty tall tale."

That was hard to deny.

She finished her drink and put the glass down. "Now I want a cigarette."

I picked up my pint and followed her out into the garden, glad she had ended the conversation.

She lit up her cigarette and took a long drag. "There was one loose end from Ryan's crew you gave us. One of his suppliers, Sally Parkes. You got any more on her?"

I struggled for a moment to recall the name—these borrowed memories fade faster than my real ones.

"Just someone he buys from sometimes, a relative of one of his girlfriends. Lives out in Millbrook."

"She's a new name to us. We're going to pay her a visit. You got the time to be around when we do it? I'm not that interested in her, but I'd like to know where she's getting her gear and she ain't gonna tell us."

"Yeah, sure." I was glad she wanted to carry on our arrangement. "Give me a call when you know when you're doing it."

"Cool. Might be Sunday. Got the warrant, but I'm waiting to see if we can get the sniffer dog. I'll let you know."

"What's going to happen to Michelle?"

She shook her head slowly. "Nothing good."

"But why? She's got no connection to the second murder. They must see that."

"She's all they've got. So they'll keep leaning on her until they get something."

"What would make them stop?"

"Solid evidence. Same as your hairy ape story." She ground out the cigarette in the sand tray. "Want another drink?"

We went back inside, Sharon to the bar while I reclaimed our table.

She returned with another diet Coke and a pint for me. "You alright, Charlie?"

"Guess so."

"Wondered if you wanted to talk about the other night?"

"What's to say? Made a prat of myself, didn't I?" I gripped my glass like it was a lifebelt.

"Yeah, well that's my fault. Didn't explain the rules, did I?" She looked at me levelly, her brown eyes serious. "You're a nice guy Charlie, but I'm not looking for a relationship. Now we can be friends, maybe even have a bit of fun, but no getting involved. No broken hearts, Charlie. Can you handle that?"

I nodded; it was a better deal than I was expecting. Any time I started feeling emotional about her I only had to bring up the memory of her with Mike Scott.

"Then cheer up," she smiled at me. "You look like your dog died."

There was an e-mail from Michelle in my inbox next morning; the timestamp was 1:30am.

"I was with the police all day. They don't believe anything. They laughed at the pictures. I want to catch this thing that killed mum. Please say you'll help. Had to wait 'til Dave went to bed to send this. I can't sleep anyway. I'll call you when I can."

She signed it M with two small Xs. I had a moment of jealousy at the thought that the troll was staying at her flat before I e-mailed her back to say I was up for it.

Catch the thing?! I wondered just how to do that. Net it maybe? We'd need a good strong net and a few hefty guys to hang on to it. And then what? A good solid cage to hold it if we wanted to keep it alive. Would that be the best thing to do? Maybe we should net it, then call the police and hand it over to them. Then hopefully they would leave Michelle alone.

I carried on thinking about it all morning in the lab, turning over various ideas in my mind, before Prof came in to take my mind off Michelle's scheme with a newly published paper he'd picked up. He seemed in a good mood and genuinely interested in my views on it rather than just tossing it at me with orders to 'try it out'.

It was nearly lunchtime when we finished talking, and sometime during our discussion I got a text from Sharon. "U on 4 tomorrow morning?" I phoned her to ask what time, but had to leave a message on her voicemail.

After lunch I went back to the lab and put on another reaction. It needed to run for at least a couple of hours and I decided that I would try to call my father in that time. I wanted to show him Michelle's pictures of the goblin and see if I could get him to tell me anything about it.

It took me about twenty minutes to get to Southampton Common which is the nearest bit of open ground, and another ten to find a quiet spot away from kids' football games and romantic couples. I settled myself in a dry spot, took out my phone and played mother's recording of the summoning song through a couple of times. Once I had it fixed in my mind I started to sing it quietly; a little self-conscious at the sound of my voice.

I reached the end and started through again. After four repeats nothing had happened and I recalled mother's comment about Otherkin being less reliable than plumbers. I sang it through a couple more times then gave it up.

Maybe it was my singing, maybe it was the metal in my phone, maybe I was still too close to built-up areas or it was just the wrong place. Or maybe he was just doing something else. There was too much about this I didn't yet understand and I wasn't going to get answers here so I headed back to the lab to see how my reaction was doing.

I was a bit pissed off when I got to the lab, but cheered up when the TLC showed me that the reaction had gone pretty well. I stayed to do the work up and columned it; it was gone six before I left and Sharon finally called.

"It's on for tomorrow morning," she said. "You still OK?"

"Sure. What time?"

"Pick you up at seven."

"OK." Could have been worse; I'd had visions of a pre-dawn operation where it was barely worth going to bed. I decided to set my alarm for half-six and go to bed early.

CHAPTER 8

It took me a minute to work out why my alarm was playing Radio Solent at half-six on a Sunday morning. I remembered and wondered what I should wear to go on a police raid. I settled on what I wore yesterday with clean pants and socks.

I had just enough time to drink a cup of instant coffee before Sharon arrived. I heard the car pull up and had the door open before she could ring the bell. She looked very business-like in a dark blue anorak, no make-up and her hair scraped back.

"Ready?" she asked.

I nodded, picked up my jacket and followed her out into the cold grey morning to a green Mondeo.

"In the back," she said. I did as I was told. She pulled away as I put my seatbelt on and was straightaway talking on her hands-free to (I presume) other members of the team.

We had the roads pretty much to ourselves and were out in Millbrook in about fifteen minutes; Sharon was on the phone until we were pretty much there.

We arrived at a roundabout, four cars and a van pulled in behind us. Sharon slowed and turned down a residential road I recognised from Ryan's memories. The convoy followed and my stomach began to tighten.

"Here's how it's going to work," she said, taking off her earpiece. "You're going to sit here while we go in. When we get her we'll put her in here beside you. You do your thing while I talk to her. We'll take her to the nick; then you can tell me what you got. OK?"

"OK."

We pulled up outside a white-painted semi. The convoy

parked around us. Up ahead a marked police car parked across the road to block any oncoming traffic. Three solid-looking men in dark anoraks and Police baseball caps got out of the car behind us, one carrying a metal-ram, and walked up the short path to the front door. More followed from the other cars and a couple went to the side gate. Sharon killed the engine and got out to join them.

The largest guy swung the ram, the doorframe crumpled and the door swung open. I could hear the yells of 'Police' as they rushed in. A dog handler brought a frisky spaniel out of the van and walked it into the house.

Nothing much happened for a quarter of an hour, then two of the anorak-wearers brought a short plump woman with bleach-blonde hair out of the house in handcuffs. Ryan's memory provided her name: Sally Parkes. Sharon followed immediately behind them. She opened the car door and they shoved Sally in beside me; one of the policemen got in pushing her up against me as she kept up a torrent of abuse. Sharon got in the front and turned around to face us.

"Shut up and listen," said Sharon. "You're in the shit and you've got one way out. I don't care about you. I want your supplier. Give him to me, and you'll get a community sentence and a rehab order. Hold out and you'll go down and lose the house."

"Fuck off, copper." There was real anger in the expression.

"Suit yourself," said Sharon and started the engine.

I grabbed Sally just above the wrist where a tattoo of a Celtic design circled her arm.

"What the fuck are you doing?" She attempted to pull away. I held on and dived into the churning data stream

Her supplier's face flared in Sally's mind and fear flooded through her like a thick fog, obscuring her every thought. I kept hold her despite her lurid protests, fishing through her mind for any detail about her supplier. It was hard because of the fog that surrounded anything to do with him and took longer, but I got enough and let her go. It was a relief to be out of the fear-filled world she'd got trapped in.

We drove into the Civic Centre police station car park. The policeman took Sally out of the car leaving Sharon and me alone.

"Whatcha got, Charlie?" said Sharon, bright-eyed and eager, pad and pen ready.

"Her supplier is a bloke called Pete, he's from Portsmouth. Sells good clean stuff, not cut with much. He seems to be able to get as much as she asks for. She orders by phone, and meets him in a car park in Portsmouth to pick up, pays cash. She's really scared of him. He's trapped her and she can't get away. Someone she knew got on the wrong side of him over money and disappeared. Pete said he's fish food now."

"You got a name?" she said as she wrote.

"Robert Jones. Welsh guy, known as Robby. Small-time dealer. She last saw him about six weeks back." I thought of the slimy body I had touched in the mortuary; that could be him.

"OK. We'll follow up on that. What else you got on Pete?"

"He's a big guy, shaven head, looks like he works out and uses sunbeds a lot. Always has a couple of minders with him. She's seen one of them with a gun."

"How did she get a connection with him?"

"Another dealer who used to be a boyfriend introduced her. Guy called Tony Timson. He's dead now. Overdosed last year." I had a brief flash of a blond guy lying naked on her bed, her grief and blind panic at the coldness of his body.

"He should be in the database. She know anyone else who buys from him?"

"No. Only her and Robby."

"Could you pick his number out of her phone?"

"Easy enough he's listed under Pete. He changes his number a lot. Did you find her stash?"

"The dog found one under the hot water tank. Did we miss any?"

"No. That's it. The money's in the back of the sofa."

"Got that too." Sharon sounded pretty pleased with herself.

"She's left more with her sister."

"Right, well we'll have that too." She scribbled another line. "I'll run this by the Drugs Squad guys and see what they've got. You got a good enough idea of this Pete guy to recognise him?"

"Yeah, should think so."

"We may have some pictures of him for you to look at. Be

good to confirm his identity." She looked at her watch. "OK. I'd better go and get the paperwork rolling. You got any plans for tonight? I owe you dinner again."

"Dinner sounds good."

She smiled and opened the car door. "I'll get you a lift back up to your place if you want."

A police car dropped me at the Somerfield supermarket on Portswood Road, and I went in to buy breakfast and a Sunday paper. From there it was a short walk home; Greg and Chloe weren't even up when I got in. I brewed some fresh coffee and settled down to read the paper and have a relaxing day with a good evening to look forward to. Just before midday I got a text from Sharon: "Scrub tonite. Been another murder."

I presumed she meant another woman out in the country had been killed, which meant our hairy beast. The only surprise was it had taken until now.

Shame about dinner, guess I needed to cook another batch of chilli.

I'd enlisted Greg to help me with my focusing, without telling him exactly what I was doing of course, and I was developing a detailed knowledge of his diet. I was almost bored enough to consider going into the lab, but the next thing I needed to do would take a minimum of six hours so I thought it could wait until tomorrow.

I cooked my chilli and ended up reading all the bits of the paper I normally ignore until Michelle phoned about half past four.

"Sorry it's taken me so long to call you, but I had to wait until Dave went to the gym. I spent all Friday with the police, and he's been a bloody pain since. I haven't forgotten I still owe you a meal, and I'll do that soon. Are you OK for trying to catch that thing next weekend?"

"Yes. Have you worked out how you're going to do it?"

"Still working on it. Guess I'm going to be the bait. I'll call my father, talk to him like usual and then see if the fucker appears." She laughed nervously. "You got any ideas on how to catch it?"

"Maybe we could try to net it. How many people have you got?"

"I like the net idea. I'll get Dave to find one. He's going to bring some mates from the gym, and there's you and me."

No shortage of muscle, but I remembered how quick the creature had been. "How did you get them to agree to it?"

"I had to beg him. I showed him the pictures and told him that it was the only way to get the police off my back, and even then he wouldn't. I had to absolutely beg him." She sounded outraged.

"What did you tell him it was?"

"I said I didn't know and we'd find out when we caught it."

"Could do with a few more bodies," I said, and a thought occurred to me. "How about I ask DS Wickens to come? You know she believes you."

There was a pause. "Do you think she'd come?"

"I think she'd do pretty much anything to catch this thing. There's been another murder." And she might be able to arrange some official transport for it, if we caught it.

"Then bring her. Let's put this thing out of business."

"OK. I'll ask her. When are we going to do this? I don't know what her shifts are."

"Saturday, if it's not chucking it down. I'll e-mail the details later."

"Right. I'm definitely in. Let's make sure we have enough flashguns for one each."

"Good thinking. See you Saturday then."

She ended the call and I put my phone down feeling irrationally pleased.

I didn't get a chance to ask Sharon until she phoned on Wednesday evening.

"Sorry I haven't called," she said. "It's been madness. There's been another murder up in the north of the county near Hartley Wintney; divorcee aged fifty three, found on Sunday morning. I've spent a lot of time on the M3."

"I wish it wasn't a surprise. Does this mean another trip to the mortuary?"

"Not this time. I can't just roll up and bring you in, it's not my patch. Someone would ask questions."

"OK. Probably wouldn't tell us anything we don't already know anyway. Is there anything new with this one?"

"Nothing. Same as the others. Everyone's running around making a lot of noise but getting nowhere. My boss is doing his nut." I could hear the frustration in her voice.

"Do you want a chance to catch this thing?"

"When? How? Fuck yeah. What do I have to do?"

"Michelle is setting a trap with herself as bait. This weekend, probably Saturday. I'm going."

"I should be able to do Saturday...if there isn't another murder. What time?"

"Don't know yet. I'll text you."

"Right. I'll pick you up and we'll catch up on that dinner I owe you."

"I'll look forward to that." I hoped we'd been in a fit state to eat dinner afterwards.

Michelle didn't e-mail until Friday morning and I spent most of Thursday going through ways to entrap the creature and then finding the flaws in them. Just thinking about facing it again scared me cold. Michelle would be taking a huge risk; I was pretty sure I knew why she was doing it, but it didn't make the risk smaller. I would have offered to do it myself, but as I hadn't actually managed to call my father yet I didn't think I could do the job.

I slept badly Thursday night and woke up far too early convinced I could smell the thing then couldn't get back to sleep so I got up and went in to the lab. Even then I wasn't first there; one of the Chinese post-docs had beaten me to it.

As I worked through the day a headache grew on me along with a sense of dread; which was not relieved by Michelle's e-mail saying that it was on for Saturday, Dave had got a net and now three mates to help. I texted the details to Sharon and got a reply back within five minutes. She was really keen so there was no backing out. No suggestion of seeing her that night either, not that I'd have been very good company the way I felt.

The headache was a real killer by six o'clock. I stumbled home and went straight to bed with a handful of ibuprofen, hoping not to dream about stinking hairy murderous beasts.

CHAPTER 9

I slept the night through and didn't dream as far as I recall. I spent the morning in the lab then did my share of the shopping before Sharon turned up in her Mini at about four, dressed in sweat shirt, jeans and trainers with her hair up. She looked damned fit, but the memory of her romp with Mike Scott was too raw for me to want to test my focus.

"Recognise this guy?" She pulled a couple of photos out of her handbag and handed them to me. I looked at them; they weren't great pictures, shot from a distance and slightly out of focus, but the memories lifted from Sally were still strong.

"Sally's dealer Pete? Could be. Looks a lot like him."

"Good boy. We haven't got much on him."

"Did you get anything from Sally?" I remembered the fear that had filled her mind with a shudder. "He's a real bastard. Be good to bring him down."

"Not a word. I've kicked it over to the drugs squad; that's what they're there for." She put the photos away. "OK. Time to roll."

We headed out for Totton.

"Any progress on the latest victim," I asked as we turned onto Portswood Road.

"No. Same as the others. I've spent four days chasing up the victim's contacts and it's a waste of time, but the boss doesn't know any other way." She sounded tired.

"If tonight works then you won't have to do it again."

"Amen to that." She accelerated the Mini hard through the amber traffic light as if to emphasise her point.

I texted Michelle to let her know we were on our way and

then sat in silence as Sharon negotiated the Saturday shopping traffic.

"You're quiet, Charlie. You alright?"

"I'm scared. I'm scared that Michelle's putting herself in front of this fucker, and the only thing we really know about it is it kills people."

"If it shows up."

"Well yeah. But I think it will."

"We'll see."

It was nearly five before we got to Michelle's flat. She was waiting at the foot of the stairs, wearing black jeans and sweatshirt, her hair tied back in a ponytail. She looked tiny and very vulnerable.

"Good to see you," she said, flicking a glance at Sharon. "Come on up. Everyone else is ready to go."

"Alright mate?" said Dave without much enthusiasm as we entered the flat. "This is Gav, Terry and Craig." His three friends looked at me with silent hostility, Stella cans around their feet. They were all a similar size to Dave and wore tight red t-shirts with Test Security in black block script across their undulating pectorals. A bunch of bouncers; so at least they should be able to handle themselves.

I looked at Sharon. She stepped forward and stuck out a hand to them. "I'm Sharon. This is Charlie."

More silent hostility until one of them, Craig I think, stuck out a slab of meat with fingers attached. Sharon shook it. I didn't really want to know what he was thinking, but took it for as short a time a possible; long enough to find he thought I was a scrawny wimp.

"Let's go," said Michelle, and we all trooped out of the flat down the stairs. The troll squad got into an unmarked blue Transit van, Dave and Michelle into her mother's Polo. We followed; I recognised the route as the way I'd gone with Michelle previously which was slightly reassuring, at least I would know the ground a bit.

"Decent bunch of lads," said Sharon. "Come across them a couple of times. Not the brightest, but should be handy if things get rough."

"I wonder if she's told them what they'll be facing?"

"Doubt it. Would you?"

I thought about it for a moment. "No. Don't know what story I'd spin, but it wouldn't be the truth. That just sounds too crazy."

"Yet here we are."

I waited for her to say something more, but she didn't. The Polo turned off the main road. I felt my stomach tighten as Sharon followed down the country lane. The Polo and the Transit pulled into the empty car park and we parked beside them. The troll force climbed out of the Transit, threw open the back doors and unpacked their gear. Several coils of rope, some wooden poles, an aluminium ladder and a bundled-up net came out along with half a dozen baseball bats.

"Follow me," said Michelle, swinging a rucksack over her shoulder. "I'll show you where."

I picked up a coil of rope, good stout nylon stuff, and followed her along with Sharon and the trolls. As I expected, Michelle had chosen the tunnel of trees for the ambush. With more leaves on the trees than the last time I was here, and a cloud bank advancing from the west to cover the sun it was pretty dim under the trees. "Here." Michelle put her rucksack down in the middle of the path. "We'll suspend the net from the trees. We'll need the ladder."

One of the trolls ran back to the van for the ladder while the others spread out the net. I watched; waiting for the opportunity to do something useful. Sharon lit a cigarette. Michelle dug a couple of small black objects out of her rucksack and gave one to each of us. I turned it over in my hand; it was a flash gun for a camera.

"The batteries should be good for three hundred flashes," said Michelle.

The trolls didn't seem to need any help and had the net, thick strong nylon like the rope with a 5cm mesh, rigged inside ten minutes; ten feet off the ground with pull ropes at each corner. They cleared away the ladder and unused poles back to the van and stood around looking pleased with themselves.

"Ok, here's what is going to happen," said Michelle. "I'm going to go over there and call." She pointed to the large oak she had used last time. "When I'm done, I'm going to come back here and wait." She scratched a circle in soil with the toe of her boot. "If the monster shows then it'll probably come straight for me. Charlie and Sharon have got flashguns to drive it towards the net if it doesn't. Otherwise keep out of its way, and get it before it gets me. Clear?"

I was impressed with her calm and wondered how real it was. I certainly didn't feel calm and hoped I had time to take a piss behind a tree.

"Makes it sound so simple," said Sharon quietly.

"'Ow big is it?" asked a troll, maybe Terry.

"Bit bigger than me," said Michelle. "And like I said, it's fast."

"No worries," said Dave. "We can handle it."

"Let's do it then," said Michelle. She put her rucksack down beside the path. "Charlie, you stand over there on the bank. Sharon, by those trees." She pointed to a clump about thirty yards away.

We moved to our positions and I took a moment to water a tree. By the time I was back in position Michelle was sitting cross-legged under the oak, singing her summoning verse. I had wondered whether her father would come with half a dozen people lurking nearby, but it appeared that he wasn't deterred because when I next looked at Michelle she was lost in shadow. I looked over at Sharon and saw the glow of a cigarette in the gloom; I gave her a thumbs-up and she waved back.

I could hear the trolls talking, I looked over at them half-expecting to see one of them texting. Michelle hadn't said to keep quiet, but it seemed the natural thing to do, and their chatter increased my anxiety that they didn't know what they could be facing.

A gush of wind rattled the leaves and I thought I caught the whiff of burnt tyres. I stiffened and sniffed again but it was gone, or it was never there. Sharon didn't seem to have noticed anything, but then she'd smoked three cigarettes in the last twenty minutes and probably couldn't smell thiophenol at six feet. The trolls didn't seem to have noticed anything either so I put it down to my imagination. I looked over to the oak where

Michelle was still enveloped in shadow; nothing was likely to happen until she emerged.

I was starting to think about being hungry when Michelle walked out of the shadow. It was noticeably darker as she hurried to the centre of ambush without looking up. All of a sudden the smell of burnt tyres was strong and persistent. Flashgun in one hand, baseball bat in the other, I tensed waiting for the creature to show itself.

Michelle reached the centre and stood, arms folded looking outwards; a small part of me marvelled at her courage. I heard a rasping exhaled breath behind me. I turned, swinging the bat but hit only branches. A dark figure rushed past me into the open. The burnt tyre smell was suddenly choking. Sharon's flash lit up the glade for a white instant. The creature advanced on Michelle, club raised. She walked slowly backwards before it, holding up her hands, drawing it into the trap. I moved quietly from my post to come in behind it. Sharon did the same, flashgun in hand.

The creature got within about ten feet of Michelle. I wanted to scream at Dave to drop the net, but she still held up her hands. It jumped. She dropped her hands and rolled backwards. The net fell catching the beast's club as it swung. It shrieked painfully loud, tried to push its way through and fell after two more steps, completely tangled.

The bouncers jumped on it and got to work with the baseball bats and their boots. I wasn't inclined to stop them and they didn't look as if they needed help so I stood and watched. The creature shrieked its head off constantly, struggled and tried to bite through the netting, but seemed otherwise unaffected by the beating.

After a couple of minutes the trolls backed off, breathing heavily, and Michelle approached the still-struggling creature. She had something in her hand. In the dim light it took a moment to realise it was a long knife; a moment longer to realise that what she was going to do was a very bad idea.

"No! Stop!" Was all I got out before she stabbed the creature with all her strength; the blade sinking deep into its body. Its scream would have woken the dead. As she heaved out the blade I ran towards her, but Dave blocked me off with an arm like a tree branch.

"Her business," he grunted.

Michelle struck again and the shrieking abruptly stopped. Michelle stood back from the corpse then took three steps to the edge of the path and threw up. Dave let go of me and loped over to her. I went and looked down at the dead creature; the knife was where she'd left it, through one eye. The stench was appalling.

Sharon came to stand beside me. "What the hell is that?" she asked.

"Fuckin' stinks," said one of the trolls. "Don't want that in my van."

"What we gonna do wiv it?" said another troll.

Good question. I looked at Sharon; maybe she would have an answer. As she crouched to look at the creature I felt the earth tremble. Sharon must have felt it too as she looked around with a puzzled expression. The rumble grew stronger, heard now as well as felt.

A group of horsemen burst through the trees at the far end of the glade at full gallop. Armed horsemen, on big dark horses, swords and shields to the front, whooping war cries like redskins in an old western. Coming straight at us, glowing orange like the heart of a bonfire.

"Run, Charlie!" Sharon lifted from her crouch like a sprinter from the blocks.

I took three strides towards the trees before something clipped my legs. I hit the ground hard and bright lights flashed in my head. I struggled for breath, facedown in the dirt. Voices yelled above the thunder of hooves, orders shouted in some language I didn't recognise. Someone screamed, shrill and long, and was answered by the blast of a trumpet. The thunder rose for a moment then faded to silence.

I sat up, head spinning, and looked around. The creature's body had gone, net and all. Sharon lay face down in the path. Michelle was crouched in the shadow under a tree. Dave and the trolls were nowhere to be seen.

I scrambled to my feet and ran to Sharon, a great cold hand

gripped my stomach as she lay too still. I knelt over her and checked her wrist. Instantly pain and her terror at being ridden down flooded into me. I let go and the vision of the horsemen pounding towards me vanished.

I pulled the arm of her sweatshirt down and felt her wrist through that. Her pulse was there; the cold hand loosened its grip a bit, but she was unconscious. I didn't know what to do. My phone was in her car back in the car park.

"Michelle. Got your phone?" I shouted across the glade. "Ambulance. Now."

She didn't move for a moment. I pushed myself up and ran towards her. This was too important to be polite. "Phone. Now."

"Bastards," said Michelle. "Bastards took them all."

There were tear tracks in the dirt down her cheeks but she wasn't crying now. She dug in her bag with bloody hands, pulled out her phone and punched in the numbers. She got through immediately, asked for the ambulance, told them where we were and then passed the phone to me.

"Is the casualty conscious?" asked the voice on the phone.

"No." I said walking towards back towards Sharon. "But her pulse is strong."

"Keep her warm and don't try to move her. There's an ambulance on the way to you." I ended the call and ran back to Sharon.

Sharon was conscious when I reached her. She tried to sit up using only her left arm but gave a little yelp and lay back down.

"You stay there." I took off my sweatshirt, rolled it up for a pillow and slid it under her head, careful to touch only hair. Michelle knelt down beside me.

"Fuck. I've got a headache," Sharon said. "What happened?"

"Bastards," said Michelle. "Fucking bastards."

"Who?" said Sharon. She massaged her temples.

"Armed horsemen straight out of the dark ages, Otherkin cavalry. They took the creature, and Dave and his mates."

"Oh shit," sighed Sharon and closed her eyes. Pretty much summed it up.

I looked at Michelle. "Ambulance will be here soon. One of us should go up to the car park to show them the way."

"I'll go." She stood up and walked briskly off into the gathering gloom.

"Car keys," said Sharon softly. "In my pocket. Take my car back."

It's not easy getting keys out of someone's pocket when they wear their jeans as tight as Sharon. Another time it might have been fun; here it was just awkward and uncomfortable.

We watched the ambulance pull out of the car park, blue lights flashing.

"What do we do now?" asked Michelle quietly.

"Right now I'm going to the hospital." I didn't want to think beyond that. I knew there would be questions; lots of questions.

"I'll come with you."

Another time I might have thought that a bit pushy, today I was glad of the company.

I drove Sharon's car and followed Michelle in the Polo back to her flat. There was nothing we could do about the Transit so we left it in the car park. It was locked up and the keys were with one of the trolls, wherever they were.

Michelle parked up, went in for a minute to wash the creature's blood off her hands and we headed in to the General across the Redbridge causeway. Michelle barely said a word which was fine by me; too much had happened and I needed to think it through before I'd be ready to talk about it. When I was ready there would be a lot to say.

The Accident and Emergency department was fairly quiet; the afternoon sportsmen and DIY-ers had all been dealt with, the Saturday night drunks were yet to come. We asked about Sharon at the reception desk and were told to take a seat in the waiting area.

We sat at the end of a row of hard plastic chairs, as far away as possible from the fat woman with the two whining toddlers. There were a couple of vending machines in one corner, but I felt like I'd never want to eat again.

"I've been waiting for you to blame me for it," said Michelle, so quietly I could barely hear her.

"Why would I blame you? You couldn't know what would

happen." Not entirely true, but throwing blame around - deserved or not - wasn't going to help anyone.

"Thank you," she whispered and took my hand. There was a long pause, a gulp and a sniff. "What are we going to do?"

"I don't know. I really don't. We've got to hope Sharon's well enough to tell the police the story. They'll be all over us to find out what happened, and they're not going to believe a word even if we tell them the truth."

"So what are we going to tell them?"

"The truth I guess. I haven't got a better story."

"I don't want to go through all that questioning again." She squeezed my hand.

"Don't think we've got a choice." She squeezed my hand again, leaned into me and I slipped an arm around her shoulders. She snuggled up to me as far as was possible across two uncomfortable chairs.

"What do you think's happened to Dave and his mates?"

I thought about that for a while. There are plenty of stories in the folklore I'd read about people who had been abducted from this world; those stories tended to end badly. I didn't think now was the time to mention that.

"They're probably being held prisoner over the other side."

"How do we get them back?"

I'd not thought about anything other than Sharon since we left the forest. "I don't know. We need to talk to our fathers, if they'll come. What did your father say this evening?"

"Not much. As soon as I told him about how we were attacked he went all quiet."

"Did you show him the pictures?"

"Yeah. He didn't want to talk about it. Got up and left just after."

"That figures. My dad was just as cagey about it."

"Do you think it's even safe to try and call them? I mean, what could come through with them? The monster was bad enough, but if the riders come through then we're really screwed."

"I can't see what else we can do. I think we have to run the risk." I really needed to talk to my father about this; my one and only attempt to reach him hadn't worked so I needed a more experienced operator. I struggled to remember mother's shifts; I thought she was working late today so there was no chance of speaking to her for another hour and a half, but maybe I could go out to her tomorrow. I wondered about asking Michelle to come with me.

"You waiting to see Sharon Wickens?" A nurse in light blue tunic and navy trousers had crept up on us while we were talking.

"Yeah." I said.

"The doctor's seen her and we're keeping her in. She was unconscious for a while and we want to monitor her in case of complications. She might need a little operation to set her arm. She'll be on E4."

"Can we see her?"

"No. She's going for X-rays on her arm and then up to the ward. Tomorrow."

"But she's going to be OK?" I asked, almost afraid of the reply.

"She'll probably be going home within the week." She turned and walked away taking about a hundredweight of anxiety with her.

"Sounds like it's time we were out of here." I said to Michelle. The clock on the wall read quarter past nine and now I knew Sharon wasn't badly hurt I was damn hungry. "You want to get something to eat?"

"Suppose so." She slipped my arm from her shoulder, stood up and pulled me to my feet.

We were just walking out, still holding hands, when I recognised the burly, broken-nosed figure of DI Brown walking in, talking on his mobile. He didn't appear to notice us and we kept walking.

I phoned mother when we got to the carpark and left a message on her voicemail, telling her that something really bad had happened and to call as soon as she got the message. We scraped up enough change to pay for the parking and then I drove us to my local curry house. I was too hungry to cook so takeaway was the only option at that time of night.

It was after ten when we got to my place. There was no sign

of Greg and Chloe so we sat in the kitchen and piled into our curries; they didn't last long.

Michelle mopped the sauce from her plate with the last scrap of naan bread and looked at me with her big brown eyes. "That was really nice," she said. "Now I owe you two dinners." She reached across the table and caught my hand. "Can I stay tonight? I don't want to be alone after everything that's happened today."

There was a pleading note in her voice that was very hard to resist, not that I was considering resisting. "There's only my room."

"That's OK isn't it?"

"If it's OK with you." I tried to remember when I had last changed the sheets on the bed; not recently was the best I could manage.

"You don't snore do you?"

"How would I know?"

"I'll tell you tomorrow," she smiled. Seemed like it was decided then.

She got up and walked around the table to me and ran her fingers through my hair. "No sex tonight though. I just need to be close to someone."

I didn't even feel disappointed. I looked up at her; she bent over, her hair falling over my face and kissed me, a long lingering kiss with an oceanful of promise. With no need to care about my focus I lost myself in the sensation. It could have been half an hour before she gently pulled back and I stood up still holding her hand, a stupid grin on my face.

"Shall we go now?" she said.

I would have left the plates and forks we'd used, but Michelle gathered them up and put them in the sink. I dumped the take-away cartons in the bin then, still holding hands, we climbed the stairs.

My room was actually halfway tidy though the bed was, of course, unmade. I closed the door, switched on the bedside light and plumped up the pillows. Michelle sat down on the bed, took her boots off, pulled her sweatshirt over her head and then, by some arcane process beneath her t-shirt, took off her bra. Then she stood up, unfastened her jeans and slipped them off revealing slim legs and dark blue panties.

"Come on, get your kit off," she said. "What are you waiting for?"

I wound my tongue back in and started to undress, my fingers fumbling with the laces on my trainers until I pulled them off still laced. Michelle watched with amusement. I took off my jeans and sweatshirt and climbed into bed with her.

"One kiss then we're going to sleep," she said.

It was a long kiss and I didn't want it to end but she pulled away and rolled over.

"You can put your arm around me here if you want." She directed my arm around her midriff and snuggled against me. "Now put out the light and go to sleep."

With my free hand I turned off the light and cuddled up to her.

It would be lovely to report that I spent a blissful night with Michelle; I'd certainly spent long enough dreaming of such a night. It would be inaccurate. I barely slept. Not surprising as I'd never shared my sleeping space with anyone before and it takes practice. I didn't know that. I buried my face in her lovely dark locks and they tickled my nose. She was only a little girl, but after a few minutes of her lying on my arm I got pins and needles in it. Then I took forever to move it for fear of waking her.

I lay beside her rerunning the day's events in my mind. Could I have done anything different to save Sharon from the cavalry charge? Maybe I'd dozed for a few minutes before I heard Greg and Chloe come in sometime around 1 am; they'd probably been to the late movie at the Union. I got up to go for a piss around 2 am, didn't dare put the light on and nearly fell over my trainers. After that I had plenty of time to think about what we could do about Dave and his mates, but produced no new insight. That's the way it goes when you can't sleep, problems get bigger not smaller and you never think of a new angle on something at 3 am.

Michelle seemed to sleep soundly all through the night. I was definitely awake when the birds started singing around

6:30. She was definitely still asleep when the doorbell rang at 8:30.

I thought it had to be someone who'd got the wrong place and would pretty soon realise their mistake and piss off, but a couple more rings were followed by heavy knocking so I had to get up, put on my jeans and go down.

I opened the door to a familiar broken-nosed face.

"Morning, Charlie," said DI Brown. "Mind if we come in?" Since he was already in the hallway having shoved his way in, my answer was academic. "I'd like to talk to you about what happened to my sergeant yesterday."

A couple of big hard-faced men, one blond the second bald, followed him in.

"Can I get dressed?" I said conscious of my bare chest. DI Brown nodded. I started to climb the stairs and the big bald guy followed. I turned to look at him; he gave me a blank stare in return but stopped halfway up. I went into my room and made a point of shutting the door.

Michelle was awake.

"Police," I whispered. "DI Brown."

I hurriedly pulled on yesterday's clothes. Michelle slipped out of the bed and got dressed too.

"I'll handle it," I said. "He doesn't know you're here, let's keep it that way."

She nodded and I left the room, closing the door behind me.

"What's going on, Charlie?" Greg stood in the doorway of his room.

"Police," I said quietly. "They want to talk to me about something that happened yesterday. Don't worry. I haven't done anything wrong. I had a friend stay over last night. Can you look after her if I have to go with them?"

"OK mate. You sure you're alright?"

"Yeah." I hurried down the stairs. DI Brown was sitting at the kitchen table his two sidekicks standing behind him.

"So, Charlie. Would you mind telling me what happened to DS Wickens yesterday?" He sounded almost reasonable.

"Sure. We were trying to catch your serial killer." I pulled up a chair and sat down. "And we succeeded."

That got his attention. "What? Where? How?"

"In the forest, out Netley Marsh way. Sharon, me, Michelle Maynard, her boyfriend and three of his mates. We set a trap for it. Michelle lured it in."

"It?" DI Brown frowned.

"Yes. It. It's an animal. It's not human." His frown deepened. "I was attacked by it before."

"If you're going to give me a load of shit about parallel worlds…"

"Do you want to know what happened to Sharon?" I cut across him and, surprisingly, he shut up.

"It was yesterday evening. Michelle lured it in. We trapped it in a net and then we killed it. Then the horsemen appeared. Fifteen maybe twenty of them. They charged at us full gallop. Sharon couldn't get out of the way. They knocked her over; they took the body and Michelle's boyfriend and his mates. Then we called the ambulance."

"So there's what, four men missing along with the body and an injured police officer, and you didn't call us immediately?"

"Yeah." He glared at me long and hard. "Didn't think we'd get much of a hearing after the last time."

I could almost hear the gears grinding behind the cold stare and decided to give him a push. "I can show you where it happened. There should be plenty for your forensics guys to find."

"Sounds like shit to me, boss," said one of the sidekicks, the bald one who had followed me upstairs.

After a long moment DI Brown stood up. "I didn't ask for your opinion. Alright, let's go."

I almost cheered; he should get a load of evidence that should make even him reconsider his view of the killings, and then he might be a little more open to the idea of fae involvement. Plus it got them out of the house without seeing Michelle. I collected my jacket in the hallway and walked with them to their car feeling much better than I had when I first opened the front door.

DI Brown sat in the front passenger seat. The blond big guy drove, the bald guy sat beside me in the back; no one talked. I had plenty of time to think about what I was going to say.

There was minimal traffic on the roads and we got out to the car park in about half an hour. The van was still there, apparently untouched.

"That was the van we used." It was reassuring to see it, just to confirm I hadn't dreamed it all.

We parked and I led them down the path towards the glade. A few yards short of the glade the earth was churned with hoof prints which led off between the trees. I thought I could catch the faint smell of burnt tyres but no one else commented, so maybe I was imagining it.

"The horsemen went that way," I said.

"Take a look and see how far you can follow them," said DI Brown to the blond guy who immediately strode off along the trail. DI Brown and the bald guy followed me to the glade.

In full daylight it was easy to see where the creature's blood had been spilled; great dark patches marked the forest floor.

"Here," I said. "We fixed up a net from those branches and dropped it on it when came after Michelle. Those patches are where it bled. The horsemen came from that way." I pointed up the glade to the trees; the mass of hoof prints confirming my tale.

The bald guy took out a digital camera and started taking pictures. DI Brown pulled out his phone and moved away a few yards as he made a call.

"Get this whole area taped off," he said to the bald guy as he finished the call. The bald guy trotted off towards the car park.

"This had better not be a load of shit," DI Brown said. "I'm sticking my neck out here on your story."

The blond guy returned. "Followed the trail for a couple of hundred yards boss, then it just disappears. I did find a big net dumped in the bushes."

"Good lad. The forensics boys will want that, they're on their way." He turned to me. "I want to see where these horsemen came from. Mind yourself, keep away from the tracks."

We followed the hoofprints in the wet ground to the edge of the trees and a little way beyond but there wasn't much to see. The trees grew too thick, and the prints just weren't there to be seen. DI Brown looked at me, frowned and shook his head;

he poked around in the undergrowth for a minute or two then walked back to the wet ground. He followed the tracks in again and stood staring at where they ended.

Go on, admit it, I thought. *You haven't got a clue.*

He said nothing and after a couple of minutes we walked back to where the other two were now taping off the scene.

"Would you recognise any of the horsemen?" he asked.

"No. Don't think so. It was getting dark and I was concentrating on getting out of their way."

"So where did they come from?"

I knew he wouldn't want to hear my true answer. "You've seen the evidence on the ground, what do you think?"

"I don't know." He looked straight at me and cracked his knuckles. "I don't understand a lot of what went on here, but I know I've got a crime scene and I understand how to investigate that. The answers will come."

And will you be prepared to recognise them when they do? I thought, but said nothing. Just then my phone rang. I pulled it out and looked at DI Brown.

"Go on," he said. "Answer it."

It was mother. "What's going on, Charlie? Are you OK? I didn't get your message 'til gone midnight, and I didn't want to wake you too early."

"I'm OK." I walked a few yards away from DI Brown and tried to keep my voice down a little. "We caught the hairy creature last night and killed it, then a load of Otherkin cavalry showed up. My friend Sharon's in the General and there's four guys missing, but I didn't get hurt. I'm with the police now out by Netley Marsh where it happened."

Silence on the phone then "Oh Charlie."

"I need to talk to Jack. We've got to find out some way of getting these guys back. I think they were taken to the other side."

A longer silence then "Oh shit, Charlie. That's not good."

"I know. I've read the stories too. That's why I need to talk to him."

"Why do you think he'll help? He's always avoided talking about over there."

"He's our only chance. I think we made a big mistake killing the creature and made things much worse. He must see that he's got to do something to restore peace."

"Maybe. I think I'll let you argue that with him."

"But you'll help me talk to him?"

"Yes. I'm working one 'til nine. It's a bit late to swap a shift but I could call in sick then come and get you."

"No. Don't do that. I've no idea how long I'm going to be with the police. I could be hours yet."

"Okay. I'm working tomorrow, but I'm off Tuesday and Wednesday."

I didn't think a day would make much difference, but I didn't want to wait until next weekend. Seemed like I'd have to risk Prof's anger and take time off during the week. "OK. I need to work on this. Maybe see you then." I ended the call.

This would be so much easier to handle if I had a car. I really couldn't use Sharon's, but Michelle had one. I could ask her to take me out to mother's. I wondered what she was doing now, whether she was on her way back to Totton. The idea of seeing her again gave me a warm glow.

As I put my phone away another one rang with the theme to The Sweeney - DI Brown's. He answered and walked back towards the other two coppers deep in conversation so I followed keeping a few yards back.

The whole area where Michelle had killed the creature and the cavalry had charged through was taped off, so I kept well clear of it and went to sit on a tree stump wishing I'd brought a heavier sweatshirt. DI Brown continued his conversation, waving his free hand to emphasise some point. The other two were deep in animated conversation with occasional glances over at me. I wondered how Sharon was. I should try to visit her today.

A matched pair of dog-walkers strolled into view down the path from the car park, their dogs bounded forward under the Police tape to sniff the area where the creature's blood had spilled.

"Get those dogs under control," yelled the bald guy. "This is a crime scene."

"There's no need to shout, young man," said the woman.

DI Brown finished his conversation abruptly and hurried

over. He pulled out his warrant card and pushed it at the dog walkers.

"DI Brown, Hampshire Police. Get these dogs out of here now."

"But we walk them here every Sunday," said the man.

"Not today you don't," said DI Brown with, I thought, great restraint.

The dog walkers called their animals to heel and walked off back down the path with stiff indignation.

"For fuck's sake. Where are uniform when you need them?" said DI Brown to the trees. He opened out his phone, punched in a number and after a moment began another earnest conversation.

After a few minutes two uniformed constables appeared from the direction of the car park.

"Right, get this area secure. I don't want any more bloody civilians getting in here, or their dogs. SOCO should be here anytime."

No soon had he spoken than four guys in white overalls, each carrying a couple of metal cases, arrived and went straight into conference with DI Brown. The conference lasted a couple of minutes then they spread out and started unpacking their gear. DI Brown beckoned to the blond guy and walked over to me.

"We don't need you here anymore. DC Wilson will take you back to the station and you can make a statement. OK?"

"OK." I followed DC Wilson down the path to the car park only too glad of the chance to get out of the cold. I hoped breakfast might be involved somewhere too.

DC Wilson didn't speak to me until we were on the Redbridge flyover.

"What really happened?" he asked quietly without looking at me.

"Exactly what I told your boss. We set a trap for the killer, you saw the net. We caught it in that and then a bunch of people on horses came and took it off us. And they took four of our team with them."

He said nothing, but I could feel the scepticism coming off him in waves.

"You know Sharon don't you?" I said.

"Yeah."

"She's a smart girl, a good copper? You trust her?"

"Yeah."

"She wouldn't go along with something like this if she didn't think it was pukka, would she?"

No reply. Maybe he thought I'd trapped him. "Look you don't have to believe me, just keep an open mind on it. Any word on how she is this morning?"

"The boss said she had a comfortable night."

Sounded encouraging. "Good. I'll try and see her later today."

That was the end of the conversation. Ten minutes later we arrived at the Civic Centre Police Station, five minutes after that I was sitting in the same interview room as Sharon had used with DC Wilson, a cup of machine coffee and a bacon sandwich.

"This will be recorded, video and audio." DC Wilson pointed up at the camera then sat down opposite me and opened a yellow legal pad to a clean page. "Right, let's have it then."

"Where do you want me to start?"

"At the beginning," he said, a sharp edge in his voice.

I picked a starting point and told him the story trying to keep the events in order. He wrote steadily with the occasional request that I hold on for him to get it all down. I reached the end of the tale with the ambulance taking Sharon to the General, then the questioning started. Not harsh or overly aggressive, but certainly demanding questioning; as bad as facing Prof when he was pissed off. I knew DC Wilson didn't like my answers from the way he snapped at me, changing direction, probing for inconsistencies. I was glad of the camera's restraining influence on him.

We went over some parts, particularly the cavalry charge, three or four times before he packed it in.

"OK. Enough for today." He closed the pad and stood up. "You can go."

I walked out of the room. He caught me at the door, just out of camera shot, and stuck his face in close to mine.

"I don't know what fucking game you're playing with this

shit," he growled, too low for the microphones. "But if you had anything to do with Sharon getting hurt, I'll see you do time for it. Now piss off."

I walked out with my heart thumping and sat on the low perimeter wall until I'd calmed down. It was twenty to twelve by my watch so I decided to go home via the supermarket and cook some lunch. I tried to call Michelle as I walked to the bus stops, but got only her voicemail. I left a message telling I was done with the police and I was going home and hoped I'd speak to her later. I did wonder what Greg and Chloe had made of her.

I found out about an hour later when I arrived home with my shopping. Greg and Chloe were sitting in the kitchen lingering over toast and coffee.

"Morning, Charlie," said Chloe putting down her mug. "What's going on?" Her hair was a pale shade of green; an improvement on last week's pink.

"Breakfast," I said unpacking my shopping. I was tired, hungry and stressed-out and really didn't want to explain, but these were my friends.

"You know that's not what I mean," said Chloe. "What about the police, and who was that girl?"

"First things first. I'm starving. Let me get some breakfast on then I'll talk."

"Are you in trouble, Charlie?" asked Greg.

"And what about that other girl?" said Chloe. "The policewoman, Sharon?"

I slit open the packet of sausages before I answered. "Her name is Michelle, and Sharon is in the hospital at the moment."

"What happened, Charlie?" said Chloe.

I thought about what I was going to say as I placed four sausages under the grill then went in search of the frying pan.

"I was helping Sharon with an investigation, stuff went wrong and she got hurt. She's in the General, but I think she's going to be OK. That's why the police were here."

"What were you doing?" asked Chloe.

"Sorry, I can't tell you until it all comes to court." I set the pan on the hob and lit the gas.

"And what's this Michelle got to do with it?" said Greg.

"She's just a victim in all this. She needed somewhere to stay."

"So you offered?" said Greg. "Nothing to do with her being cute?"

"How old is she?" said Chloe. "She looked really young."

"She's twenty."

"And Sharon's OK about her?" said Chloe.

"Yes, no problem." She certainly should be after her 'no relationships' speech. I pulled out the grill pan to turn my sausages and place the rashers of bacon beside them.

"You're not in any trouble with this are you, Charlie?" asked Greg. "Those coppers this morning looked pretty heavy."

"No. We're all on the same side." I hoped DI Brown would agree.

"Just let us know if there's anything we can help with," said Greg. "Even if you can't explain what's going on."

"Thanks. I might need to call that in sometime. Is there any coffee left?"

"I'll make some more," said Chloe and got up to fill the kettle.

Greg stood up from the chair and stretched. "Come on Chlo. We gotta go, Charlie. Practice this afternoon for the big game next month. We'll see you later."

I was kinda glad to see them go; they were my best mates and I didn't like deceiving them about what was going on, but it just wasn't a runner to tell them.

I decided that I would drop Sharon's car back to her place and leave it there. I shouldn't really drive it at all, but it would be easier to get a bus to the General from there. Visiting started at three; in the meantime I needed a shave, a shower and some clean clothes.

I got down to Sharon's and parked up with no problem, but must have just missed a bus because I waited twenty five minutes until one came along. Plenty of time to worry about whether Sharon was going to be alright, whether she would blame me for what happened, and to think about what I was going to do next about Michelle, my father, Dave and his kidnapped mates. Lots of thought: conclusions none.

Sharon was in a six-bed bay of a fourth floor ward in a bed next to the window. She was reading a magazine when I walked in and didn't spot me until I reached the end of her bed then her face lit up.

"Charlie!" She tossed aside her magazine. "God, it's good to see you. I've been so bored and they won't let me have a fag."

"You're feeling better then?" A truckload of anxiety slid from my shoulders.

"Yeah. Got a headache, but really I've had worse hangovers." She looked pale with dark circles under her eyes.

"They letting you out soon then?"

"Seeing the consultant tomorrow." She held up her left arm which had a fingers-to-elbow cast. "I might need an operation to pin it."

"Sounds painful, are you going to be able to use it?"

"Aches a bit, but I should get full use back in a few weeks. What happened to my car, Charlie?"

I gave her the car keys and sat down in the chair beside her bed. "I left it back at your place."

"Thanks." She put the keys in the drawer of her bedside cabinet and then turned to face me.

"What happened yesterday, Charlie?" she said quietly. "I can't remember."

She sounded very young and a little frightened and her dark eyes seemed very wide.

"What's the last thing you do remember?"

"I remember parking the car out in the forest."

"You remember why we were there?"

"Yeah. We were hunting your killer ape."

"And we caught it." I told her everything I remembered from yesterday. I kept my voice down so that the visitors around the other beds didn't have anything to get nosey about.

"Jesus, Charlie," she said when I had finished. "Sounds like we're lucky anyone came out of that. Who were those guys on horses?"

"Otherkin. My father's people."

"I've heard that name before." Sharon frowned. "Don't know where. Who are they?"

"The Devil's hunt, faery cavalry, whatever. Myths about them turn up all over northern Europe. If they took the creature's body, that makes them Otherkin."

"Yeah. That makes sense. What about Michelle's boyfriend and his mates?"

"Took them with them. There're lots of folk stories of people being taken like that. That's the most likely thing since there's no sign of them."

"Not going to be easy to get them back then." Sharon looked serious for a moment and then grinned. "Think they'd open up if we got a search warrant?"

"Maybe. Want to run it by your boss?"

She screwed her face up. "Not yet. I'll give it a few days."

"I was out where it happened with him this morning. He's got a full forensic team going over it. There should be plenty to find, there was that creature's blood all over the ground."

"Good. Maybe they'll find enough to convince him."

"You think it's possible?"

"Yeah. He's stubborn but he's not stupid. Show him enough evidence and he'll come round, and I'll make sure he sees the evidence when I get back."

"Yeah? Can't happen quickly enough for me. I've got a very bad feeling about this. I think we've made things worse."

"Worse than a supernatural serial killer?"

"An armoured cavalry raiding party?"

That silenced her for a while.

"You think they'll come back?" she asked eventually.

"The folklore books I looked at all mentioned raids by them. Burning farms, stealing cattle, taking slaves. Even if only half the stories are true, they're a bad lot to get the wrong side of, very big on revenge."

"I hope you're wrong."

"So do I." Didn't think I was though. I suddenly felt very tired.

"You all right, Charlie?"

"Tired. Didn't sleep much last night. Just feel like everything's got out of control suddenly."

"Not your fault."

"No. But I'm still in the middle of it."

"But you're not on your own." She reached out and squeezed my hand. Taken by surprise, the rush of thoughts caught me unfocused; pain and worry about her future washed over me. I pulled my hand back sharply.

"Sorry. Forgot," she said with a nervous smile then she turned her head to look away.

I turned to see what she was looking at. Two men, one carrying a bunch of flowers, were standing at the entrance to the bay. I recognised the flower-bearer as the other of DI Brown's sidekicks from the morning, the DC who had found the net. The mud on his trousers said he had come straight here. Sharon waved to them and they walked over to stand beside her bed, eyeing me suspiciously.

Seemed like a good time for me to leave; I stood up and offered the chair to them.

"You going, Charlie?" There was disappointment in her voice.

"'Fraid so. These boys'll keep you entertained, and I'll come again tomorrow."

I felt a bit bad about leaving, but Sharon would undoubtedly get more from them about the investigation if I wasn't there. And I really did need to go home and sleep.

There was an voicemail from Michelle when I switched my phone back on thanking me for looking after her, apologising for having to scoot off as she had to work and saying she'd call me tomorrow. I realised I had no idea of what she did for a job, and her mother's faded memories offered no clue. I tried to call her but got her voicemail again. I left a message to tell her that Sharon seemed okay and I looked forward to talking to her tomorrow.

It was after six when I got home. There was no sign of Greg and Chloe, for which I was grateful; I really didn't want to answer more questions right now. I cooked up a batch of beef stew for the week then settled down to watch TV. The ringing of my phone woke me just after ten; it was mother.

"You wanted to see Jack. Well he's here, and he says he can't go back."

CHAPTER 10

I don't normally pay that much attention to what the radio is talking about first thing in the morning; it's just something to wake me up gently. I woke up pretty quickly at the news of two people dead and three missing after a fire overnight at a farm in the New Forest. I returned to Radio Solent, but got nothing more than police and fire investigators would be looking into the cause. Could be a coincidence, but equally it could be the next strike of Otherkin revenge.

I would have liked to go straight out to Mother's, but there were two solid reasons why I couldn't. Prof would have expected me in the lab if the Martians had landed, and I was also down to supervise an undergraduate practical session.

So the lab it had to be; once there I got onto the BBC Hampshire webpage and kept it open for updates to see if my suspicions about the farm fire were going to be confirmed. The farm was isolated and there were currently no witnesses or survivors; it seemed more and more possible. By midday the updates had slowed and the fire was being treated as suspicious. I went to lunch convinced it was the work of the Otherkin. On the way to the canteen I phoned the hospital; Sharon was still there, and they reminded me that visiting finished at eight.

Michelle phoned while I was at lunch to ask if I'd heard the news. We agreed that it sounded like an Otherkin raid. Then I told her about Jack.

"Oh shit, that sounds serious," was all she said; an accurate assessment in my opinion.

"I'll know more when I've talked to him," I said. "I'm going to try to get out there tonight. I'll call you after. I don't know when I'll be able to see you, but I'll try to make it soon."

"I'd like to see you too. I don't like being on my own." There was a catch in her voice as she said it that made me want to reach down the phone and cuddle her.

"This week, I promise." I didn't know how I would manage it, but the memory of her kisses made damn sure I'd try.

The undergrads kept me busy until after six. I checked the news on The Echo website, there was no further information on the fire. I sent a text to mother to tell her I was coming out and wanted to stay over. I knew she was at work and should not be phoned except in complete emergency. She replied inside ten minutes that that was fine.

It was gone seven before I got to Sharon's ward. She was sitting up in bed reading a newspaper, the remains of her dinner on a tray in front of her.

"How's the food?" I asked.

"Charlie." Big smile. "You made it. I'd nearly given up on you." She had more colour in her cheeks today.

"Sorry I'm late. I had to look after the baby chemists today. How's the headache?" I sat down in the chair next to her bed.

"Nearly gone." She put down the newspaper and leaned towards me. "Charlie," she said quiet and low. "I remember. I remember seeing the ape thing."

"That's great. Do you remember the horsemen?"

She looked puzzled. "No. Not yet."

"Maybe that'll come back too. Looks like they did."

"What do you mean?"

"You didn't hear about the fire?" I looked at the paper she'd been reading; yesterday's Mail on Sunday. I should have bought a copy of tonight's Echo.

"What fire?"

I filled her in on what I knew.

"Could be," she said when I'd finished. "But equally there are plenty of other explanations. They'll be able to tell what caused the fire pretty exactly, you know."

"I doubt the Otherkin understand forensics. There'll be evidence all over the place, just nobody to arrest."

"That'll piss the boss off even more. He wasn't happy with

yesterday's show. The boys told me he gave everyone a hard time after you'd left."

That I could believe. "Guess you won't have to worry about him for a week or two."

"I don't know. I should be out of here tomorrow. They decided my arm doesn't need pinning. I'd like to be back at work by the end of the week."

"Really?"

"Yeah. Charlie, this is turning into the most interesting case I've ever worked on. I don't want to miss out on it."

"But you'll be signed off."

"Officially yes, but I can drop in to talk to my colleagues. And someone needs to stop the boss from making a prat of himself with the travellers, because that's the first thought he'll have if there's horses involved."

"You think you can stop him?"

"Someone's got to try. Just like someone's got to try and get Michelle's boyfriend and his mates back."

I felt a stab of guilt; it had suited me well enough that Dave wasn't around.

"I've been thinking about that. I should see my father tonight. I'll ask him what we can do."

"You sure you'll see him? He hasn't always been reliable about showing up has he?"

"Should be OK this time. He's staying with my mother." I paused. "She says he can't go back to the other side. That sounds pretty serious. I guess that's tied up with the Otherkin cavalry coming through."

"That figures. All the more reason for me to get back in the office."

"Do you think you can really make a difference?"

"Like I said, gotta try and no one else is gonna do it."

"Will you get into trouble for this?"

"Probably get a bollocking for getting hurt, but no more than that."

A nurse came to the entrance to the bay and called. "Five minutes until the ending of visiting time."

I stood up. "Call me when you're home. I'll tell you what I

got from my father."

I had lots of thinking time on the way out to mother's; waiting for buses, sitting on buses. I was deeply relieved that Sharon wasn't badly hurt; we'd been lucky and it looked like we'd made things worse. The best thing to come out of it was that she now believed me about the beast, but the price had been too high. That led me to thinking about how to get Dave the troll and his mates back and stop the raiding, but I had so little information about how things work over there that any speculation was pointless. Hopefully Jack would open up and supply some of that information tonight; if he didn't then we were truly screwed, though not as screwed as Dave and his mates.

I ended up thinking about Michelle and there I had even less idea of what was going on. I could barely comprehend what she had gone through in the last few weeks; it was remarkable she was still walking around and not under sedation in a psychiatric ward. It seemed to me the best thing I could do was make no assumptions, no demands on her and keep my promises to her. Not easy when there was a wild visceral attraction that drove me to her which was completely different from how I'd felt about Sharon.

I sat at the back of the sparsely-populated lower deck, sent mother a text and then watched the road go by thinking how much simpler life had been a few weeks ago, dull but simpler. I was hungry; I always get pissed off if my blood sugar gets too low. It should have occurred to me to buy something to eat on the way and my own stupidity pissed me off even more.

It was half past ten and I was starving when I got to Mother's. There was no answer to my knock even though there were lights on. On a hunch I walked around the side of the house to the back garden, soft yellow light shone out through the open door of the garden shed and I heard my mother's laughter from within.

"Hello," I called. I really didn't want to walk in on them enjoying a romantic interlude.

"Charlie." A few moments later my mother came out of the shed, her hair loose and tousled, Jack behind her. Mother had clearly found him some normal clothes; I recognised his shirt as one of my old ones. I wondered where his trousers had come from; mine wouldn't have fit him.

She reached out and hugged me, I hugged back careful to avoid bare skin.

"You must be hungry," she said. "I've got steak and kidney on the hob. Won't take a minute to mash the potatoes."

She released me and hurried off into the house. I turned to face Jack. There was so much I wanted to say, but I was unsure where to start. How would he react?

He made it easy. "So my son, you slew the High Lord's servant." He held out his hand to me. "That was a brave deed, but it brings a great storm behind it."

I took his hand and gripped it with relief. "You're not angry?"

"Why be angry? I told them it would come to this. They understand so little of this world now, but they did not listen."

"But now you can't go back."

"Being angry will not change that. I am sad this has happened, it will bring much suffering and pointless bloodshed." He released my hand.

"It already has. A farm was burned last night, people taken."

He sighed and looked away. "And now you seek my help to return the taken to their rightful place."

I had forgotten that he too could read minds on skin contact. "Seems like we're the only people who can do anything. No one else on this side understands what's happening."

"What would you have us do?"

"We can't just leave them there. We have to try to bring them back."

"You do not understand what you are facing."

"Then tell me."

He looked at me levelly as if calculating what to say. I felt the momentum with me and pressed on. "You need to understand some things too, if you're thinking of staying here. I'm sure mother is happy to have you around, but everything you eat and drink has to be bought and paid for by her, and she doesn't earn much." I felt the echoes of mother's words to my sixteen year-old self. "If you're going to stay you have to contribute."

"I can work."

"As what? You don't know how this world works. You can't simply turn up and get a day's work without identity documents. Those kind of jobs don't exist anymore around here." Well they did, but you wouldn't want to do them; a Chinese takeaway that I used to use in town was busted a couple of months ago for using illegal immigrants.

"I have some skill with animals."

"The farms around here are run by Cadland and Exbury estates. They don't take casual workers without National Insurance numbers."

He looked at me levelly again. I thought I caught an echo of sadness in his gaze. "You should go and eat. We will talk more after."

Mother called out 'dinner's ready' from the kitchen so I went in, leaving him by the shed.

"How's your friend that was hurt?" asked mother as she served up.

"She's coming out tomorrow. Got a cast on her arm and sore ribs, but otherwise OK."

"She was lucky by the sound of it."

"I think so. I thought she was a goner when the horses went over her." I shivered at the memory.

"You should bring her round sometime. I'd like to meet her."

She laid a full plate of steak and kidney with mashed potato and peas in front of me which ended conversation for a while. I ate while she bustled around the kitchen, emptying the dishwasher and making tea.

I finished my meal and picked up my mug of tea to go back out to the shed.

"Take this to him." She held out another steaming mug. "I'll be out in a minute, and Charlie." She paused. "Be careful with him. I know he seems fine now, but he wasn't when he first turned up. He was frightened, and I've never seen him like that before."

Jack was sitting cross-legged on a rug on the floor of the shed. I put the mugs of tea down beside the candle lantern that usually was the centrepiece of our Christmas decorations.

"Did you eat well?" he asked. "She is a good cook."

"Very well." I sat down beside him. "So, you were going to tell me what we're facing."

He reached out and picked up his mug and looked into for a long moment as if working out what to say. "To understand what is happening, you need to understand the land itself."

He took a sip of tea; I waited for him to continue.

"Our earliest stories tell of the gods leading us there from this world, choosing us to rule the land. Only a hundred or so were chosen; from these all of us are descended."

"So there aren't that many Otherkin?"

"There are some thousands now. We've had a long time to breed, but fewer children are born there now than in the old times, and that is at the heart of the problem. Some of us, like me, come back to this world to take lovers, and sometimes we bring our children back with us. There are others who would forbid this, and argue that we are diluting the chosen race and this is why our magics grow weaker."

"So they sent the creature?"

He nodded. "They have become powerful. Many of the Great are in their party. The High Lord Faniel, the King's son is with them. They would not attack the half-born and those who stand with them openly. That would be too obvious a breaking of the ancient law, though I fear it will come in time. Instead they chose a softer target and sent this servant to kill our lovers. By killing it you delivered a deadly insult to some of the highest in the land."

"An excuse for war?"

"Just so. Among the Great with them are those still strong enough to open the way for the raiding parties to ravage as they did long ago."

I didn't quite understand this, but it didn't sound good. "Why is this happening now?"

"The King grows old and weak. Lord Faniel feels his time is near, and is impatient to have his way. Even the Great who do not hold his view feel it is a bad time to oppose him."

"So he sent the creature?"

"I doubt it was him personally, but certainly he knew of it and approved."

"And his followers would have the prisoners?"

"Most likely. The prisoners are the property of whoever captured them."

"So they might not be all in the same place?" That would make it even more difficult.

"Most likely not. Do you begin to see the difficulties now?"

I did, but I didn't want to give up. "There must be something we can do. Could we ransom them?"

"Possibly. They might consider it if enough gold was offered."

"How much would be enough?"

"Hard to know." He shrugged. "It would be a lot."

I had feared it would be. "I don't know how we could get our hands on that. Is there anything else they might want?"

"Cattle or horses perhaps, but again a lot."

"So we're left with trying to take them back, or abandoning them." I didn't like either option. "How well guarded would they be?"

"Probably not at all, but to get them to leave you would have to break the compulsion."

"What compulsion?"

"Our magics work mostly on the minds of others, with illusions and compulsions. If whoever holds a prisoner puts a compulsion on them, then they would not be able to think of leaving."

"Can you break that compulsion?"

"It depends." He shrugged. "Depends on who laid the compulsion, how long ago and what type it is. If one of the Great laid it, then no."

"Why?" I felt like a four year old asking how everything works.

"The Great are the strongest magicians in the land; that is how you become one of the Great. I am not that strong."

"So you're not one of the Great?" I wasn't actually disappointed.

"I turned aside from that road. I was not made to study." He grinned wistfully.

"You said you were a prince," said mother. I looked up to see her standing in the doorway and wondered how long she had been there.

"I did not." Jack sounded outraged.

"Gotcha!" she laughed. "You should see the look on your face." She slid down beside him, wrapped her arms around him and they kissed.

I waited, feeling awkward, until they had finished.

"So if the prisoners have a compulsion on them then we have to drag them away?"

"That could harm them greatly," said my father. "Much better to get the compulsion removed."

"Would a compulsion laid over there still work over here?" I said.

"I don't know, it is possible."

"So have you decided what you're going to do?" asked mother.

I looked at Jack, but he said nothing.

"Someone has to put a stop to this before it gets any bigger," said mother. "I just heard about another farm fire on Radio Solent."

"Oh shit," I said, and for a moment saw again the riders charging out of the trees.

Still Jack said nothing.

"Someone in authority is going to figure it out eventually," said mother. "The police may lack imagination, but they are very methodical. They'll get there in the end, and when they do there'll be hell to pay."

Jack frowned deeply but still kept silent.

"You always wanted to take him," said mother. "Now you have the chance. Take him, and find a way to stop this."

"I'm a marked man over there," he said. "It would not be safe."

"If this goes on, your world won't be safe," said mother. "You don't know how good this world has become at war. Your cavalry won't stand a chance."

I wondered if you could get a helicopter gunship through a portal, or a tank. Maybe not, but you surely could get a squad of SAS men through.

"If you ever want to go back there, then you have to do

something to stop this." I recognised her 'do not argue with me' tone from my teenage years.

"Very well," said Jack. "Though I cannot see what I can do. Do you wish to do this now?"

I glanced at mother then looked at my watch; it was after midnight.

"If it is as urgent as you say then we should not delay," said Jack.

He had a point; we had argued so strongly for action that we could hardly put it off.

"How long will we be?" I asked. He shrugged in reply.

"Time is different over there, isn't it?" said mother. "A few hours there could be days here."

"Yes. It seems so," said Jack.

"If I'm going to be gone for a while I need to send some texts. Tell some people I'm going to be away." I turned to mother. "You'll need to call Prof. Tell him I'm taking some holiday. He'll kick up about it, but I haven't taken any holiday since I started so he can't really complain."

"I'll speak to him tomorrow, first thing."

I went into the house, took my mobile from my jacket and tapped out messages to Sharon and Michelle. "Going with my father. Could be gone a while." I sent it then wrote another to Greg. "Staying with mother 4 a few days."

I put my jacket on, left the phone and my watch on the table and went back outside. I could hear raised voices as soon as I opened the back door.

"He may look like a grown man to you, but he is still a child in many ways so I expect you to look after him," said mother. Thanks mum.

"Of course I will," said Jack. "How could I do otherwise? But it is dangerous. Those looking for me are not gentle."

I walked quickly into the shed trying to give no sign that I had heard them. "Ready."

"Bring nothing with you that is iron. The doorway will not allow anything iron to pass through. And we need a gift for you to bring." He stood up and turned to mother. "Have you any more chocolate?"

"None left," said mother.

He thought for a moment. "Do you have any of those little sticks that make fire?"

"Matches?" said mother. "There's some in the kitchen."

I followed her back indoors. She found me a couple of boxes of matches which I slipped into a jacket pocket.

"I wish I was coming with you. I've always wanted to know what its like over there," she said quietly. "Maybe next time."

We walked around the side of the house and out into the lane. She threw her arms around me and hugged me fiercely.

"You be careful," she said before going back into the cottage.

Even though it was a mild night with enough sky light for me to follow Jack without too many stumbles I did wish I had a torch; I didn't want to have to abort my first visit to his world because of a sprained ankle.

"What should I call you?" I asked as we walked down the lane. "You're my father, but I don't know your name."

"A name is a powerful thing," he said. "To know the true name of something is to have power over it."

"I've read that, but I need to call you something."

"Your mother calls me Jack, that will do for now."

I had presumed we would go to somewhere near the stream where he had first appeared and this was correct. We stopped in a small grove of trees, their branches outlined against the orange glow of the refinery; the stream chuckled away nearby.

"Is this it?" I asked. "Where's the gateway?"

"It is hidden," Jack said. "A simple little spell."

He took my hand, for a moment his words echoed in my ears. When he let go I could see a slightly glowing oval ahead of me, the edges outlined in blue, where previously had been only darkness.

"Do you see it now?"

"Yes."

"Follow me closely and keep walking."

He reached out a hand and caught my wrist and led me through the gateway. There was a moment's chill on my skin as I crossed the threshold and everything went dark.

A current surged through my mind similar to someone's

thoughts at first touch, but without the structure and coherence, a multitude of voices each asking a different question.

"Do you feel it?" said Jack. "This is the place between."

With the wind roaring through my brain it was all I could do to answer. I made myself keep walking through the mind-storm and then it was gone and we were standing in a wood, sunlight dappling through the leaves.

"So this is it?" I looked around us and saw nothing extraordinary, just trees and grass.

"Welcome to my home," said Jack with a smile. He looked older; difficult to say how old but no longer like a teenager and he was back in his brown and green kit. I looked down at my own clothes; they were unchanged.

"I wish you were visiting at a better time." His smile faded. "We should move from here. Our arrival may have been observed."

A faint path wound between the trees. I looked around; it did not seem to lead on, proof enough that though this gateway was established it wasn't used often.

I followed Jack along the path through the wood. I'm no botanist, but the trees and vegetation looked pretty similar to home, nothing terribly different except that there was more birdsong and maybe the air seemed sweeter. I should have been tired, instead I felt full of energy and excitement to the point where I almost burst out laughing.

"Do you feel it?" asked Jack. "The very essence of the land all around you?" He spread his arms wide like a sun-worshipper greeting the dawn. "I feel better already."

"I certainly feel something and it's good."

He smiled at me, dark eyes sparkling. "That is what makes this place what it is. I love to visit your world, but if I stay too long it drains the life out of me and I have to come home. You have the power within you. This place can nurture it and bring it to flower."

"If they don't kill me first."

"True." The sparkles faded. "Come. I cannot take you to my house. That will be watched but there are other places. People I trust."

He strode off down the path. I followed, my blood still singing. I wondered about his house and life here. Did he have a wife? Children? What was his place in this world? It didn't feel right to ask him directly, but I hoped he would drop some clues.

A few hundred yards on we reached a broader more established path. After a moment's thought Jack led us down to the left. Another mile or so brought us to the edge of the wood. Used as I was to the wide fields of Hampshire, the tiny fields were a surprise. The second surprise was the creatures labouring in them. Maybe four feet tall and ape-like, smaller versions of the beast Michelle had killed; they mowed the long grass with scythes while others behind them raked it into rows. About a dozen of them marched in step slowly across a field which wouldn't have held a decent game of football; not one paid us any attention.

"What are they?" I pointed at the labourers.

"Gwasannath. Servants. Simple creatures with enough brain to follow a compulsion. We use them for much of the work here."

"They look like that thing that attacked mother and me, only smaller."

"Yes. Very likely. Some of the Great breed them to suit particular purposes, warriors among them."

I shivered despite the warmth of the air; the idea that I might meet more of the stinking murderous things was deeply unappealing.

"These gwasannath belong to my brother, this is his land. His house is beyond that hill." He pointed to a gentle slope that rose away to our right. "He is closer to the court than I, and will likely know more of what Lord Faniel intends."

"So where is your house?"

"Far from here. To go anywhere near would invite trouble."

"So the gateway we've just used isn't the one you usually use?"

"No, not at all. I've never used it before, but I knew it was here."

"How did you get us here then?"

"Did you hear the place between in your mind? If you have

the power and you answer it with who, or where you wish to go, then you will come to the nearest gateway."

I wanted to ask him more about the gateways, but he strode off up the slope along the edge of the wood and I had to hurry to keep up with him.

It was pretty warm out in the direct sun and I was sweating a bit when we reached the top of the hill. The countryside was spread out below us in a broad valley; a lazy river meandered through it in the middle distance, smoke rose from a scatter of farmhouse chimneys. It looked well-ordered and prosperous, much like north Hampshire apart from the tiny fields, each edged by a thick hedge. Part of me was disappointed; I don't really know what I had expected, something more different perhaps, but this rural idyll seemed too much like home.

"That is my brother's house." Jack pointed across the fields. "What do you see?"

"A long white building with a thatched roof, a couple of other buildings that look like barns, all surrounded by a big hedge. Why?"

He smiled at me. "My brother will be embarrassed."

"Why?"

"He has laid a glamour on the house. You should see shining walls and a golden roof. It says much for your strength that, untrained as you are, you see past it."

"Oh!" That made me feel rather pleased with myself.

We followed a well-worn path towards the house, crossing the hedges by stiles set beside the wooden gates. In one field we came across a half-dozen black cattle about the size of a Shetland pony. First the tiny fields now miniature cattle; I stood and stared in amazement.

"What are you looking at? They will not hurt you," said Jack. "Have you not seen cattle before?"

"Not this size. They're much bigger back home."

His turn to look at me with amazement. Clearly in his visits he hadn't noticed any cattle, but then I don't think that was what he came for.

We crossed the deep dry ditch and entered the farmyard through the open gate to the cries of children playing somewhere out of sight. A pair of large dogs leapt out from their kennel beside the well barking furiously and I hoped the tethers restraining them were stout. The door of the main house opened; a man in a knee-length smock stepped into the yard, shorter and plumper than Jack but with the same eyes and curly hair. I felt a little thrill of excitement that this was another relative I didn't know I had.

He threw his arms wide in welcome and said something in a lilting liquid tongue that sounded a bit like Welsh then turned to me and bowed.

"He says we are welcome in his house, and asks if I have brought him another nephew," said Jack.

Another nephew? Much as I suspected. I smiled, wondering what I should call him and how many other relatives I had over here. Probably lots; which made the place feel a little less strange.

Jack replied in the same lilting language.

"Welcome, son of my brother. Welcome in my hall," my uncle said in thick halting English.

We followed him into the house along a straw-strewn corridor, a half-dozen spears stood in a rack behind the door, the broad bronze heads looked freshly cleaned and sharpened. He showed us into a small room with a pair of wooden settles against the walls. Sunlight filtered through the half-open shutter and a faint scent of beeswax filled the dusty air. Two child faces framed by dark curls appeared around the door for a moment and withdrew silently.

We sat on the settles and he opened a polished wooden cabinet, took out a dark earthenware flagon and three wooden goblets. He drew out the stopper, poured generous portions of a purple liquid and handed us the goblets. I took a smell of it; a bit like port but with added plums.

My uncle spoke a few words that sounded like a toast and lifted his goblet. I raised mine in reply and took a mouthful; definitely like port, but sweeter and fruitier. Be worth taking some back if I could.

My uncle sat down next to Jack and they began talking in their own language. From the low tone of their voices and their grave expressions it was clearly a serious discussion; at one point Jack leapt from the settle with what I assumed to be a series of swear words. I watched them and sipped my drink and wondered if it would be impolite to pour myself another. I was still buzzing from the essence of the land or whatever it was in the air, but looking around I was a bit disappointed. From the manual labour in the fields to the thatched roof and beaten clay floor of the house and the rough-woven smock my uncle wore, the Otherworld seemed more like a visit to a medieval theme park than anything else. So far I hadn't seen anything that looked like it was iron. I wondered what the mowers were using for their scythes; bronze possibly, or maybe even flint. That fitted, I guess, with the riders, who had looked like a Dark Ages cavalry charge because that's exactly what they were. Bronze swords may not be as good as iron; but they will still kill you if someone stabs you with one.

The conversation finished and Jack turned to me. "The prisoners are all at the King's hall guarded by followers of Lord Faniel. He has decided to bring back the old ritual of the Midsummer Offering. The prisoners will be his offering."

"What does that mean?" It certainly didn't sound good.

"The Midsummer Offering is a tradition from our earliest forefathers to give thanks to the Gods for our home here. The blood of the sacrifice renews our bond with the land."

"You mean they're going to be killed?"

"Yes. Understand, this has not been done since before my grandfather's time. It is a measure of Lord Faniel that he intends to return to the old ways."

"What about the King, his father? Can't he stop him?"

"The King is a sick man. He has no strength for anything, he cannot catch his breath, and the merest effort brings him pain. He swoons often and falls asleep at any time. He will do nothing to oppose Lord Faniel."

"Then we have to get them out. How long is it until Midsummer?"

He looked at me for a moment as if I was an idiot. "Twenty days."

"How long is that on the other side?"

He shrugged. "I do not know. Time moves differently there."

"Can we get them now? Or at least see where they're being held?"

He chewed his lip in thought for a moment then spoke to my uncle.

"They are guarded by only a few men," he said turning back to me. "But if they carry a compulsion laid on by Lord Faniel, as is likely, then we will not be able to break it."

"We need to have a look, see if we can work out some way of getting them out."

More lip chewing followed by another consultation with my uncle.

"How well do you ride?"

"I've never been on a horse."

"Then we walk." He turned back and spoke to my uncle, presumably declining his offer of horses, then stood up and drained his goblet.

I followed him out to the yard and the dogs immediately starting barking. My uncle joined us a few seconds later, handed me a rolled-up woollen cloak, said a few incomprehensible words and embraced Jack.

"He says come back and see him in better times," said Jack. "Put the cloak on. It will hide your clothes that do not belong here." He looked at my t-shirt then down at my jeans and scuffed Nike trainers. "If there was more time I would teach you how to conjure a glamour to hide those."

"How hard is it to learn?"

"Put on the cloak, I will try to explain as we walk." I unrolled the cloak and put it on; it had a hood and horn buttons that fastened it across the front. I bowed to my uncle in farewell. We crossed the yard and walked away, without looking back, down to the lane that served the farm.

I was already feeling too hot by the time the dogs were out of earshot and would have gladly shed the cloak. "How does this glamour spell work then?"

"This is something you should have been taught years ago. It is a simple enough spell, the difficulty lies is maintaining it and that takes practice. Some small part of your thought has always to be thinking of it, otherwise it fades."

I could see how that would need practice. "What's the basic spell?"

"To convince anyone else of the appearance you must first convince yourself. Build a picture in your head as detailed as you can, of what you want them to see then send it out to the world."

"OK. I understand about building the picture you want other people to see, but how do I send it out?"

He stopped walking and faced me. "As an exercise then imagine you are wearing boots like mine."

I looked down at his plain brown leather boots, trying to capture the scuffs and sheen of dust in my mind, to feel them on my own feet.

"When you are happy that you have the image, hold out your hand. You have a sweet food in your world that you chew and blow bubbles with. That is what you are going to do with the picture. I will show you."

I nearly lost the picture over the thought of mother giving him bubble gum. I struggled to compose myself then reached out my right hand. He took it and for a moment I swear I saw and felt a scuffed pair of brown boots on my feet.

"Keep thinking of the boots," he said and released my hand.

We walked on and I kept thinking about the boots. There was so much I wanted to ask him, but the determined way he was striding ahead suggested he wasn't in a talking frame of mind. I also had no idea of what he had done, so if I started a conversation and the glamour slipped, I didn't think I could replicate it.

They were waiting for us where the lane met a wider road. Whether my glamour worked or not was irrelevant because they knew who they were looking for. Their leader was a hefty young guy in a polished bronze breastplate over mail and with a sword; not a big sword but it looked damned serious. He had four foot-soldiers with him in leather armour carrying broad-headed spears like those in my uncle's house, and half a dozen gwasannath. The gwasannath were noticeably bigger than my uncle's mowers, the smell of them nearly choked me.

They came at us from three directions. The gwasannath swarmed over the hedges that lined the lane behind us, the spearmen from either side, their spears thrust toward us. I didn't have time to react before there was a spear point six inches from my face.

Their leader yelled something incomprehensible; probably stand still or hands up. I stood still and raised my hands just in case. He walked up to us, stuck his sword point under Jack's nose and spoke to him. I didn't understand a word, but from the look of defiant hostility on Jack's face it was "Lord Faniel's going to be so pleased to see you" or similar. Jack didn't say anything which seemed to annoy him. He threw a command over his shoulder and turned his attention to me as two of the soldiers kept my father covered with their spears while the gwasannath encircled us.

I lowered my hands and looked him in the eye as he approached sheathing his sword. He didn't seem to like me looking at him because he barked out an order. The man behind me dropped his weapon, grabbed my hands and forced my arms fiercely up behind me. I had no time to focus on him because his leader took hold of my jaw and snarled gibberish at me, twisting my head to one side with his thick forearm, digging the rings on his fingers painfully into my face. His will powered into my mind, focused as a firehose, sluicing away my will.

I lashed out at the invasion, pushing his flow back on itself towards him, gaining strength from my pain and anger. For a moment everything flashed red followed by an intense black. When the light came back the leader was lying on his face in the road in front of me. The spearman who had been behind me was ten feet away crumpled under the hedge, the front of his breeches dark from where he had pissed himself. The other three spearmen stood around Jack with their mouths hanging open.

I stared at the leader, my head spinning, everything too bright like I'd been looking into the sun. Fuck, I did that. But what did I do?

"Run, Charlie," yelled Jack. "Run for the gate."

He twisted around and grabbed one of the spearman beside

him around the neck. The man folded up like a ragdoll. The soldier behind him swung the butt of his spear at him. He rolled away from the stroke, but it caught him a glancing blow in the small of the back. He tumbled to the ground with a yell of pain and then, as the spearman raised his weapon to strike again, vanished.

"Run, Charlie." His voice came from everywhere.

I looked at the ring of gwasannath; they were just standing there blank-eyed. I took a couple of steps towards a gap between them, they didn't react. I threw off the cloak and ran like hell up the road, a spear crashing into the hedge beside me. I vaulted the first gate I came to and fled across the fields.

I ran until the breath burned in my chest before I risked a look behind; nothing chasing me. I knew damn well I couldn't outrun the gwasannath so it was obvious that they hadn't come after me. I was more concerned about the spearmen; either I had outrun them or, more likely, they had decided to pursue their more valuable prisoner. There was no telling how easily they could summon reinforcements; even now the cavalry could be assembling. I wondered briefly about their leader; whether I'd just stunned him, or damaged him more permanently. If I'd really hurt him then I definitely didn't want to face their payback.

I took a look around to see where I had gotten to. By pure good fortune I had jumped the right gate, and was now close to the top of the ridge above my uncle's farm. I briefly contemplated going back to try and free Jack. Two things decided me against doing it: he had told me to run for the gateway, and I had no idea of how easily the squad of gwasannath could be brought back into action. The gateway it was; all I had to do was find it and then make it work for me—easy then.

Actually the first part was straightforward enough; climb the ridge then walk along the edge of the wood. I considered trying to put on a glamour, but had no confidence in my ability and reckoned that a badly done glamour made me more conspicuous than none at all.

I reached the crest of the ridge with no obvious pursuit and relaxed a little. My uncle's gwasannath still marched mindlessly across the fields, their new-mown handiwork guiding me to where the path entered the wood. From there it was more difficult; on our way in we had walked a long way down this path, joining it from a much fainter path. Trying to spot the minor path was hard. I hadn't really been paying attention when we arrived, caught up as I had been by the energy of the place; now I struggled to find it. Several times I turned off along what looked like a path, every time I ended up retracing my steps. It was getting dark under the trees and I was getting more and more stressed, thinking I might have to spend the night out here. I wished I had Sharon with me, or Michelle; Sharon would surely have had the sense to pick out a landmark or two.

The path when I found it was fairly obvious, just much further along than I remembered. I nearly cried at the sight of it. Following the path, I was able to see where we had pushed through undergrowth a few hours earlier. The glow of the portal was more visible now in the gloaming, its light an almost purple blue.

I was about to run to it in relief when I caught the smell of burnt rubber. I ducked into the undergrowth and crawled carefully forward. The gwasannath had beaten me to it; three of them stood silhouetted against the blue oval.

Hardly daring to breathe I crept away from the portal until I found a little hollow to hunker down in and collect my thoughts. Recalling Jack's words about how the portal worked I reckoned I could use it. Think clearly of who, or where you want to go, and it'll take you there seemed to be the essence of it. That should be easy; I really wanted to go home.

There was one problem, or rather one problem cubed. There was no way I could physically confront one of the smelly bastards, let alone three. *Simple creatures with enough brain to follow a compulsion,* Jack had said, and Michelle had scared one with a camera flash so I needed something to scare them off. A decent glamour would do it for Jack, but I couldn't even reliably conceal my trainers so it had to be something else.

I thought hard about it and came up with nothing. Maybe I could find my way back to my uncle's farm and hide up there, but it was probably crawling with hostile soldiers by now.

Thinking of my uncle I thought of the matches I should have given to him. I put my hands in my pockets and found the box.

I was sitting under a pine tree, the ground was littered with dry fallen branches which would burn really well; definite possibilities. I quietly gathered up an armful of dry bracken and wound it around a five-foot pine branch.

I made my way back to the path with my unlit brand to a point where I could see the gwasannath lit by the glow of the portal. With shaking hands I took out the matches; if I was wrong about this then I was in for a whole world of shit.

The first match snapped off without striking. I paused for a moment thinking about what I was about to do. There really didn't seem to be any alternative; I wouldn't last long as a fugitive over here. I struck a second match. It flared and the bracken caught alight. After a couple of seconds the pine needles began to catch. I ran down the path straight towards the glowing blue oval the burning branch held out in front of me, blazing clumps dropping from it.

Two of the gwasannath shrieked and ran, the third stood its ground. I thrust the burning branch at its ugly monkey face. I felt the impact and the scream nearly burst my eardrums as it went down.

I kept on full tilt into the blue glow. I dropped the branch as the chill hit me and the voices slid into my mind. I tried to summon the strongest images I could of mother and home: her gentle smile, the sound of her voice, the smell of grilled bacon for breakfast, the taste of her chicken soup. Everything went dark and the chill spread across me as if I had dived into a cold swimming pool. I clung to my images of mother as a tumult of voices rushed through my mind and kept running.

It was dark on the other side; I only realised I'd come through when my shin made contact with something solid and I fell headlong. I looked around; the tree branches were outlined against an orange glow across a quarter of the sky. A wave of relief flooded through me; I'd never been so glad to see the lights of the refinery.

It took me a while and some pain to find my way to the lane. It was an overcast night and the refinery's glow didn't provide much illumination to pick my way through the wood to the riverbank. It had clearly rained recently leaving puddles invisible in the low light which I invariably found; I nearly slipped into the river at one point.

It must have taken nearly an hour to travel what would be a gentle ten minute stroll in daylight, groping my way through the trees. I was pissed off, cold and muddy when I reached mother's house. There was no one around, no traffic noise from the main road and the house was dark. I knocked long and loud, hoping like hell that she wasn't working a night shift. After an endless couple of minutes a light came on upstairs, the bedroom window opened and mother stuck her head out, her hair loose and tousled.

"Who is it?" she called down. I realised she wouldn't be able to see me until I stepped back from the door.

"It's me, Charlie."

"I'll be right down." She closed the window and a few seconds later the light came on in the hallway. The front door opened, she came flying out and grabbed me in a big tight hug; I didn't need skin contact to feel her relief.

"Charlie. I've been so worried." She hadn't hugged me like that for about ten years.

She loosened her grip and looked up at me. "What happened? Where's Jack?"

"Still on the other side. They were waiting for us. He got away, I think."

Her face froze for a moment, but only a moment, then she looked down at the state of me. "You need a shower and some clean clothes. Then you're going to tell me everything about it."

I wasn't going to argue with that. I left my filthy trainers on the doorstep and went upstairs to the bathroom. The long-case clock on the landing said quarter to three which sparked a sudden thought.

"What day is this?" I called down the stairs.

"Thursday, well Friday now. You were gone three days."

She couldn't have surprised me more if she'd slapped me. "Three days? It felt like three or four hours."

"Wow. I've always known time works differently there but

still. Have your shower then we'll talk about it."

I thought about it as I warmed up under the shower. I had twenty days of Otherworld time to organise a rescue; that could be as much as a couple of months over here. Good news, because I reckoned I'd need every day of it to come up with a workable plan.

Swaddled in a big fluffy bathrobe with my hair still wet I went down to the kitchen and sat at the table. Mother handed me a big mug of hot chocolate.

"I'm not going to bed until you've told me everything," she said. "What did you mean, he vanished?"

So I told her everything that I could remember, though some bits got out of order. She asked lots of questions, I remembered more stuff, we kept talking and then it was morning and I realised I should be going to the lab.

"I spoke to your professor," said mother. "I told him your father had turned up unexpectedly and wanted to spend some time with you. He's given you some time off, but he didn't sound very happy. I pointed out that you are entitled to holidays, and you hadn't taken any since you started there. I hope I haven't made things worse."

In spite of myself I yawned. If I could cope with gwasannath then I'd find a way of coping with Prof.

She looked at me and then at the clock on the oven. "Past your bedtime, and mine too."

Hard to disagree with that. I picked up my phone from the table to text Sharon and Michelle that I'd made it back before I went to bed. "Call me at two. I've got stuff to do," I said.

Mother smiled at me. "Like organising a rescue from the other side?"

"That too."

CHAPTER 11

It was nearly four when I woke and checked my phone; there were messages on the voicemail from Sharon and Michelle. Both said approximately the same thing—they wanted to know all about where I'd been. I decided to have something to eat before calling them.

Mother must have been up some time because she had a beef and vegetable stew simmering on the hob. "Hungry?"

"Yeah. You should have woken me earlier."

"I thought you needed to sleep." Hard to argue with that under the circumstances.

She ladled a plateful of stew and carved two doorsteps from a white loaf to go with it; I presumed she had eaten earlier.

"I was thinking about what we can do," she said while I ate. "Because we have to do something, there was another raid while you were gone."

"Anyone taken?"

"Four."

"More victims for Lord Faniel's big show."

"Yes, and it's down to us to stop it happening. If we wait for the police to figure it out those people are dead."

"True." If DI Brown had changed his attitude Sharon would have said.

"So what are we going to do?"

"My uncle said the prisoners aren't heavily guarded. I think I know enough about using the gateway to get a rescue team to the other side."

"OK, but you do realise if we grab them back that isn't the end of it. They'll just come and take some more. They might easily see it as a provocation, then you've made it worse."

I thought about it a moment while I chewed a wedge of gravy-soaked bread. "Yes, but at least we'll have a bunch of people who can tell their story to the police and then they'll have to listen. What else can we do?"

"But that's not going to stop it. The police can't exactly go over there and arrest Lord Faniel, can they? We need some way of convincing him to stop. What about his father, the King?"

"He's a sick man. They said he doesn't have the strength to stand up to Lord Faniel."

"So take a doctor over there." She made a steeple of her slim fingers. "What did they say's wrong with him? Maybe it's something curable."

I took a moment to remember my uncle's words. "He has no strength for anything and cannot catch his breath. He faints and falls asleep at any time of day, the merest effort brings him pain."

Mother nodded. "I see a lot of them like that in the nursing home. Dad was just like that before he had his bypass."

My grandfather died when I was eleven so I'd only known him in his declining years as the cancer ate him; grandma was his second, much younger, wife. This cottage had belonged to his older sister.

"I didn't know he'd had a bypass. I thought he died of prostate cancer."

"He did, and he had a bypass two years before you turned up. It kept him alive long enough to know you," she said with a weary tone to her voice. "They told us it was a ten year fix so he did well out of it. I remember the state he was in waiting for the op and he was just like the king. He couldn't do anything; the least effort gave him angina. We had the ambulance out to him three times in two months. He was dying in front of our eyes. He had the bypass, came out of hospital a new man. He was back playing golf within a month."

"I didn't know any of that."

"We never had the right time to talk about it, and now isn't it either. You want to get a doctor to look at the King. He's the only person who can stop this. What else can we do? Kill Lord

Faniel? That would just make things ten times worse."

I thought for a while; everything I knew about the Otherkin, the way they'd reacted to the killing of the gwasannath, suggested she was right about making things worse. As a plan it had a logic to it, plus a load of difficulties; such as finding a doctor who believed in parallel worlds.

"Know any doctors who might be persuadable?"

"None of the ones round here. How about a medical student?"

"Maybe." I didn't actually know any, but Chloe might; she seemed to have an unlimited network of friends. "But we have to have Jack to make it work. The language over there is really different and not many of them seem to speak any English. Which brings us back to a rescue team."

"Or someone else from that side. What about that girl in Totton's father?"

"Michelle? Maybe, I don't know much about him."

"But he must be in a similar situation."

"Worth trying. I'll ask her." The prospect of seeing Michelle gave me a warm feeling. I reached for my phone, selected her name out of the address book and keyed call. She picked up after three rings.

"Hi Michelle."

"Charlie. Where are you?"

"I'm calling from the other side." I couldn't resist the wind-up.

Her shriek almost made me drop the phone.

"What's it like? I always wanted to go. Tell me!" There was a pause then. "You said you were back. Can you get mobile reception over there?" Another pause. "You're winding me up, aren't you? Where are you really?"

"I'm at my mother's. Seemed like I was over there for two or three hours, turns out it was four days."

"Did you find Dave and his mates?"

"No. But I did find out about them." I didn't want to tell her what I'd found over the phone. "There's a lot to tell you. I need to talk to you about your father."

"My father?" There was a pause which made me think I'd

made a mistake. "Come on over. I still owe you a meal."

"I just had dinner here so don't worry about the meal. I'll be an hour or so. I'll text you when I'm on the bus." I ended the call.

"You need to hurry if you're going to get the bus," said mother. There was wistfulness in her expression which made me think that she wanted me to stay longer. "I scrubbed your trainers, but they're still damp."

She fetched them from beside the back door and pulled out the scrunched-up newspaper she had put in to dry them. I put them on; they were indeed still damp. I picked up my phone and jacket. Mother followed me to the front door.

"You go careful and keep in touch," she said. I smiled at her and then ran for the bus stop.

I sent the text to Michelle once I was on the bus then phoned Sharon and got her voicemail. I left a brief message to say I'd call her later. She called back ten minutes later; I told her there was plenty to talk about and arranged to see her tomorrow. It was nearly six; the bus had quickly filled up and I didn't want to have a detailed conversation about the Otherkin with two dozen eavesdroppers.

Michelle must have been watching for me from her window because she opened the door while I was still twenty yards short of it and ran out to me with a happy smile.

"Charlie! I was so worried about you" She spread her arms wide in welcome, we hugged and then, still entwined, went up to her flat.

"I've hardly slept since Monday," she said. "I kept thinking that you'd just disappear like Dave."

A reminder, if I needed one, of the news I had to tell her; not that she seemed to be missing her troll too much to judge from her arm curled around my waist.

We settled on the little sofa facing each other. She took my hands in hers and looked at me, dark eyes wide. "What did you find out over there?"

"My father took me to meet his brother, who is close enough to the people behind the raids to know what they plan to do." I tried to keep my voice calm and authoritative, as if I was reading out an instruction manual. "Dave and the other prisoners are going to be sacrificed at midsummer as an offering to their gods. They're planning a big ceremony to mark the new regime. We've got about twenty days, Otherworld time, to stop them. That's why we need to speak to your father."

Her face crumpled in distress. "I've tried to call him every day, but he hasn't come. Can't your father help?"

"They came looking for us. He got away, but I don't know how long he can hide from them."

Her face crumpled further and she squeezed my hand hard. "Oh shit, Charlie. What're we going to do?"

I took a moment to think about it. "Try to get them out. I think I can use the gateway to take people over there. I may be able to get us close to my dad. After that then... we're just trusting to luck."

"That sounds really dangerous. We could all get killed."

I couldn't deny the truth of that. "I don't see what else we can do. There's no-one else going to help us, and if we don't do something they'll die."

She said nothing for a while, just gripped my hand and looked at me with moist eyes. I wanted to reach for her but held back.

"How did we get here?" she whispered. "What the fuck happened, Charlie? I always thought the Otherworld was a peaceful and happy place."

"It's all down to Lord Faniel."

"Who's he?"

So I told her what I knew of Lord Faniel and his plans to cleanse those who dilute Otherkin blood.

"That's just disgusting," she said. "He's like the Otherworld BNP."

"Yeah. But he has support over there, and the opposition have no leader."

"We're screwed, Charlie. We're so screwed."

A tear trickled down her cheek and then I did reach for her. She came to me and I held her as she wept, hoping that she was wrong and not believing it.

It seemed a long time before she raised her face, looked at me with red-rimmed eyes then kissed me. After a few seconds

I felt her tongue exploring my lips, I opened to her and raised a hand to tangle my fingers in her thick dark hair. We held the kiss for what felt like minutes before she pulled back.

"I should go call my father again," she said. "Come with me?"

"Of course."

She put on her big black coat and we walked down hand-in-hand to where the Polo was parked.

As before she seemed to need all her concentration for driving, so I kept quiet and thought about what to say to her father as we made our hesitant way out through Netley Marsh. There was no one around when we got to the car park in the forest; we parked and walked down into the little valley where Michelle had killed the gwasannath. I climbed up the bank and looked around for the characteristic glow of a portal.

"What are you looking for?" Michelle asked.

"A gateway. Must be one around here somewhere."

"Can you see it? What does it look like?"

"They're normally hidden. My father did something so that I can see them."

I walked a few paces into the forest and a faint glow caught my eye between a couple of pine trees. "It's over there."

She climbed up beside me and we walked over to it.

"I don't see anything," she said.

"It's hidden, and I don't know how to reveal it. Here." I took her hand and gently directed it through the glowing surface of the portal.

"Oh!" she squeaked and pulled her hand back. "That feels weird. Like I put my hand in a freezer."

"That's it. That's the way to the Otherworld. " I took a couple of steps away from the glowing surface. "Not safe to go there at the moment, but this is where your father comes through."

She stood a moment by the portal.

"One day," she said then slipped an arm around me. We walked back down into the valley. She sat down cross-legged before her usual tree and began her song. It was bit like the song mother had taught me in its lilt, but had a different melody.

I moved away out of earshot then stood and watched her,

my hopes fading with the light as the minutes ticked by. After twenty minutes or so she stood up and walked over to me.

"Do you want to try now?" she said.

"Give it a go," I said. I thought it pretty unlikely Jack would respond, but there was nothing to be lost by trying.

I sat under Michelle's oak and sang my summoning song through a dozen times before giving up on it. Wherever he was, he wasn't able to come to me. I could think of several reasons why, none of them good.

We walked back to the car in silence, arms around each other. I was glad of the comfort she offered in a world that seemed increasingly hostile.

"What are we going to do, Charlie?" asked Michelle when we got to the car.

"Go home and think of another plan." I knew it wasn't the answer she was looking for, but it was the best I could do.

"Do you want to stop and get a drink on the way back?" she asked.

"Not really." I had too much on my mind to enjoy even the quietest pint. She started the engine and drove unsteadily out of the carpark.

"What's your father like?" she asked when we reached the tarmac of the lane.

"Hard for me to say really. I've only met him three times. Has yours always been around?"

"Pretty much. I remember mum taking me out into the forest to meet him when I was little."

I felt a stab of jealousy. "When did you start seeing him on your own?"

"I was around eleven, I guess. He taught me my own song to call him. He always seemed happy to talk to me."

"I wish I'd had that. I could have so done with someone to talk to when I was a kid. Did he come most times when you called?"

"I think so. That's why it's so strange that he won't come now."

"It must be that he can't. Lord Faniel's men are guarding the portals or something."

We reached the main road. While we waited for a gap in the traffic, two fire engines came roaring up from Totton, blue lights blazing and sirens howling.

"Do you think there's been another raid?" Michelle asked.

"It could be something completely unrelated. But yeah, I think there'll be more raids. There's no reason for them to stop."

She turned hesitantly onto the main road and I kept quiet as she negotiated the traffic. An ambulance on blue lights came speeding up from Totton in the middle of the road. Michelle had to pull in to the kerb to avoid it. My feeling that there had been another raid increased.

Another ambulance and a police van, both on blue lights, came through before we reached Michelle's place.

"Do you want a cup of tea?" asked Michelle as she locked the car.

"Yes, sure." There was plenty of time before my last train.

We hurried in out of the rain and I went to the bathroom while she put the kettle on. When I came out she was standing by the fridge holding a container of milk listening to the radio.

"There's been another raid," she said. "Out past Cadnam. It was just on Radio Solent."

"Oh shit." There didn't seem to be anything else to say.

She put down the milk and came close to me.

"Can you stay tonight?" she asked, in almost a whisper. "I really don't want to be alone."

I reached out to her and pulled her close. "Of course I'll stay."

She raised her face to me and we kissed until the kettle boiled but the tea never got made. She untangled herself just enough to lead me to the bedroom door and push it open. A freshly-made double bed took up most of the room. The room was tidy and there was no sign of anything that looked like it belonged to Dave the troll.

She released me to draw the curtains, put on the bedside light and then started to undress. With no theatricality she took off her black jumper, hung it on a hanger and then unclipped the light bra underneath. Her breasts were a surprise; the baggy jumpers and T-shirts had hidden a well-shaped pair with small dark nipples. She unzipped her jeans and slid them down her slim legs, carefully folded them and laid them on a chair. Finally she took off her dark green panties, tossed them into the wash-basket and turned to look at me.

I hadn't moved, my eyes caught by the dark triangle at the top of her thighs; it is possible my mouth may have been hanging open.

"Aren't you going to get undressed, Charlie?" She grinned at me, mischief in her eyes. "Would you like some help?"

She stepped around the bed, reached up and kissed me very gently on the lips. Her hands went to my waistband and unfastened my jeans. I jumped as her fingers touched my stomach.

"Ticklish?" She ran her hand upwards drawing my t-shirt with it and I raised my arms to help her take it off. I was quivering as her hands returned to my waist.

"Relax," she whispered and slid her thumbs into the waistband of my boxers. I held my breath as she slipped them down. I couldn't speak for fear of breaking the spell as I stepped out of my boxers. She turned back the duvet with one hand and drew me to her with the other. We lay back on the bed, her soft skin like warm velvet on mine.

"Turn off the light, Charlie," she breathed in my ear.

I slept much better this time, but still woke early. I was lying on my back with Michelle's head on my shoulder and my first thought was that I must have snored. Michelle was still asleep and I lay there in drowsy contentment enjoying her closeness and trying not to think ahead. Eventually I had to break the spell, get up and take a piss. Michelle was awake when I got back.

"You alright, Charlie?" She propped herself up on one elbow and brushed her hair off her face.

"Never better." Damn true; I felt like I'd swallowed a sunrise.

I climbed back in beside her and she plumped up the pillows so we could sit up and she settled herself comfortably against my chest.

"I knew you'd be nice when I first saw you," she said. "And I was right. How come you haven't got a girlfriend?"

"How do you know I haven't?"

"Cos you're too nice, you'd have said something."

Which begged the really big question. "What about Dave then?"

She was quiet for a while. "I've been with him since I was fifteen. He was my first boyfriend. He was nice at the beginning. I thought I loved him. But he's changed ever since he joined that gym. He's not interested in what I want; I'm just a possession to him. He was just horrible when Mum died."

There an edge of sadness in her voice so I gave her a squeeze to reassure her that she wasn't just a possession to me. She raised her head looking for a kiss so I helped her find one.

"What are you going to do if we get him back?"

"I don't know. He's not going to just let it go."

"We'll worry about that when we rescue them." Which at the moment seemed as remote as the moon.

"Let's not talk about that now. I've got to go to work in a couple of hours. We've got time for a bit of fun before then haven't we?" Her hand reached down to my groin.

I decided to go home, have a shower and a change of clothes; that would give me a bit more time to get my head together before I went to see Sharon. I floated down to Totton station with Michelle's parting kiss on my lips.

The house was empty when I reached Arnold Road for which I was grateful. My shelf of the fridge was empty too; Chloe must have thrown out my stuff which had gone off while I was away. I'd only had coffee and a slice of toast with Michelle so I had to go out again and make a trip to the supermarket. I knew now why she was so slim; she didn't eat anything.

After shopping, a shower and change of clothes, I cooked myself breakfast and then called Sharon.

She picked up within a couple of rings. "Charlie! Where are you?"

"Arnold Road. Just had breakfast. I was wondering what you're doing today? I'm presuming you're out of the hospital."

"Waiting to see you. I've been home for days. Sounds like there's a lot to talk about. When are you coming round?" She sounded like she was back to her old self.

"How about right now?"

"I'll put the kettle on."

It is two changes of bus, or a solidly long walk over to her place so I called a taxi, and didn't think it too extravagant to pay seven quid to get there in twenty minutes.

Sharon opened the door with a broad smile on her face and a new lighter cast on her left arm. We went into the kitchen and, scorning my help, she made coffee one-handed.

"So tell me about the other side." She passed me my coffee. "What's it like? What's going on over there?"

I sat on the sofa beside her and recounted my experience. Sharon kept her eyes on me, sipped her coffee and didn't interrupt.

"So it all revolves around this Lord Faniel?" she said when I'd finished.

"Right."

"Any way we can get to him?"

"Not without my father. We can't even talk to him because they speak a different language over there."

"I wasn't thinking of speaking with him."

"He's got a lot of people around him, some powerful magicians. It'd be very difficult to get anywhere near him without an intro."

She stared into the bottom of her mug while I drank my coffee. "Any idea how long we've got until their midsummer party?"

I shrugged. "It was twenty days away when I was there, but time moves differently between there and here. It felt like I was over there two or three hours, and I was gone four days. I'd guess we've got a few weeks."

"Shit, Charlie. I think we're screwed."

Much as Michelle had said but Sharon didn't start to cry, just clenched her jaw and looked determined. "You gotta plan?"

"Not much of one. I think I can use the gateway to get close to my dad. I could maybe take a rescue team through with me. I'd need a team though." I was hoping she might have some names for the team.

"You're right. That's not much of plan." She chewed her lip for a moment. "What about the other murder victims? Maybe someone close to them would know how to contact their Otherkin lovers."

"Longshot, but worth asking."

"I'll do some digging on Monday. Never know what I might run up."

"You making any progress with your boss?"

"A little. Forensics came back with confirmation of the hair samples matching from the murder sites and where the horsemen hit us. That's made him think, but he can't live with the conclusion yet. There's a lot of pressure going down. One of the farms that got hit belongs to the brother-in-law of a cabinet minister. The Chief Constable had the Home Secretary demanding a personal briefing on the situation."

"That's serious shit."

"Oh yes."

"It does mean he should be able to get whatever resources he needs though." A platoon of Royal Marines perhaps?

"Maybe. There's a lot of high level people he would need to convince first. That's not going to encourage him to stick his neck out."

"We need something more." I thought about it for a moment. "I could take him over there."

A moment of silence suggested she was seriously considering it. "Maybe. I'll look for a way to put it to him, but I want to come too."

"Fair enough." Thinking about it I wanted her along too; if only to keep DI Brown in order. "Can't do it yet though. Think about the time difference. It's like I just left an hour ago over there. They'll be stinking hairy beasts all around the gateway."

"That's OK. He's not ready to go for it yet. We can make sure we're tooled up to deal with them when it happens."

"Should at least convince him if he comes face-to-face with one."

"That would probably do it." She grinned at me. "Don't know what we'd need for the senior brass though. More coffee?"

She gathered up my mug and went to put the kettle on again.

"I spent a lot of time on the computer last week," she said. "Looking for what we've got on that dealer you turned up over Portsmouth way. There's surprisingly little for someone who seems like a major player."

I'd been so preoccupied with the problems of the Otherworld that Pete the scary dealer had slipped right off my radar.

"What did DI Scott say?"

"Hadn't heard of him, which I guess reflects what's in the database, but I'm still surprised. Said he'd ask around, but I could tell he wasn't that interested."

"Yeah? I'm surprised. I thought after we cleaned up Tommy Rowe he'd be well up for anything we put his way."

"Well yeah. But he's funny sometimes, very political. Maybe he thought I was trying too hard to raise my profile with his bosses."

"Were you?"

"No. Don't think so. Just doing my job. Doing what my objectives say I'm supposed to do, improve inter-functional links."

"Your boss didn't strike me as someone who'd be big on objectives?"

"No." Another grin. "But his boss is."

"What are you thinking of doing? Going after him yourself?"

"Can't easily do that, he's off my patch. I'll keep digging for a while. Might need you to read some people for me. I'm seeing Mike tonight, so I'll try to work on him."

The stolen memory of her last night with him flashed across the front of my mind, giving my stomach a little kick of remembered pain. I had no doubt tonight would finish up the same way.

"Yeah, of course, whenever." I remembered how scared Sally Parkes had been; someone who could inspire that level of fear needed to be stopped.

I left Sharon to get ready for her night out around six; Michelle got off work then and I wanted to give her time to wind down before I got there. I bought two bottles of wine at an off-licence on Shirley High Street then took a bus down to the Central Station and caught the train to Totton. I sent her a text from the bus to confirm I was coming and got a big smiley straight back.

Michelle answered the door in a big fluffy white dressing gown, her hair still damp from the shower. She closed the door before flinging her arms around me. I kissed her carefully as I still had a wine bottle in each hand.

"I was thinking about you all day," she said.

"Me too." Not completely true; I was thinking about scary bastard Pete the dealer some of the time.

"I was going to get a takeaway in tonight," she said over her shoulder as we climbed the stairs. "Is that OK?"

"Yeah, fine." If she'd said we were going to eat wallpaper tonight I'd have said yes. "I brought wine. I didn't know if you prefer red or white so I got both."

"I'll drink both."

She opened the door at the top of the stairs, candlelight spilled out and soft music played. I caught the scent of joss sticks as I stepped into the flat. She took the bottles from me and put the white in the fridge while I took off my jacket and trainers. She opened the red, poured two glasses and brought them over to the little sofa.

I snuggled down beside her. She picked up the phone.

"Let's order the takeaway now," she said. "Then we've got all night."

"So how come you've only just started seeing your father?" Michelle asked. We were lying naked on the sofa wrapped in a duvet watching the omnibus edition of 'Eastenders'.

"My mum kept me away from him when I was a kid."

"But why?"

"He wanted to take me over there."

"Really? Why?"

I paused for about a quarter of a second before deciding that I was going to tell her about my talent. After all we had just shared the best night of my life.

"Because I have a talent. I can do their magic." I tried very hard not to sound pleased with myself.

She pulled away from me and sat up. "What do you mean? What can you do?"

"I'm touch telepathic. I can read people's minds when I touch them."

"Show me."

"I can't. It doesn't work on you."

She stared at me with wide dark eyes. "Why not?"

"I don't know." I'd thought about this a fair bit, but reached no conclusion. "You're the only one, apart from my dad. So I guess you must have some magic that prevents it." She looked pleased. "With anyone else I can get what they're thinking with just a brief skin to skin contact."

"What's it like when you read someone's mind."

"I get everything they're thinking, but not in a controlled way, at least not yet. It's like sticking my face in front of a fire-hose, there's just so much stuff that comes at me. That's why I didn't have another girlfriend. I couldn't stop it happening."

"And it works on everyone?"

I nodded. "Even the recently dead. That's how I ended up working with Sharon."

"Wow! That's really weird. How did you get into that?"

I told her the whole story starting with me finding Karen; it took a while because she kept interrupting with questions. As I reached the end she went quiet and stayed that way when I finished explaining.

"You read mum, didn't you?" she said quietly. "That's how you knew what killed her."

"Yes I did. Sharon took me to the mortuary the morning they found her."

Michelle didn't speak; the brimming tears in her eyes spoke for her.

"It was very quick. One of her last thoughts were of you."

The tears brimmed over. There wasn't really anything I could say. I held her as she cried, trying not to remember her mother's last moments.

"Promise me, we'll get the people who did it," she whispered.

"I promise," I said even though I had no idea how I would keep it.

I would have stayed the night with Michelle, but she had an early start at the supermarket so I caught a train back to Swaythling. I got back to the house in Arnold Rd about half-past ten. Greg and Chloe were sitting in the kitchen eating a Chinese takeaway.

"Charlie! So you are still alive," said Chloe through a mouthful of spring roll. "We got your text. Where have you been?"

"Like I said I was with my mother." Not actually a lie. "There was some family stuff I had to deal with." Again, not actually untrue. "Then I was with Michelle."

"Ooh!" said Chloe. "Is this significant?"

"Yes. I think so." I tried to keep the grin off my face.

"You mean you've finally got a girlfriend?" said Greg.

I nodded and the grin took over.

"Cool," said Chloe. "When do we get to meet her properly?"

"I don't know. I've only just started seeing her. I don't want you guys frightening her off."

"As if we would!" said Chloe.

"Give it a few weeks then we'll see." I looked forward to a time when Michelle meeting my friends was the biggest thing I had to worry about. I just couldn't see how to get there from where I was.

My phone buzzed with a new message. It was from Michelle. I opened it. All it said was 'goodnight' followed by a line of kisses.

"Is that from her?" asked Chloe. I guess the smile must have given me away.

"Yeah. Just wishing me goodnight."

I left their grins and questions then and headed for my room feeling like I'd just scored the winner in the FA Cup Final.

CHAPTER 12

I got into the lab at my usual time and tried to pick up the threads of what I'd been working on. At ten thirty the Professor came into the lab and asked me to come to his office. His tone suggested this was not going to be a good-natured chat.

"Close the door and sit down, Charles. We need to talk about the future of you and your project."

He never called me Charles unless it was serious; filled with foreboding, I sat and waited as he tidied the scatter of papers on his desk. He squared off the stack and looked at me as if I was a well-precedented reaction that had failed to work.

"It's around this time of year I usually advise students to start applying if they want to post-doc abroad, until recently I was going to advise you to. You've done well so far, but something has changed in the last month and I'd like to know about it. I don't like my students taking unplanned absences, it disrupts the smooth running of the lab, and particularly don't like arguing with their mothers about it. What's going on, Charles?"

Where to start? Or more to the point, how much to tell? Not the whole truth for damn sure.

"Until about a month ago I'd never met my father." I paused, thinking of how to phrase it. "He's now established contact and I've been trying to spend time with him. It's been difficult. I grew up with a lot of anger about him." All true; I waited to see how he would respond.

He stared at his fingers for twenty seconds or so. "You're an adult Charles, doing a responsible job. It's down to you to resolve any issues you have with your father, and keep them out of the lab. It's called being professional. I can't write a reference to Buchwald or Carreira if I don't think you'll do a decent job for them." His American accent, picked up during his years at MIT, was stronger than usual. "You need to think very seriously about this and apply yourself. This is your career in science at stake."

He was right, which was annoying. "Yes, Prof."

"I want to see you taking more responsibility in the project. You need to read more and develop your own ideas."

"Yes, Prof." I thought I'd been doing that, but there was no sense in arguing the point.

"We wouldn't be having this conversation if I didn't think you were good enough, Charles. I'm glad to hear that you're still committed to your chemistry and haven't decided to become a financial analyst." The way he phrased it underlined his contempt. "Now what I would like you to do is go away and prepare three alternate strategies for the last stage of our synthesis, full referenced, and we'll talk them through on Thursday."

"Yes, Prof." That had sounded like the end of the conversation so I stood up.

"Oh and Charles, you will tell me about any more time off in the future, won't you?"

"Yes, Prof."

I walked back to the lab thinking about what he'd said. I hadn't really given much thought to the future beyond the immediate horizon of getting the hostages back, but clearly things weren't going to go back to the way they had been. One thing was certain though; I'd worked damned hard to get here, and I didn't intend to blow it now. I would still need a job when I finished the PhD, so I needed to dig in and work harder. The sort of pharma research job that sounded my best option needed almost as good a reference as a post-doc with a big name group, even contracting needed a solid one.

I honestly was resigning myself to an evening in the library when I got Michelle's text. She had bought the stuff to cook me dinner and wanted to know what time I would be there, so the literature would have to wait. I thought that we should go out to Netley Marsh and try to call our fathers again too. In the meantime there was a backlog of reactions to be cleaned up.

It was just past six when I left the campus. I called Michelle to tell her I was heading out to Totton. She hurried me along by telling me what she would do when we were alone.

I had just reached the end of Arnold Road when my phone rang. I pulled it out and looked at the screen, 'unknown number'.

I keyed answer. "Hullo?"

"Charlie?" I didn't recognise the voice.

"Yeah. Who's this?"

The call cut off. I stood staring at the phone in confusion.

A big black car pulled in beside me. Three big guys piled out. They were on me before I realised what was happening. Two of them grabbed me by the shoulders. One I vaguely recognised took my phone. A red panel van pulled up beside the car. The side door opened, they dragged me in and dumped me face down on the plastic sheet that lined the floor. Heavy weights immobilised my right arm and legs and a bag was pulled over my head. The door slammed shut and the van accelerated away. I felt something cold and sharp against my neck.

"You just shut up and sit still," one of them said.

I did exactly that, my heart thumping like crazy. The van slowed for a junction and I kept very still. I remembered where I recognised one of the guys from; Sally Parkes' stolen memories. He was one of the minders that worked for Pete the scary dealer.

The realisation hit me like a litre of liquid nitrogen. These guys were utterly ruthless, the fact that they had snatched me off the street in broad daylight showed that, and they had killed before. Little Welsh Robbie, poor bastard; Sally's memories supplied the name and the epitaph.

I lost it for a while, a fit of shaking took me and I pissed myself. The guys holding me laughed, but didn't loosen their grips and the van drove on.

I have no idea how long we drove for, it could have been an hour. Long enough that I passed through blind panic and raw terror to a place where I could think clearly about how to survive this. Not that I came up with much; run like hell first chance I got was the best I could do.

The van braked, changed gear, turned and then carried on

in low gear up a much rougher road. After about five minutes it stopped. I heard the side door open. Then I was dragged out by my legs. I hit the ground with a thump that knocked the air out of my lungs. The bag was snatched from my head and I looked up at my surroundings.

We were in a clearing, trees all around, very quiet not even birdsong. I eyed the three men and the woods beyond. They were big bulky guys; I reckoned I might be faster across the ground, but first I had to get past them. I backed away from them and thought for a moment of rolling under the van, but decided I wouldn't be quick enough to get away.

"Get up." The biggest guy growled and kicked me hard in the ribs.

It hurt like hell and I yelled out in pain. He bent down to grab me. I twisted away from him and caught his meaty wrist with my right hand just below the 'Pompey til I die' tattoo. The instant his thoughts reached me I pushed them back, thrusting my anger, pain and terror into his mind. He gasped; his eyes opened wide showing white all around the iris then rolled back into his head. I kept pushing; squeezing his thoughts down into darkness just as I had done with the young Otherkin soldier, but this time it was a conscious act. I held onto him as he collapsed sideways, almost falling across me, his consciousness draining away under my pressure.

Then I was up and moving. The other two guys were standing open-mouthed. I dodged past them and sprinted for the woods. There was a narrow path leading from the clearing into the trees, I pelted down it for all I was worth. There were a series of loud pops behind me, something went crack past me and split a tree branch a few feet off the path. It took me a moment to realise they were shooting at me.

I dodged off the path to try and put something solid between my back and the guns. It was dark under the trees and there wasn't much undergrowth, just lots of fallen timber; big enough to trip over but not hide behind. I swerved around the larger trees and crashed through banks of green bluebells a week or so from flowering. The ground rose ahead of me to a ridge, by the time I'd reached the crest my chest was burning.

I risked a glance behind me hoping that my pursuers would be a long way behind. They weren't, they were about forty yards back; too busy with trying to catch me to shoot at me. I put my head down and tried to speed up and ignore the stitch in my side.

The ground fell away from the ridge more steeply on this side and there looked to be more undergrowth at the bottom. I zig-zagged my way down the slope knowing that a trip could be very costly.

One of the guys behind obviously thought it would be quicker to come directly down the slope and cut me off. I heard a yell and breaking wood then he tumbled past me to finish up about ten yards away in a bush. He landed pretty hard; I hoped he'd done himself serious damage, but he got up and launched himself at me. His fingers skimmed my shoulder, but I twisted away from them and ran. He must have taken some damage because I got clear of him easily enough, but it had cost me time and his mate was much closer now.

There was a faint path leading up the little valley. I sprinted up it, lungs burning, wishing I'd been more diligent about going to the gym. There was another pop; a bullet cracked past me and hit a tree. I could hear the guy behind me snorting and gasping for breath and expected him to tackle me at any moment. I really, really needed something good to happen like him tripping over a tree root or getting attacked by a rabid fox or running into a couple of dogwalkers. Why weren't there any dogwalkers around? There's dogwalkers in every wood in England, why not here?

There was more cover around me as I got further up the valley, but the guy was still too close behind for me to consider trying to hide. I swerved around a clump of holly trees and saw my salvation shining blue right in front of me. Hanging in the air between two trees was a portal. I ran straight for it; my pursuer still close enough behind me that I could hear his gasping breaths.

The chill washed over me as the light died away and the random rushing filled my mind. I was close to puking with the effort, but some part of my brain worked enough to remember that I couldn't use the portal that led to my uncle's farm. I grabbed onto the image of Jack as I'd last seen him and held that in my mind as I stumbled forward.

I collapsed out of the portal and lay gasping on the ground trying to get enough air into my lungs. The extra sweetness of the air and the kick in my spirit told me I'd made it through. I was still in woodland but it was night-time dark and there was silvery light in the sky somewhere ahead of me. I wondered briefly what had happened to my pursuer; had he run into the portal, or was he standing in the wood back in Hampshire wondering what the fuck had happened? Not that I cared that much; he hadn't followed me so that was all that mattered.

After a few minutes I had recovered enough to sit up. Nothing much was making any sound near me so I reasoned that this portal was unguarded. I should probably have gone straight back through the portal to mother's, but I wanted to see if I could find Jack and the silvery light intrigued me.

I pushed my way slowly and cautiously through the trees; just because I hadn't heard anything wasn't any reason to start making a row. The light grew stronger until I came through the screen of trees and saw the source.

About five hundred yards away rising from sweeping lawns, a palace shone with crystal light like a chandelier. Silver walls shimmered, impossibly pointed towers twinkled against the velvet sky, and flute music flowed gently through the night air. I stood open-mouthed in amazement; this was like a Disney version of Fairyland. The contrast between it and my uncle's farmhouse was just too big to take in, then the penny dropped; it was an illusion. Somebody was pouring an awful lot of effort into one huge glamour. I wondered what it really looked like, probably wooden and thatched.

Somewhere in there was Jack, the portal wouldn't have brought me here if he wasn't nearby and I had no idea of how to find him. I couldn't see an entrance or doorway from here, but that didn't mean there wasn't one. There were no guards patrolling that I could see but, I presumed, there would be wards and other magical barriers against intruders. I remembered what Jack had said about the hostages: 'they are guarded by only a few men, but if they carry a compulsion they cannot leave'.

Would that apply to him too? I wished I could ask him; then it occurred to me that I did have a way of getting in touch with him.

I sat down at the foot of a tree and began to sing his summoning song. I figured it might take a while for him to wake up and respond if he could, so I kept singing the tune over and over, all the time watching the palace. Keeping the rhythm of it going against the insidious music of the glamour gave me continual difficulty.

I was singing a long time before I saw the figure making his way down towards me. He was halfway across the lawn when I first saw him; perhaps that is where he emerged from the spell that wove the illusion of the palace. A huge slab of anxiety slid off me at the sight of him.

I stood up and hurried out to meet him.

"What are you doing here, Charlie?" His face seemed strangely colourless in the silver light. "How did you get here?"

"I was being chased through the woods and I found a portal. It brought me here. They would have killed me."

"Who was chasing you? Did they follow you?" He glanced over his shoulder at the palace. "We should not be out in the open like this. This is not a safe place for you."

"Drug dealers. Criminals back home. They didn't follow me. They wouldn't be able to see the portal or understand how it works."

"That's one less trouble then. Come, let us get out of plain view. Lord Faniel's men ride tonight, we would not wish to meet them."

I certainly didn't want to meet them again without a machine gun in my hands. We hurried into the cover of the trees. "This is as far as I may go," said Jack.

"Why? What do you mean?"

"This is the limit of my prison. Lord Faniel himself laid the compulsion on me to remain within sight of the palace."

"Oh right. So they caught you? Are you alright?" He looked undamaged, but that could be a glamour.

"I'm unharmed." He shrugged. "It is not possible to evade the Great for long."

"How come you're here? Aren't they guarding you?"

"No. So far I am free to do as I please within my prison. Lord Faniel thinks that I can do nothing to hinder him if I cannot leave the palace. They do not have the resources to guard me full time."

"Have you seen the hostages?"

"I have. They are at the palace."

"Can you take me to see them?" Maybe something useful could come out of this fucked-up day.

"They are guarded."

"I thought they would be. I need to get a look at where they're being held, and how many guards there are."

There was a pause before he spoke. "What is in your mind?"

"Rescuing the hostages. Bringing an army through that portal and getting them out." An army was a bit of an exaggeration, but the rest was serious.

"They will carry compulsions against leaving."

"How do we deal with that?"

He didn't reply immediately.

"We're running out of choices," I said. "If we do nothing they die."

"Without the person who laid the compulsion, it is hard to remove," he said without looking at me, his face hidden in shadow.

"But it can be done? Can you do it?"

Another pause. "It depends who laid the compulsion, but some of them, most of them, I could remove."

"Then that's what we have to do. We bust them out, bring them to you, you remove the compulsion and then we take them home." That made it sound easy, which I was pretty sure it wouldn't be; busting them out was sure to involve fighting.

"This puts me in danger," he said, still not looking at me. "I cannot leave here, and it will go hard for me if Lord Faniel learns that I did this."

"Can you hide from him?"

"Here? No."

"What about the King?"

He shook his head. "He's a dying man. He has strength for nothing."

"But would he stop Faniel if he wasn't ill?"

"Yes, I think so. He steered us away from tangling with your world."

"Then he is our way to deal with this." I remembered mother's theory about his heart condition which looked pretty sound in the light of the Google searches I'd run. "If we can get him to come over, the doctors in my world will be able to give him another ten years or more. Do you think he would come? Could you convince him?" This sounded marginally easier than convincing a medic from home to come here.

"Your people can truly do this?" I could hear the wonder in his voice.

"If I'm right about what's wrong with him, then yes. He would be almost back to his old strength. My grandfather had it done. It's a common thing." Provided we could get someone to pay for it, of course.

"He would regain a measure of his strength? Then I think he would come. Who would not wish to live for another ten years?"

"Can you get to him to ask him?"

"Yes. They know who I am. The queen is…a cousin."

"Then that's the plan. Could we go and see them now?"

"In the middle of the night? No, let me pick the time. It is important that this is done the right way. But now would be a good time to look at the prisoners. I will conjure a glamour to conceal you from the guards. Do not speak if they come close."

We stepped out from the cover of the trees and walked up the grassy slope towards the palace.

"What do you see?" He asked me.

"A huge palace with silver walls and pointed towers. A glamour, I guess, but it's a good one."

"It is a glamour. Once it was the work of one man to cast it, now it takes three. You do well to recognise it, but it is a fine building none the less."

He lead me around to one side of the palace with the, by now annoying, music following us all the way. It all still appeared to be silver and crystal, though I suspected we were walking through outbuildings and storage sheds. A couple of times he pulled me into the shadows before patrols of gwasannath walked past. I don't know how he knew they were coming; I hadn't even smelled them and would have walked straight into them.

He halted us at the corner of a building. We peeked around the corner at a two-storey building some fifty yards away that faced onto a wide grassed open area.

"This is as close as we dare go." He pointed at the human guard armed with a short spear and leather breastplate slouching in front of the double doors that appeared to be made of opal. "This is the Royal stables. There wasn't any other building large enough to put them in. All the horses have been moved out."

"Is this the only way in?"

"No, there's a door at the back that leads to a midden, and there's also an entrance to the hayloft up above."

"Is he the only guard?"

"Wait." We waited huddled against the wall.

Boots crunched on gravel and two more guards appeared around the corner of the stable block and approached the spearman. There was a brief conversation before the spearman changed places with one of the new arrivals and the two marched off again around the block.

"That's all there is to see. They'll be back around soon."

He turned away from the stable block and I followed him back across the palace grounds towards the portal.

"What will you do when you go back?"

Where to begin? "I have an army to gather, and I have to deal with the people who tried to kill me. That's just for starters. I'll probably be back here soon, later today even, figuring for how time runs differently here. There're people who'll need to see this before they'll believe it's real. A look at that palace should do it. Will you be able to slip away and meet me?"

"Who knows?" He shrugged. "Possibly. I don't think that portal is watched, but I could be wrong."

Whatever I was going to say next was lost as he yelled. "Get down!" and dropped to the turf. As I followed there was a flash of blue light and, a few seconds later, the thunder of hooves.

"Keep your head down." He must have known I was about to take a look at what was happening.

The thunder ceased, voices called out in triumph and laughter; the cavalry had returned after another successful raid. The glamour Jack had woven worked well enough, or perhaps the horseman had no mind to be watchful, and after a couple of minutes they trotted off towards the palace.

"Fuck! What was that flash?" I asked once they were out of sight

"One of the Great opening the way. There are few now who still have the power to open such a gateway."

"Like the portals we've been using?"

"No. Not at all, these work by a different kind of magic and exist for only a short time. No one knows how to create a lasting portal."

"Ah right. So where did the portals we use come from?

"Who knows? They've always been there." He stood up and looked around. "Clear enough, they've gone."

"With more prisoners for the party?"

"Probably. Lord Faniel has lost sight of all sense in this. He and his circle have no thought for the consequences."

We walked towards the portal glancing frequently over our shoulders in the direction of the palace. Nothing disturbed us and we reached the edge of the woods in a few minutes. I turned to Jack, short of something to say. He reached out and took my hands.

"You should go now, Charlie. Your mother is calling to me. Tell her how it is over here."

I nodded then he turned and walked back towards the palace.

"You be careful," he called over his shoulder.

I watched him go for a minute before going into the woods back towards the portal, within a few yards I could see its soft blue light shining through the trees. I hurried to it and took a moment to think of mother and her cottage before I stepped through the shining blue oval.

I stepped out into full daylight and could immediately hear my mother singing somewhere nearby. I hurried down to meet her by the river where I knew she would be.

I couldn't move as quietly as Jack through the undergrowth, so she was on her feet and moving towards me when I saw her. She screamed, dropped her pickaxe handle and broke into a run as soon as she saw me.

"Charlie!" She caught me up in a wide hug and gripped me so firmly I could scarcely breathe. "I've been worried half to death."

I wondered how long I'd been gone; hadn't seemed a long time, but then on the evidence of my last trip it was probably days. "What day is it?"

"Wednesday," said mother, easing her grip on me.

Shit, the whole of Tuesday, and more gone in what felt like an hour or so over there.

"Where've you been, Charlie?"

"Over there. I saw Jack."

"Your friend Sharon came to see me. You didn't tell me she was in the police." There was a warning in her quiet restrained tone. "What have you been doing, Charlie? She said they'd had a report of someone getting dragged into a van near your place. Someone who looked like you."

"I've been helping her with some stuff."

"Is there a connection?"

"Yes," I said reluctantly. I knew I wouldn't get away with anything less than full disclosure. "I was grabbed by a bunch of guys who work for a big drug dealer who's one of her targets. I got away from them and went through a portal." That made it sound much easier and less frightening that it had been.

"Big drug dealer? That sounds very dangerous, Charlie." She shook her head. "I don't like people knowing about what you can do. You shouldn't have told her."

"I didn't have much choice."

"How come?"

I gave her a brief rundown of how I'd read poor Karen and incriminated myself with my statement.

"So she trapped you into telling her?"

"I suppose so, but it was my choice to keep working with her. I wanted to do something useful with it."

"And see where it's got you. Onto a drug dealer's deathlist."

She turned away and walked determinedly towards the path. After a moment I followed her. We headed towards home in single file along the riverbank; the ground was damp and slippery from recent rain. I wished I was wearing boots like her.

"You saw Jack over there?" said mother when we reached the track.

"Yeah, I did. He's…er…confined."

"What does that mean? Is he alright?"

"He's fine. He just can't go anywhere out of sight of the royal palace. It's a compulsion they laid on him."

"So he can't get away at all?" said mother.

"No. Not until the compulsion is removed, but he can walk around the palace and the grounds. He heard you calling and asked me to tell you how things are over there, and why he couldn't come."

"I guess I'll forgive him for not turning up this time then." The way she said 'this time' made me think there had been plenty of other times.

We reached the track and marched for home. As I trailed behind her, I hoped mother wouldn't ask me to stop working with Sharon. I wasn't going to, but I didn't want to go against her wishes.

We reached the cottage and mother reclaimed the key from under the geranium pot. She went inside while I paused to take off my muddy trainers. My hand went instinctively to my pocket for my phone to call Michelle and Sharon, then I remembered who had it.

"Bollocks." Without my phone I didn't know Michelle's number or Sharon's.

I went into the kitchen where mother was putting the kettle on. She turned to look at me, tears streaming down her face.

"Oh Charlie. I thought I'd lost you. When Sharon told me about you getting dragged into a van, I thought you were gone."

She reached out, wrapped her arms around me and hugged me, reminding me of my bruised ribs. I felt awkward as I held her; she'd never done this before, and it was an uncomfortable reminder of how high the stakes were and how close I'd come to the edge. I clung on to her for a couple of minutes before she composed herself.

"Have you told Sharon you're back?" she asked.

"No. They took my phone. It's got all my numbers on it, I can't remember hers."

"I've got it. She left me a card. Now where did I put it?"

She poked around in a couple of drawers before finding it under a shopping list secured to the fridge door by a lobster-shaped magnet.

Sharon answered after half a dozen rings.

"Charlie! Where are you?" she practically screamed down the phone.

"I'm at my mother's."

"Stay where you are. I'll come and get you."

"Yeah. Ok. Why?"

"We'll talk about this later. I'll need a full statement. First I gotta phone the boss and let him know you've turned up. I'll see you in an hour." She ended the call before I could ask her for Michelle's number.

Sharon took a lot less than an hour to get to us; thirty five minutes which means she pushed her luck hard along the A326. During that time I told mother about what I'd seen: the shining palace, how the prisoners were guarded and how Jack was. It seemed like no time at all before Sharon arrived.

"Charlie, thank God you're safe," Sharon said as soon as she saw me. Mother glared at her but she still hugged me.

"I was so worried about you, Charlie," she whispered.

"With good reason." I said quietly, not wanting mother to hear. "They had guns."

"Doesn't surprise me," she said after a pause.

"That's very touching now," said mother. "But you put him in danger in the first place."

"What?" Sharon couldn't have been more surprised if mother had slapped her, which she looked about ready to do. "I didn't do anything."

"Right! You didn't do anything to protect him from a dangerous drug dealer."

"It wasn't like that," said Sharon.

"Really? Well let me tell you what it looks like from here," said mother. "It looks like you've exploited him and his talent very nicely then hung him out to dry when the going got tough."

"No. That's not what happened," said Sharon.

"No it isn't," I said, deeply embarrassed at what mother was saying. "You're wrong. I put myself up for doing it."

"And what choice did you have?" said mother. "That, or a murder charge?"

"No, it was my choice," I said. "It was always my choice."

"Really? Then I want you to stop."

"But what he's doing is really important," said Sharon.

"Your opinion doesn't count," said mother. "In fact, I think you should leave."

Sharon took her car keys out of her pocket and looked at me. The decision wasn't hard to make. I moved towards my muddy trainers beside the door.

"Where are you going?" asked mother.

"With Sharon." I bent down, turning my back to her, and put on my trainers. I felt like I was sixteen again and didn't want to make eye contact with her. "I'll call you when I've got a new phone."

I didn't bother to tie up my laces and walked out to Sharon's car without looking back. Sharon got in and started the engine. We didn't speak until we reached Blackfield crossroads.

"You OK, Charlie?" she asked.

"I'll live," I said. "It's only because she's scared. It makes her angry. She'll be fine in a day or two. We've had much worse arguments." Which was true, but I'd hoped they were all behind us.

"You don't think I'm exploiting you then?"

"No. I wouldn't be here if I did, would I?"

"Good. Why don't you tell me what happened then? You'll need to give a full statement later, but I need to know what happened now."

"OK, but can I borrow your phone first. I want to give Michelle a call. I was supposed to be going to see her when they grabbed me and they took my phone."

"That could be handy if they've still got it."

"Doubt it. Probably long gone. These guys knew what they were doing."

"Maybe. What makes you connect them to a dealer? You're talking about Pete from Portsmouth, right?"

"I recognised one of them from Sally Parkes's memories. He left a big impression on her."

"OK. Phone's in my bag. Her number should be in the address book."

I dragged her bag off the backseat, found the phone and flipped it open. Michelle's number was in the address book.

She answered on the third ring.

"Hi Michelle. It's Charlie." Her reply was an incoherent happy squeal.

"I'm okay, but a lot's happened. I'm using Sharon's phone because mine was stolen."

"Where've you been? I was so worried."

"It's a long story. I'll e-mail you the full version, but I was over there for a bit. I've seen where they're keeping the hostages."

"When can I see you?"

"I don't know, soon." I felt reluctant to say more in front of Sharon, even though we were now just friends. "I'll call you when I know more, I promise." I ended the call feeling that I had so much more to say, but now wasn't the time.

Sharon kept her eyes on the road. "So tell me what happened."

I told my story, from my leaving the lab on Monday, trying to leave nothing out. Sharon didn't interrupt but frowned a lot.

"You sure these guys belonged to Pete?" she said, when I'd finished.

"Like I said, I recognised one of them from Sally Parkes' memories."

She pursed her lips and frowned again.

"What bothers me is why grab you now? You haven't gone anywhere near him. He doesn't know about you."

"He must do. I remember I got this weird phone call just before they grabbed me. My phone rang. I didn't recognise the number and someone said 'Charlie' then rang off when I said 'yes'. Then they grabbed me."

"Be pretty easy to find out the number that call came from, but where did they get your number?"

"Good question. My friends have it, but it's not like it's on my Facebook page."

"Which makes it a problem, least ways I think so. I think I know why they chose now to grab you. I think it was because I started digging into the files and asking questions. The timing fits exactly."

"So what are you saying?"

"Someone passed the information on and I think I know who. I'd like to be wrong, but I don't think I am."

"Who?"

"Mike Scott. He's the only person I've told about you."

I felt a brief stab of anger at his name; that made a nasty kind of sense. "Where did he get my number?"

"It's in the system, Charlie. It'll be tied to the statements you made. It wouldn't be hard for him to find it."

"So what're you gonna do?"

"I don't know." She fell silent for a while and I didn't intrude on her thoughts. "I don't think he's dirty. He probably got trapped by doing something outside the guidelines that he's being threatened with now and he can't get out. If I go to the internal investigators they'll turn him inside out then hang him out to dry. I think...hope he deserves better than that. It's difficult because we've been more than friends."

Which I knew only too well. "I should be able to tell you how dirty he is."

"He knows about your ability. He was interested in using you on an operation, so I told him. I'm sorry, Charlie." She sounded sorry too.

"He knows I have to be able to touch people to get information. Doesn't mean he can stop me."

"Would you do that, Charlie? Maybe we can find him a way out."

"Depends on how dirty he is." My memory of Pete's crew plus that surge of anger had left me disinclined to be sympathetic. "He set me up. How dirty is that? Those guys weren't messing around."

"We don't know what he did, or how much he knew about what they were going to do. Maybe I'm wrong, but I still think he's a good copper."

I tried to moderate my inner caveman. "Then we need to find out before we make any other plans."

"OK. But here's the thing, you can't go back to your house in Arnold Road. They may try again."

I hadn't thought of that.

"Shit! Where can I go?" Greg had already established how flexible our landlord was about our rental contract; having to rent somewhere else too would put a severe strain on my finances. I quickly ran through a list of my mates who might have crash space and came up blank. "I don't have anywhere else to go. I have to get to the lab every day. I just got a bollocking from Prof about my attendance and this isn't going to help."

We drove on in silence for a minute or two.

"I've got a spare room at mine," said Sharon.

"Are you sure?"

"Yeah." Sharon smiled a tight little smile. "You're house-trained aren't you?"

"I'll need to go back to Arnold Road and pick up some stuff," I said. "And talk to my housemates. How long am I going to need somewhere else?"

"Could be a while," said Sharon. "Until he loses interest in you, or we put him out of business."

"So how long's that going to be? Have you got enough to go after him?"

"Nothing like enough." Sharon shook her head. "Best place to start is to find the phone that made the call to you just before you were snatched. I can look at footage from the traffic cameras too, see if I can identify the van they used. Then see if I can find anything to tie it to them. You can look at the photos on file. There ought to be something on Pete's known associates."

"That sounds pretty low level."

"That's the only way it's going to happen," said Sharon. "So much resource is going into these cavalry raids, everything else is on hold."

"But they tried to fucking kill me."

"And they've probably killed before. We know of at least one person who was probably killed by them."

"That's not reassuring."

"Best I can do."

I looked at her profile as she drove and regretted the harshness of my tone; if she was going to put me up in her flat then the least I could do was to speak nicely to her.

"Did you find out how long we've got left while you were over there?" she asked.

"Bollocks no! Clean forgot. I did see where they're keeping the hostages though, and it isn't heavily guarded."

"You think it's still viable to go in and pull them out?"

"Yeah, and there's more. How difficult would it be to arrange for someone from over there to get a heart bypass here?"

"I've no idea." She paused as she thought about it. "It would have to go a long way up. Why?"

"That's the way to stop the raids. I told you the guy behind them is Lord Faniel. He's the heir to the throne, and his father, the King, is sick. It sounds like he's got a heart condition, and hasn't got the strength to control Lord Faniel. My father reckons he could be persuaded to come over here for treatment. If we can sort him out, then he can go back and take control."

"I've no idea who could authorise it. Chief Constable maybe? Or Home Office."

"It's got to be cheaper than all the police overtime that's going into investigating the raids."

"For sure, but it's on a different budget. Maybe in the past senior officers had slush funds to do stuff like this but they don't now. It's all too closely monitored."

"Somebody must be able to make it happen."

"I'll try to find out who, but they'll take some convincing."

"I think I can show them something over there that'll be pretty convincing." Even if it is an illusion.

"Could be a whole committee."

"Perhaps we should run a coach tour."

Sharon laughed; a welcome break in the serious atmosphere.

"Has your boss, or anyone, got any closer to accepting what's really going on?"

"No one has said anything to me."

"But someone must be questioning the existing theories."

"Maybe, but no one's prepared to stick their neck out."

"Shit! What does it take?" I thought for a moment. "Know any journalists?"

"Yeah," she said cautiously. "Don't know that I'd trust any of them. That's a risky way to go."

"I think we have to take some risks otherwise the hostages are dead."

"Yeah." She paused. "Let me think about it."

"I could get in touch with them directly, leave you out of it."

"The ones I know wouldn't take you seriously."

I wondered if that was entirely true, but decided not to pursue the point just now. We went past the turn-off for Totton which reminded me about Michelle. The thought of her gave me a solid dig deep in my groin and I wondered if I would be safe spending time with her. I didn't think there was any way Mike Scott could know I was seeing her, but the last thing I wanted was to lead Pete's crew to her.

Chloe and Greg were in when we got to Arnold Road and were all over me in an instant demanding to know what was going on. I didn't want to tell them and Sharon dug me out of the hole by saying it was an operational matter, but I had to promise the full story later.

I collected a few changes of clothes and my laptop and found the insurance paperwork for my phone. I could always come back for more if I needed to, not that I had a lot. I hoped it wasn't going to be for too long. I like to have my own space sometimes and crashing with Sharon wasn't going to be like sharing a student house.

"Is that all you're bringing?" said Sharon when I came downstairs.

"You want me to bring more? I can go and get some."

"No. You'll do as you are."

I put the gear in the car and left Greg and Chloe with a promise to get in touch tomorrow.

It was just short of ten o'clock when we got to Sharon's flat. Her spare room was surprisingly tidy; three or four plastic storage crates, labelled with their contents, stacked in one corner, the bed already made up.

"Nice room," I said. "Have you got a wireless network?"

"I swear I'll never understand blokes," said Sharon, hands on hips. "Here you are in a girl's bedroom for the first time, and all you want to know about is the wireless network."

She looked at me, her head tilted to one side, and I recognised the challenge in her eyes. I remembered her suggestion that we could still have some fun together, but now that I had Michelle the idea didn't appeal. It was a complication I didn't need, but I did need the network.

"So what's the password?"

"I'll write it down for you." The look was gone from her eyes and I hoped she wasn't too pissed off. "Do you want a coffee?"

"That would be nice, thank you."

Getting my laptop to talk to her network was surprisingly easy; I'd endured hours of frustration enough times before that the cybergods owed me and they paid up for once. I sat down to work my way through the accumulated e-mails, and then compose my message to Michelle.

"You hungry?" asked Sharon when she brought the coffee.

"Yes." I'd only had a sandwich at Mother's since I got back. The moment Sharon asked I was ravenous.

"What do you fancy? Pizza?" She passed me a menu from a takeaway.

I glanced down the list. "American hot. D'you want some money towards it?"

"No, my treat. I owe you a couple of meals at least."

She went to phone in the order and then set the table leaving me to my laptop. I started my message briefly setting out what had happened, then moved on to more detail about what I'd seen on the other side. I described the building and the guards holding the hostages and the King's illness. Then I outlined what I had talked over with Jack; bringing through a rescue team and bringing the King back here.

Set out like that it made clear the magnitude of the task before me: find a team competent to handle opposition and prepared to follow me through the portal, rescue the prisoners and organise an operation for the King. All within an undefined, but short, time, otherwise a load of people die.

Simple then!

Except I had no team, almost no one believed me about the existence of the Otherworld and I didn't know any cardiac surgeons. Oh, and a major drug dealer wanted me dead.

I read the message back, changed a couple of words, then the doorbell rang.

"That sounds like dinner," called Sharon from the kitchen. I read the message through once more, added a line about seeing her very soon and hit 'send'.

Sharon produced a bottle of red wine and we sat down to eat. I couldn't afford to be a connoisseur of takeaway pizzas, but this seemed a good one to me, though too small.

When it was finished we sat on the sofa with the rest of the wine watching trash TV. My head was too full with all the problems for me to follow what was on the screen. I closed my eyes to concentrate better.

"You should go to bed, Charlie."

"What? I'm fine."

"You were snoring."

OK, maybe she had a point; I blamed the red wine. I left her to the incomprehensible plotlines and went to my new bed.

CHAPTER 13

Sharon woke me with coffee just before seven.

"Did you sleep OK?" She sat on the end of the bed, her damp hair tied up in a towel, a dressing gown covering her only to mid-thigh. It was difficult to ignore that she had very nice legs.

"Like a log. This bed is better than the one at my place."

"Good, then you'll have plenty of energy. We've got a busy day ahead of us."

"So what's in our busy day, and does it include breakfast?"

"I can do you toast, there isn't enough milk for cereal. We can get something at the canteen down at Central. I need you to do a statement then we can look at some mugshots, and I'll see if we can track your phone."

"Guess I'll need a crime number for the phone insurance."

"We can do that too." She stood up. "Do you want a shower?"

"Yeah." Then I realised I hadn't brought a towel. "Got a towel?"

She looked at me pityingly. "Sure. In the cupboard beside the bathroom. There's shower gel there too." She left the room closing the door behind her.

Two slices of toast with a thin covering of low fat spread weren't my idea of breakfast, but it would have been out of order to say anything so I suppressed my hunger until we could get to the canteen. That seemed like a long time away once we got started on the statement in the interview room. Sharon was as thorough as before, even though she'd already heard the story a couple of times. We took an hour and a half to reach my escape from Pete's heavy crew.

"So what should I say here? That I escaped through a doorway into a parallel world?"

She thought about it for a minute. "Guess so. Anything you make up and gets disproved later fucks the whole statement."

"And talking about portals doesn't?"

Another minute's thought. "I think it's always better to tell the truth."

So I did. I typed it out exactly as I remembered it, we printed it out and I signed it.

"What now?" I asked. "And does it involve food?"

She looked at her watch. "Yeah. Trip to the canteen then we'll look at some pictures, see if you can identify those gorillas."

Fortified by coffee and bacon rolls we went to another office, Sharon logged on to the computer and pulled up a series of photos on the screen.

"Just tell me if you recognise anyone." She started scrolling through them.

A couple of dozen pictures went by, then I spotted him.

"That's one!" A big cold hand gripped my stomach as I stared at the jug-eared broken-nosed face.

"That's the guy who I..." How to describe it? What had I actually done? I couldn't answer that, but I hoped it had damaged him. "That's the guy who was in charge."

"You sure?"

"Yeah. Not going to forget him easily." The cold hand relaxed before it endangered my bacon roll.

"That figures." She clicked on a link and another page opened up. "Tony 'Tonka' Wheeler. Age thirty four, sometime amateur boxer and nightclub doorman, done time for assault. Nothing about him being an associate of Pete Murphy, which is kinda strange in itself. Right, let's see who he hangs out with, and if you recognise them."

I'd had much less of a look at the other guys and none of the pictures jumped out at me like Tony Wheeler's. We spent another twenty minutes looking at pictures of villains which produced nothing.

"Right. I need a cigarette break," said Sharon. "Then I'll get you a crime number and take you back to school."

It didn't seem worth responding to the school comment. "You could have a talk with my Professor, tell him what's been going on. That would help a lot."

"Guess I can do that. We informed him you were missing, so it won't be too much of a surprise."

"Thanks. Gets me off the hook."

It was half-eleven when I got to the lab. Sharon went off to talk to Prof and I logged on to pick up my e-mail. There was a reply from Michelle—one line: 'I just want to see you' signed off with a line of kisses. A warm glow of horniness started in my groin and spread up my body to my face where it bloomed into a broad grin before my brain squashed it with a reminder of the practicalities of seeing her alone. Then one of my labmates came in and instantly demanded to know where I'd been. I hate lying to my friends even though I've been doing it most of my life, so I fended off the questions by saying it was a police matter and I couldn't talk about it now, which didn't satisfy him one bit. I knew I faced a dozen similar conversations through the day.

Prof came in about fifteen minutes later and took me to one side where we couldn't be overheard.

"DS Wickens has told me how you've become involved in an important police operation, and I want you to know that time is not a problem. If you have to be absent from the lab, I understand. I hope it resolves soon and we can have you back full-time. Be careful, we don't want to lose you, and if you need to talk then my door is always open."

I was so surprised that all I could do was gurgle 'thank you' as he left the lab. I wondered what Sharon had said to him.

I had lunch in the canteen and spent the afternoon cleaning up a reaction and trying to get some sense out of my insurance company and phone provider while thinking about how to raise a rescue team. My initial idea had been to ask some of Greg's role-playing mates, but the problem was they knew too much. I'd hung out with these guys and some of them were serious scholars of medieval warfare. They'd done courses on medieval swordsmanship, and knew all about the damage a bronze sword could do. They simply wouldn't go for anything that risked real fighting against trained warriors; I could just hear them saying it. They could be useful for the planning though.

By six I had a gram and a half of product and the promise of a new phone tomorrow but no rescue team. Sharon hadn't made any arrangement about picking me up, but had given me a key so I joined the queue at the bus stop thinking that even Pete Murphy wouldn't try to grab me in a crowd. I was very keen to go and see Michelle; I sent her a text to see if she was free, but she texted back to say she was working until ten.

Sharon turned up at the flat just before seven alight with excitement.

"I think I've found someone who can cut through all the red tape and get things done. I got a call from the Chief Super when I got back from dropping you off. He told me this guy was coming to talk to me, and I should answer all his questions. He didn't say precisely who he works for, but he's some kind of spook. So he turned up and asked me a load of questions about when I got hurt by the cavalry. I told him everything, and said he really needed to talk to you. He said he wants to talk to you as soon as possible. That OK with you?"

"Oh yeah." Damn right it was; finally the prospect of someone in authority believing us.

She reached for her phone out of her bag; she took out a card along with the phone and keyed in a number. She turned away so I couldn't hear the conversation but it didn't last long.

"He'll see us now. He's staying at Jury's Inn. Let's go."

Fifteen minutes later we were in an anonymous room in the hotel. The man we'd come to meet was almost as anonymous as the room; average height, pale blue shirt, dark trousers, neat mid-brown hair. I guess you don't want intelligence officers who stand out in a crowd.

"Glad you could make it, Mr. Somes." He had no trace of a regional accent. "Call me Nigel. DS Wickens said you can shed some light on the attacks that have been occurring across the region recently. What can you tell me?"

I looked around for somewhere to sit down; Nigel had the only chair so I sat on the beige bedspread.

"The raiders are from a parallel world. They've been sent by the crown prince, Lord Faniel, as revenge. The missing people are being held hostage and they'll be killed at midsummer over there as a sacrifice to their gods." I watched his face as I spoke, but his expression didn't change.

"How do you know this?" he asked mildly. He wasn't taking notes so I assumed we were being recorded.

"My father comes from over there. He and my uncle told me. I've been over there. I've seen where they're being held." I tried to sound confident and authoritative, not sure I succeeded.

"You said these raids are revenge, revenge for what?"

"The killing of one of Lord Faniel's servants. Before the raids started there were a series of murders of women out in the country. They were killed by this servant after meeting lovers who'd come from over there. The night Sharon was injured we caught this creature and killed it, that's when the raiders first came through."

"Who's we?"

"Sharon and me. A girl called Michelle Maynard, her boyfriend Dave and three of his mates. Michelle's mother was the first murder victim. Dave and his mates got taken by the raiders."

"And what kind of creature was it you killed?" He might have been asking me what colour car I drove.

"Ape-like, nearly man-size, very strong. They found its hair at all the murder scenes didn't they?" I looked over at Sharon for confirmation.

"That's right," said Sharon.

"You saw this creature too?" asked Nigel, looking at her.

"Yes," said Sharon. "We caught it in a net, Michelle Maynard stabbed it. Then the cavalry came."

He was silent a moment as if absorbing the information, but nothing showed on his face; he would be a superb poker player. "The cavalry from…er…over there? How are they getting here?"

I too paused a moment to consider my reply. "There seems to be two ways to get here. They have magicians who can open a big, but temporary passage between the worlds. That's what the raiders use. But there are smaller permanent passages. I've used a couple of these smaller ones to go there."

"Is there any way to block them from coming?"

"Not directly that I know of, but we have a plan to remove Lord Faniel from power. His father, the King, is ill, but if we bring him over here and get him an operation then he can take charge again, and he'll stop the raids."

I looked for any sign of his buying into the idea; there was none.

"You said you've seen where the missing people are being held. Can you find it again?"

"Yes." A moment of inspiration struck me. "Do you want me to take you there?" If that didn't convince him nothing would.

"Is that possible?" Was there a flicker of enthusiasm?

I glanced at my watch. It wasn't yet eight; that gave us another hour's light.

"We can do it now if you want." I willed him to agree.

He also glanced at his watch. "No, that won't be necessary. Thank you for your time."

He stood up, went to the door and held it open. I didn't need to touch him to know that he hadn't believed a word. We walked back to the car in a deflated silence.

"He was never going to buy it, was he?" said Sharon as we drove away.

"I don't know. He didn't seem to react to anything much. I don't see what more we could have done. I told him everything and it wasn't enough. If he'd agreed to go and see it then I don't see how he could've denied it."

"Did you notice how he avoided touching you? Didn't shake your hand, even though he shook mine. Did someone tip him off about you?"

"No. I didn't spot that." But I should have, I thought. "How many people know about me?"

"I don't know, there aren't many. Maybe it's nothing, but I've got a bad feeling about this."

We had to stop for a red light at the London Road junction. "Do you want to stop in Bedford Place and get a takeaway?" I'd been hungry before we came to see Nigel.

"If you want. I'm not really hungry."

I bought cod and chips, resisting the temptation to eat until we got back to the flat. Sharon went outside with a pack of cigarettes while I ate.

I'd finished and was washing up the plate when she came back in.

"The more I think about it, the more this smells like a stitch-up," she said, sounding grim.

"But I don't understand why?" I said. "Aren't they interested in finding out who's behind the raids. And what about the prisoners? They're gonna be killed."

"If they don't believe us about the raiders, then why would they believe the prisoners are going to be killed?"

"So we're not going to get any help getting them out?" I already knew the answer. "Know anybody who might want to come along?"

Sharon shook her head. "No one on the force'll touch it. Severely career limiting if it goes wrong. You got anyone?"

"Thought I might have, but it seems less likely now." I told her about Greg and the LARPers and my doubts about them getting involved.

"Why would they do it?" asked Sharon. "They've got no stake. They don't know any of the prisoners, and they won't get paid. I wouldn't do it if I were them."

"No. Now that you put it that way, neither would I. So we need someone who has got a stake." I thought about it for a bit. "How about Dave's mates from the gym and the security company?"

"They sound like a better bet. At least they know some of the prisoners, and they'll probably be more use than your student mates if things get ugly."

"Right. I'll look into getting in touch with them tomorrow. Michelle might well know some of them. I'll e-mail her tonight and ask."

"Do it. We're not going to get any official back-up unless we can show them way more evidence."

I would really have liked to talk to Michelle, but I wasn't getting a new phone until tomorrow and I didn't want ask Sharon if I could use hers, so e-mail it had to be. I retreated to my room, fired up my laptop and wrote her a long message describing the meeting with Nigel then asking about Dave's mates. I signed off with a line of kisses. I pissed around online for a while waiting to see if I would get a reply, but none came so I went to bed.

I didn't get my reply until I logged on in the lab next morning. Michelle's e-mail said she knew some of Dave's mates and the gym where they worked out. If I wanted to talk to them, I needed to get over there early in the evening because most of them would be working as it was Friday night. She reckoned six would be a good time. I replied to say I'd be at her place at half past five.

I left the department after the visiting speaker's lecture and caught the Unilink into the centre of town. By four o'clock I had my new phone. I sent texts to Sharon, mother and Michelle to let them know I was connected again, then headed for the station.

Michelle was so pleased to see me that we were a bit late getting to the gym. I'd rather expected that it would be a shiny new building with lots of glass and chrome, but it could hardly have been more different. When Michelle parked up outside it, I thought it was scruffy warehouse in a rundown industrial estate beside Eling wharf. There was no reception desk, just a pair of heavy duty rubber doors that I struggled to push through into a low ceilinged room. There were no mirrors or dance music playing, just a series of metal installations on a bare concrete floor filled with a dozen or so big guys moving lumps of metal around. It looked like an industrial workshop. No one paid us much attention for a while.

"Can I help you?" We turned to see an older guy with a shaved head wearing a grubby tracksuit over a Test Security t-shirt. His neck looked about three times thicker than mine. Behind him stood a much younger guy, maybe only nineteen or twenty, but still built like a brick shithouse. They must have come in the doors behind us.

"What do you want?" the older guy said when we turned to him.

"I want to talk to anyone who knows Dave and the other missing guys," I said.

"That's pretty much everyone." He waved a meaty arm to

the whole room. "You can talk to me. This is my gym."

I'd thought about how to approach this conversation and decided that direct was best. I also thought it would have come better from Michelle, but she insisted she didn't want to do it so it was down to me.

"We know where they are and we need a team to get them back."

"So why not go straight to the police?"

"They don't believe us," said Michelle.

"Why should we?" He'd clearly had a lot of practice at being the hostile doorman who kept out the undesirable punters.

"Don't." I said. "Just keep an open mind long enough for us to take you there."

He took a moment to think about it, but I didn't get the feeling that he was any closer to believing me. He just hadn't thrown us out yet.

"Where are they then?"

"You know all those farm raids that have been going on?" I really didn't think he could have been unaware of them considering the press and TV coverage. "It's the same people doing them have got the boys. And they're gonna kill them if we don't get them out soon, along with the people they took from the farms."

"And what's it got to do with you?" The hostility was back in his voice.

"I was there when they were taken. I'm the only person who knows where they are."

"Yeah, really? Well I think you're a nutter. Now piss off before I throw you out."

He was about three times the size of me so I wasn't going to argue. Anything more I said was just going to get me into trouble so I just shrugged and turned to push through the rubber door.

"Bastard," said Michelle when we got outside. "Now what?"

"Don't know. Go home and think about it, I guess."

We were halfway back to the car when there was a shout behind us.

"Hey, wait a minute." It was the younger guy running to

catch up with us.

"You're Craig's brother, aren't you?" said Michelle when he reached us.

"Yeah. I'm Warren," he said. "Look my mum's going crazy with worry about Craig. Police haven't done fuck all, we haven't even seen them for a week. I'll do anything to get him back. Do you really know where he is?"

"Yes," I said.

"And they're really going to kill him?"

"Yes."

"Well I'll come with you. Some of the other guys will come too. I'll get them. And you can take us there?"

"Yes," I said. "But you'll need a few hours."

He looked at his watch. "I've got to work tonight. How about tomorrow?"

"Sure." I said. "Name a time."

"How long we gonna need? I'm working again tomorrow night. Midday?"

"Midday's fine."

"I'll talk to the other guys. I'm sure some of them'll want to come."

"Great. Bring as many as want to come. We'll meet you here at midday."

"This had better not be a wind-up." He sounded desperate.

"You decide when you've seen it." I was pretty sure that the sight of the palace would prove convincing. "Do you want my number in case you need to change anything?"

"Yeah. OK."

We exchanged mobile numbers and then he walked back to the gym.

"See you tomorrow," I said to his broad back.

"Looks like we may have the beginnings of a team," I said as we walked to the Polo.

"I think a lot of them will come," said Michelle. "I recognised most of them there."

I was relieved more than pleased but she was right, it had gone pretty well from a most unpromising start.

We had just reached the Polo when my phone rang. I didn't

recognise the ringtone and was confused for a moment. I looked at Michelle, thinking it might be her phone.

"That's your phone isn't it?" she said.

I took it out feeling a bit of an idiot. The call was from Sharon though it was difficult to make out what she was saying because she sounded so distraught. In between sobs the words stitched-up, Nigel and bastard came through.

"Are you at home?" I asked. The reply sounded fairly close to yes.

"I'll be there as soon as I can," I said and ended the call.

"Can you drop me to the station," I said to Michelle.

"You got to go?" She pouted. "I was going to cook you that dinner I owe you."

"It'll have to wait. Something bad has happened to Sharon. I'm not sure what, but I need to go."

She pouted a bit more but opened up the car. It only took a few minutes to get to the station. There was a train due in five minutes so we had a goodbye kiss and I promised to call her when I found out what had happened to Sharon. I only just caught the train; the kiss went on longer than I'd planned.

On the short train journey and the longer bus ride I thought about what could have happened to reduce Sharon to incoherence. She usually seemed so sorted and cynical that I couldn't imagine anything getting to her that much, but something had.

The curtains in the flat were drawn when I got there which struck me as strange because we hadn't left them closed. I opened the door with the key Sharon had given me; the hallway was dark, but there was a subdued light on in the living room.

"Hello," I called out, wondering what the hell I was going to find.

A noise somewhere between a sigh and a mew came from the living room in reply. I closed the door and went in. Sharon lay flopped across the sofa, an empty bottle of vodka on the floor beside her.

I knelt beside her. "What's up?"

"I've been suspended pending psychiatric evaluation." She pronounced the words with exaggerated precision.

"That's my career screwed, Charlie." She started to cry.

I reached for her and held her as she wept; her anger and frustration washing through my mind. I wanted to pull back, to distance myself from her pain, but she needed me, so I found a place to put it where I could stand aside and it didn't hurt me. The anger helped; hers and mine, at Nigel who had stitched her up. I wanted to take him through the portal and leave him to the gwasannath.

I held her as she cried and thought murderous thoughts about Nigel for what felt like a long time then I gently lifted her head.

"How much of that bottle did you drink?"

"Most of it," she whispered. Not good news. I wondered whether to call an ambulance, or if she would be OK if I simply put her to bed. I decided to take the chance on putting her to bed. I'd need to stay with her in case she got sick, but it would save her further embarrassment and I'd seen mates who had drunk more just sleep it off. She'd feel like shit tomorrow though.

"I need you to stand up for me, Sharon."

"Where we going?"

"Bed."

"You goin' to fuck me?"

"Not in your state."

"Shame."

I got my feet under me and, with my arms around her chest, tried to lift her. I got her halfway up, but she sagged against me.

"I feel dizzy." I hoped she wasn't going to get sick.

"Put your feet down. You'll be OK when you can feel the floor."

She slid her feet off the sofa and would have fallen if I hadn't held on to her. With my support, she tottered to her bedroom and flopped onto the double bed face-up.

"Get yourself undressed; I'll be back in a minute." I thought it would be a good idea to have a bowl in case she got sick so I left her to find one. The nearest I could manage was the waste paper bin, I brought that and left it beside the bed.

She had managed to take one shoe off. I removed the other and thought about taking off her trousers. They were her good work trousers and would be badly creased if she slept in them.

I unfastened the waistband and put a hand in the small of her back.

"Lift up."

She raised her hips and sighed. I pulled the trousers down past her buttocks revealing black panties. I moved my hand to slide her trousers down her bare legs and her unfocused lust washed through my mind. I tried hard to push it into a corner, remembering my pain at her casual fling with Mike Scott, but it was strong and nearly overwhelmed me. I pulled the trousers over her feet and was glad to break the contact. I rolled her onto her side so that if she did vomit she wouldn't inhale it then hung up the trousers.

It was nearly eight by now and I was pretty hungry. Sharon wasn't going to be eating so I poured myself a big bowl of Rice Krispies and ate it sitting watching her. She was snoring gently by then; I shifted the duvet to cover her and went to watch TV for a bit. I sent Michelle a text to tell her Sharon was very drunk and I'd fill her in tomorrow

After an hour of getting up to check on her every five minutes I gave it up as a bad job, and climbed in beside her. I kept my clothes on to minimise the skin contact. She was far away over the midnight ocean and didn't notice. I cuddled up to her and put out the light.

I slept poorly, waking up frequently to check if Sharon was alright and hadn't thrown up. She slept through, and somewhere in the small hours as I chewed over what we could do I had a bit of inspiration.

I got up about seven and left Sharon to sleep on; it was clear that she was past any danger now but still had a massive hangover ahead of her. I fetched a jug of water, glass and a pack of paracetamol which I left on the bedside table for when she woke and went to make coffee. There wasn't much to eat beyond Rice Krispies so I had another bowl as I checked through my e-mail.

I clicked onto the BBC South website; the news headline was of another farm burned and people missing, Lord Faniel's followers without doubt.

Sharon was still snoring happily so I headed out to the shops to stock up; we needed more milk and Rice Krispies.

She was awake when I got back weighed down with two large bags of groceries.

"I feel like shit," she said. She was sitting up in the bed holding a glass of water with both hands. "Where were you?"

"No wonder with all you drank last night. I was shopping, but I'm guessing you won't want breakfast."

She grimaced and shook her head slowly. "Was I really out of order last night?"

"Yeah. But you had good reason."

"I'm sorry." There was such sadness in her voice that I had to give her a hug, avoiding skin contact because I really didn't want to experience her hangover.

"But what're we gonna do?" she whispered.

"I had an idea. Could you get hold of the contact details for the next of kin of the hostages?"

She thought about it for a moment. "Why?

"Thought we could go and talk to some of them. Tell them what's really going on. Maybe they might get your bosses to take it seriously. Didn't you say one of them is the brother of a cabinet minister?"

"Yeah, that's right." She paused for a while. "You'll have to do this on your own Charlie. I don't think it would look good if I went with you. I can probably get you the details though. I'll make some calls when this headache eases off."

"No hurry. Can't do anything about it today."

"Why? What's happening today?"

"I've found a rescue team and I'm taking them through the portal this afternoon to convince them it's real."

"Oh. Right." She groaned and lay back. "Who are they?"

"Dave's pals from the gym."

"How many you got?"

"Don't know until I see who turns up."

"What time you meeting them?"

"Midday. But I don't think you're fit for it."

Another groan.

"Bugger. I wanted to go over there."

"There'll be other chances," I said. "At least if we're successful. Look, I bought a load of stuff and I'll put it in the fridge, so you won't starve. I was going to cook breakfast and then head off. Do you want anything?"

"Bit of toast maybe."

I put away the shopping and started cooking myself the full works breakfast. After a few minutes Sharon demanded I close the bedroom door because the smell was making her sick.

I polished off breakfast, took Sharon her toast, then checked my e-mail one last time and headed off for Totton.

I got to Michelle's about quarter to twelve and we hurried straight out to the gym in the Polo to see who had turned up; I hoped it wasn't just Warren. On the way I told Michelle about Sharon's suspension.

"It must have been that guy Nigel," she said. "I'll bet they already know about the Otherworld and they're trying to keep it quiet."

"Makes sense to me. It would be hard to believe that no one in authority knows about it after all the time people have been coming through. There must have been thousands of half-breed kids over the years."

Warren had five mates waiting for us at the gym and two more arrived just after us. I could have wished for more, but was grateful to see that many. Rather than explain immediately I told them to follow us out to Netley Marsh. We waited a few minutes to see if anyone else was going to show up, then set out with a convoy of cars behind us.

We got to Netley Marsh just after half past twelve without losing anyone and parked up in the car park. Warren and his mates quickly gathered round demanding to know what we were going to do. I stood up on an old tree stump facing them.

"Right, I'm Charlie and rather than explain where Dave and the boys are, I'm just going to take you there. We can talk about it after. Anyone got a problem with that?"

"But where are we going?" asked a guy in a blue track suit with tattoos covering most of his forearms.

"Where they're being held." I didn't want to say anything about portals or parallel worlds. No one else spoke up so I continued.

"Now there's a few things you need to know. First, we're going for a short visit, we're not going to try and get them back. We need to be tooled up for that. Second, the gateway will reject anything made of iron, so if you've got something leave it here. That means leave your phones behind. Third, it's dangerous over there. There's a war going on. No one's going to talk or make a row. Clear?

I scanned their faces, inviting questions. There was a short delay while some of them put their phones back in their cars.

"Right then follow me," I said and led them down the path out of the car park into the forest towards the two pine trees that marked the portal. I brought them right up to it, though of course they couldn't see it, and stood facing them.

"So where are we going?" Same tattooed guy.

"This way," I said and took Michelle's hand. "Join hands and stay together. It'll be cold and dark for a bit, but keep hold. If anyone gets detached and goes off on their own, then I'm not going to come and get you."

I waited half a minute while everyone joined up. I squeezed Michelle's hand and walked slowly towards the glowing oval of the portal. Behind Michelle was Warren and then tattooed guy. The icy ripple of the portal washed over me, then the wind and voices whirled through my mind, though the tone was softer than before, almost welcoming.

I visualised the palace and kept walking until I felt rain on my face. *How much time has passed since I was last here?* I wondered. *Is Lord Faniel's cavalry still around?* I took a deep breath, savouring the richness of the air and kept moving, pulling the chain of people out of the portal. I turned to Michelle to see her reaction; by the silver light of the palace I could see a broad grin across her face and I put a finger to my lips to stop her speaking.

Once everyone was through the portal I drew them, still holding hands, towards the light of the palace. A gentle rain was falling and the sky was light away on the horizon to my left. It must be just after dawn, I thought; I hope the palace guards are warming themselves in the guardhouse.

The impact of the palace in the grey light was breath-taking.

I could hear the gasps from just about everyone. I gave them a couple of minutes to take it in then headed back to the portal.

"Everybody still holding on?" I called on the threshold. "No one missing?"

There wasn't so I stepped into the portal with Michelle close behind. The sun was low in the sky when we emerged back in the forest.

"That was amazing," whispered Michelle, her arm tight around my waist. "I want to go again."

I led the group down to the dell where Michelle had killed the gwasannath then turned to face them.

"Right. Let's talk about what we saw. That shiny place is the King's palace. That's where the boys are being held."

"Where were we?" asked Warren. He, like several of the others, was looking around as if he expected to still be able to see the palace.

"We went through a gateway into another world," I said. "Like Narnia only it wasn't in a wardrobe."

"So Narnia is real?" said one of the guys, a six foot four chunk of muscle with a surprisingly soft voice.

"That wasn't Narnia, but it was a parallel world" I said. "We were just there. It seemed real enough, didn't it?"

"Can they do magic and stuff?"

"They can do things I can't explain any other way."

"How do you know this stuff?"

"My father's from there."

Half a dozen of them asked questions at once. I held up my hands.

"I'll answer all your questions, but what I need to know is now that you've seen where they are, who's up for trying to get the lads back?"

Warren's hand went up straight away, the others more slowly but everyone raised a hand.

"You said they were going to kill my brother and the others," said Warren. "What's going on? Why's this happening?"

"There's a war going on, just our side hasn't realised it." I gave them a brief rundown of Lord Faniel's world view and intentions finishing up with: "so we have to get the hostages out then bring the king over here, and maybe we can end it."

"What's the opposition going to be?" asked the tattooed guy.

"There's not many guards," I said. "They are armed though. Swords and spears. I haven't seen any bows. Plus they have squads of these big smelly apes. They're really strong and fast, but not too smart."

"We got some stab vests," said Warren.

"Good, bring them," I said. "The idea is to get in and out without contact, but if we can't then we'll need them."

"How long have we got before they kill them?" asked another big bloke with a biceps like my thighs.

"I don't exactly know. It's due to happen on Midsummer's Day, but time moves differently over there." I looked at my watch. "We went through the portal just before one. It felt like we were there a couple of minutes, but it's now half past six."

"Shit I'm working at eight," said the tattooed guy. Several other voices echoed him.

"OK," I said. "We'll break it up now, but I'll need your contact details. I don't exactly know when we'll be going in to rescue them, but soon."

We walked back to the cars with them still asking questions. I took out the notebook I'd brought and collected contact details for all of them. Once they had signed up they headed off until Michelle and I were alone. She slipped one hand into the back pocket of my jeans.

"You did great," she whispered and squeezed my backside. I turned and kissed her for a couple of minutes.

"The palace was just amazing," said Michelle. "And the portal felt so weird."

"Really? How did it feel?" I had often wondered if Michelle had any magic about her, beyond the sexual she possessed in abundance.

"It was like it was talking to me inside my head. Is that what it's like for you?"

"Yeah, only there's so many voices, it's more like sticking my head into fast-moving water."

She unlocked the Polo and we got in. She started the engine and drove cautiously out of the car park while I wondered about her powers.

"So if there's lots of portals around, why don't loads of people end up over there?" she said. "I mean, anyone could just walk through one without knowing it."

I thought about it as she drove slowly down the gravel track to the lane. "I don't know for sure. Maybe you need to have a bit of magical ability to even hear the voices. Even if you have and you walk into one, you're suddenly somewhere cold and dark with weird feelings in your head. Your first reaction is going to be to try and get out. Maybe the portal just spits you straight out again. You have to go in with a clear intent. You concentrate on where you want to go and it takes you there. If you don't give it that it rejects you."

"That makes a kind of sense. So if I went in thinking about my dad it would take me to him?"

"Worked for me." She steered us down the lane towards the main road.

"I'd like to go and see him, see where he lives. Surprise him." She went quiet for a minute or so. "How long do you think we've got until they kill the hostages?"

Did telepathy feature among her powers? "No idea. I'm really confused by the way time works between here and there, but it can't be long." I wondered if she was worried about Dave the troll.

"Do you think we'll be able to get them out? Have we got enough people?"

I thought about it for a minute, remembering the small squad of guards I'd seen. "Yeah. If we take them by surprise."

"And if we don't?"

"That's not good to think about." A bunch of bouncers and body-builders against soldiers who'd grown up in a warrior society - ugly. We'd need something more than surprise to give us an edge. "I'd really hoped we were going to get some professional assistance by now."

"And we're not?"

"No prospect of it, not now that Sharon's been suspended. We're on our own."

She stopped for the T-junction with the main road and she put her hand on my arm. I expected her to say something but she didn't. We both knew how high the stakes had grown.

We drove in silence into Totton and parked outside her flat.

"You coming in?" she asked, her voice deep and smoky with invitation.

"OK, but I can't stay." Enticing though the prospect was, I had to get back to Sharon.

"I'll put the kettle on."

I never did get my cup of tea; we had each other's clothes off within two minutes of getting into the flat and I lost track of time.

Some time later we were lying on her bed in a sweaty exhausted tangle.

"I've never felt this way about anyone before," she said.

Laying there beside her it was hard to disagree that something special was happening. I wondered if I would ever be able to feel this comfortable with someone else. "Not Dave?"

"No." There was a catch in her voice that made me hug her. "He was my first boyfriend. I know mum didn't like him, but I just did what I thought I was supposed to do. It was fine at first, but he got really possessive. I was going to do nursing, but he didn't want me to go away. He doesn't even like me working in Tesco, but I've gotta do something."

I was liking Dave less and less. It was pretty well certain things would get messy when he got back; if he got back, and I didn't think I was enough of a bastard to ensure he didn't.

"Has he ever hit you?"

"Couple of times."

That didn't surprise me, but still made me angry.

"Don't want to talk about him anyway." She ran her fingers through my hair. "You sure you can't stay?"

"I'd love to, but I can't. Sharon'll think I've been grabbed again if I don't turn up."

"You could call her."

"But then I'd have to lie to her, and I'm really bad at lying."

She pouted and looked at me with baby-seal eyes and I nearly changed my mind. I picked up my watch and saw it was nearly eleven.

"Time to go."

Thankfully she quit trying to get me to stay then, and as

I dressed we talked about what needed to be done to get our little army ready for the raid. It seemed a long list to me and she picked up on several things that I'd missed. I wished I had someone to run it for me; someone with a military background would be ideal, but a scoutmaster would probably do.

"Will I see you tomorrow?" she asked at the top of the stairs.

"I don't know. There's so much to do, I can't promise." I kissed her one more time then walked down the stairs and out into the night.

I walked down to the station too full of things to think about to think straight. It was easier to concentrate on all the things I had to do to mount the raid than analyse how I felt about Michelle. I sent mother a text from the train to tell her that I had a rescue team and then tried to think about how we would actually approach the job.

Sharon was in bed but still awake when I got in.

"You're late," she called from her bedroom. "How did it go?"

"I took them through the portal and now we've got ourselves a team. Not a big team but enough, I think. How are you feeling?" I stood at the door unsure about going in.

"Bit rough still. I made some calls though. I've got you that contact list."

"Result."

"Yeah. Still got some friends," she said with a bitter edge. "You can come in. I won't bite."

I went and sat on her bed because that's what I'd normally do. She was sitting up in bed in an old T-shirt, her hair falling untidily to her shoulders. Dark circles under bloodshot eyes was not a good look for her.

"Thanks for looking after me, Charlie. I won't make a habit of it, promise."

"Understandable considering."

"Yeah." She looked away. "Need this to work, Charlie or I'm an ex-detective."

"You could always go private," I said. "I'd still work with you."

She looked at me through narrowed eyes. "Thanks."

"You wanted sympathy? I thought you coppers were a hard

lot and beyond all that. Or is that just a front?"

"It's all a front. But seriously, I don't want to lose my job."

"You won't. We're gonna show them it's real, because it is real."

"Yeah, course we are."

"You'll feel better about it in the morning." I stood up. "I'm going to bed. See you for breakfast."

She groaned at the mention of breakfast and I shut the door.

CHAPTER 14

I didn't sleep too well with all that I had on my mind and was up, showered and making breakfast when Sharon appeared. She was pretty much recovered, the dark circles were gone and she was very hungry. We had breakfast. Then she printed out the contact list for the next-of-kin of the missing people.

"Which one's the brother of the cabinet minister?" I asked, thinking we might as well start at the top.

"Brother-in-law." She pointed out an address in Beaulieu. "The farm was burned out. One dead, two missing."

I looked at my watch; eleven forty. I wondered briefly if they were church-going people before reaching for the phone. What to say was one of the things I'd thought about in the small hours. I keyed in the number and waited, holding my breath, as it rang.

"Hello." Cut-glass upper-class English.

"Can I speak to Alice Barrett," I said.

"This is Alice Barrett. Who is this?"

"My name is Charlie Somes. I know where your husband is."

Gasp and a pause. "What do you want? Money?"

"No. This isn't about money. I want your help to get your husband back. I have friends missing too." Stretching it to describe them as friends, but otherwise true.

"Where is he?"

"That's what I want to talk about. The explanation is not easy and will take time. I'd rather not do it on the phone."

Another pause and I prayed she wouldn't hang up on me, conscious of Sharon watching me.

"Can you come to the house?"

"Sure. What time?"

The phone was muted for a few seconds.

"Come after lunch. Three o'clock. Do you have the address?"

"Yes. I'll see you then." I hung up and breathed a deep sigh of relief.

"I didn't realise how stressful that was going to be."

"You did good," said Sharon. "I suppose you're going to want me to drive you out there."

"Er yeah. Is that a problem?"

"I can't be seen to have anything to do with an active case while I'm suspended. Not if I hope to have any career after this. I'll drop you somewhere near and you'll have to walk the rest. You can call me when you're done."

"OK." I could totally understand her reasons, but it left me disappointed; I'd have felt a lot more confident with her alongside me. "Could be a long wait if I have to make another trip over there to convince someone."

"I've done enough surveillance operations. I can do long waits."

"You could go up to the Royal Oak, they're open all afternoon."

"That's sounds like a good option. Think I'll stay on coffee though."

Sharon went to have a shower and I opened up my laptop. I sent a message to Michelle, telling her I was going to see Mrs. Barrett. Then I set up a new e-mail group with my list of volunteers

I pissed around on the net while Sharon was washing her hair six times, or whatever it is that woman do in the bathroom. I read the news, waiting to see if I would get a reply from Michelle. There was nothing to suggest that Lord Faniel's cavalry had raided again which made me suspicious; did that mean that he had enough sacrifices? Was it midsummer over there?

Sharon dropped me halfway up the hill out of Beaulieu. I'd always wondered where the gravel roads went that led off into the woods on either side of the road. To large expensive houses I'd presumed and I was right; I passed two that I'd be happy to live in as I followed the road in the gloomy drizzle, then spotted something most unexpected. Shining softly between the trees uphill from the road was a faint blue light. I climbed up the bank to get a better look; no doubt about it, it was a portal. I looked at my watch, five to three; no time to investigate further.

The substantial red-brick house at the end of the road was just as impressive as the two I'd passed. I walked past a this years' plate BMW 6 series, went to the front door and rang the bell, reminding myself that people will die if I don't do this.

The door was opened by a blonde woman of about 50. Twenty five years ago she was probably beautiful, now she was too thin and the shadows under her blue eyes too pronounced; losing your husband to the Otherworld raiders will do that to you.

"Mister Somes?" she asked.

"Yes. I'm Charlie Somes." I didn't offer her my hand; I reckoned I could guess most of what she was thinking without it.

"Do come in."

I followed through the hallway and into a small sitting room with a couple of armchairs. Another woman of about fifty was standing by the fireplace; Mrs. Barrett's sister from the look of her.

"This is Margaret," said Mrs Barrett. "She's going to listen to what you have to say."

Margaret looked at me with a firm level gaze and didn't offer her hand. She was a bit plumper than Mrs Barrett, maybe a bit younger and dressed in the same casual look that you don't buy in chain stores.

I sat in one of the chairs and Mrs. Barrett sat down facing me. Margaret came and stood behind her chair.

"So, what has happened to my husband?"

I'd rehearsed that one. "He has been taken by a group of horsemen who intend to sacrifice him and the others at a midsummer ceremony. I've seen the building they are being held in."

"Why haven't you told the police?"

"I have. They've chosen to ignore me."

"Why?"

"The truth is inconvenient to them."

"Why is that?"

"Because the truth is that these horsemen come from a parallel world, and that is where you husband is." I watched their faces, waiting for their reaction; this was where they'd throw me out if they were going to.

Mrs Barrett said nothing, looked up at Margaret as if asking for her opinion.

"You said you've seen where he's being held." said Margaret. "Do you have any proof of this?"

"Yes. I can take you there." I consciously polished my syllables in their presence. "There's a gateway between the worlds nearby."

Mrs. Barrett looked at Margaret again. "I can see why the police have chosen to ignore you," she said and stood up. "Would you excuse us a moment, Mister Somes?"

She and Margaret left the room and closed the door. I wondered where I'd gone wrong and what was going to happen next. I half expected a couple of coppers to appear.

They returned after a couple of long minutes both wearing dark green Barbours.

"Would you show us this gateway, Mister Somes?" said Mrs. Barrett.

I don't know which God I'd been praying to, but I thanked them.

"Happy to," I said.

"Is this gateway walking distance, or are we driving?" asked Margaret.

"Walking distance. It's off in the woods halfway down the drive."

"Really?" She glanced at Mrs. Barrett and some message passed between them.

"They're hidden by a concealment spell," I said, knowing it wasn't going to help.

"I see," said Mrs. Barrett. "So how can you see it?"

"My father taught me." Not strictly true as I had no idea what he had done.

"Naturally," said Margaret.

We went out and Margaret closed the front door behind us.

"Time moves differently over there," I said. "Even with a brief visit, we'll be gone several hours."

"Really?" Margaret looked at me, scepticism personified. "Why are you doing this?"

"The short answer is because people will die if I don't."

"Is there a long answer?" said Mrs. Barrett.

"Yes. My father comes from that otherworld, and the people behind these raids are his enemies. They'll stop him coming here and me going there. I've only just got to know him. I don't want to lose him again." It was actually the first time I'd articulated the thought. "Don't bring anything made of iron with you. The gateway will reject it."

"I don't think we have anything," said Mrs Barrett. "I think the zips on these jackets are brass."

We walked down the gravel drive in the rain until the gateway came into sight between the trees about thirty yards away uphill.

"Up there." I followed a vague path up the bank then scrambled over the two-strand wire fence, sliding on the wet leaves underfoot. The ladies followed with an athletic ease that surprised me. The gateway hung in a dip between two trees, shining with a soft blue light. I walked up to it and slipped my hand over the threshold. It tickled like a cold mountain stream and the wind of it whispered through my mind. I pulled my hand back and turned to them.

"This is it."

"But of course it is," said Mrs. Barrett. I stared at her gobsmacked.

"This is the spot isn't it, Mags?"

"Pretty much," said Margaret.

"Well then I see no reason to stand in the rain anymore," said Mrs. Barrett. "Let's go back inside."

I followed Mrs. Barrett and Margaret back to the house in a stunned silence.

"Would you like tea?" Mrs. Barrett asked as she took off her coat.

"Yeah, tea would be nice," I said completely bemused.

"Sit yourself down." Mrs Barrett said, opening the door of the little sitting room.

Mrs. Barrett and Margaret left, presumably for the kitchen and a sisterly chat. I sat down and wondered what the hell had happened. I'd thought the minimum for them to believe me would be passage through the portal and sight of the palace, but here I was.

The ladies returned. Mrs. Barrett sat opposite me; Margaret behind her chair as before.

"I've confused you, haven't I, Mister Somes?" said Mrs. Barrett.

"Yes, actually you have, Mrs. Barrett."

"Call me Alice," she smiled. "When we were young girls, fifteen or sixteen and living in this house, we had a friend named Mary Brooks. She would go out into the woods here and call up a boy she said was a faery. We went with her several times and met him. I never really liked him, he was strange and he made me feel uncomfortable. But the point is she called him from the place you took us to, and he was certainly not of this world, was he Mags?"

"Oh no," said Margaret. "Funny fellow. I didn't like him at all. It's no wonder she got into trouble with him."

"So you see, we know about this other world," Mrs. Barrett said. "And if they've turned nasty then I'm not surprised. So what do you want of us, Mr. Somes?"

I was so relieved it took me a moment to reply. "Influence. You can persuade the people with the power to get things done to help us. Me and my friends are planning a raid to get the prisoners back. There's reason to believe there's not much time before they're going to be sacrificed. We could really do with some trained people coming with us. SAS, or something like them."

"Well I don't know if I can help you with that," said Mrs. Barrett.

"That's only half the job though," I said. "If we get the hostages out, they'll just come back and take some more and we'll have made things worse."

"What's the alternative?" she asked.

"To end it we need to bring their king over here. He's a sick man and it's his son that's responsible for the raids. From what I've been told, he sounds like a classic cardiac patient. If I'm right, and we can get him a bypass or something, then send him back strong enough to control his son, we can stop the raids."

"That I can definitely help with, "she said, her face lighting up. "One of my neighbours is a cardiac surgeon. He works at the General and the Chalybeate. I'm sure he'd be able to arrange that for you. The money won't be a problem."

At last, a bit of luck running our way.

"When are you planning on going in?" asked Margaret.

"I don't know exactly how long we've got, but it will have to be soon. I think it would be good to start the process now." I didn't want them to feel I was telling them what to do, even though I actually was.

"I'll go and give Alexander a call now," said Mrs. Barrett. She stood up and left the room.

Margaret took over her chair.

"The people you're going in with," she said. "Have they got any experience?"

"No," I said, embarrassed at the answer I was about to give. "They're bodybuilders and doormen."

"Oh! I see."

"That's all I've got. No one official wants to believe me."

"That's no surprise. They're useless the lot of them. But your people could suffer badly if things go wrong."

"I know, but what else can I do? Stand back and let them die?"

"Of course not. I'm glad someone is doing something for poor Alice. The last few weeks have been very difficult, and the police haven't been any help. You're a very courageous young man."

I didn't feel like it at the time.

Mrs. Barrett came back in.

"I've spoken to Alexander, and he can arrange everything for your patient."

"That's great. Thank you." A small wave of relief washed through me.

"He was very helpful," she smiled again. "I've known him a

long time. He's been a good friend."

"How much notice does he need?"

"Not very much, I would think. He was only saying last week how the Chalybeate is less than half full."

"I'll still try to give him a day or two's notice."

The door opened; a young woman came in carrying a tray laden with teapot, cups and a plate of scones.

"Thank you, Anna," said Mrs. Barrett and reached for the tea pot.

She poured the tea; we ate scones and made polite relaxed conversation for twenty minutes or so before it seemed like time to go.

"Thank you for coming, Charlie. I'm sorry we were so suspicious," she said at the front door. "If you need anything else, just phone me."

Margaret held out her hand, I shook it briefly and was pleased to find she had no remaining doubts about me. I walked out into the rain and took my phone out to call Sharon. Then I called Michelle to let her know how it had gone, she didn't pick up so I left a voicemail.

Sharon was waiting for me when I got to the end of the gravel road.

"How did it go?" she asked as soon as I opened the door.

"Pretty damn good." I sat back in the seat and let the tension drain out of me. "She already knew about the Otherkin, and her neighbour is a surgeon at the Chalybeate. He'll do the King's op if we can get him there."

"Sounds like a result." She started the car. I took out my phone to text mother an update and realised she hadn't replied to my last text or the previous one. That rang a little alarm bell in my mind.

"Do you mind if we drop by my mum's place? It's less than ten minutes away."

"Sure." She accelerated away up the hill.

"She hasn't replied to the last couple of texts I sent her, she normally does."

"You think there's a problem?"

"It's probably nothing." Except that little alarm bell was still there.

I was right about how long it took to get there. Sharon parked up just around the corner.

"Considering how things played out last time, I'll wait here," she said.

I walked down the lane dodging the puddles; mother's rickety Fiesta was parked in its usual spot. Despite the gloom, no lights were showing from the cottage windows. The alarm bell got louder. I knocked at the front door and called out; no answer. The door was locked and the key wasn't under the geranium pot.

I went around to the back, a cold hand gripping my stomach. The back door was hanging by one hinge, the lock smashed. Through the doorway, I could see the kitchen table overturned. The cold hand squeezed hard.

I stood there for a long cold minute not wanting to believe what I saw, the rain running down my face, then ran for Sharon.

Sharon came and took one look then phoned for the local police.

"Best stay out and let SOCO do their job," she said. We retreated to the car to wait for them in the dryness.

"Got to be Lord Faniel's men," I said.

"Shouldn't assume anything, but yeah," said Sharon. "This sort of shit doesn't happen by chance. The only other candidate would be Pete Murphy, but there's no reason for him to connect her to you."

"It's another way for Lord Faniel to control my father."

Sharon nodded. "Fits all the way down."

"I hope she didn't fight them, they could hurt her badly." The overturned table suggested that she hadn't gone without resistance.

The first police car took less than ten minutes to arrive with two constables on board. We showed them the broken door then I answered all their obvious questions as patiently as I could manage as more cars turned up. At one point they took me into the cottage to see if I could tell if anything was missing; nothing was apart from mother. After that there was a lot of miserable frustrating hanging around while the SOCO team did their thing, then another long wait until a couple of blokes in a red Transit turned up to fix a bit of plywood over the broken door. Sharon got through half a packet of cigarettes; I was tempted to ask her for one.

"This changes nothing," said Sharon as we drove back. "We stick to the plan such as it is."

I knew she was right even though I wanted to go straight to a portal and go in search of mother.

"It doesn't help anyone if you get captured, or put them on their guard. We need the surprise."

As we drove back up the A326, we talked over how much there was still to do. Making plans made me feel that I was at least doing something constructive and slightly eased the knot of frustration in my mind. I tried to call Michelle again as we approached Totton, but it went to voicemail and I didn't leave a second message. I felt uneasy that she hadn't picked up or replied to my first message; it seemed unlikely that Lord Faniel's men could have found her too, but that didn't stop me stressing about it.

"You want to stop and get a takeaway?" asked Sharon as we came through Millbrook.

"Not hungry," I said. "Just want to get things rolling."

I went straight to my laptop when we got back to the flat and sent out an e-mail to my little volunteer army to set up a meeting. I couldn't think of anywhere else to meet so I used the gym carpark. Next I sent a short message to Greg to tell him I wanted to call in that promise he'd made about helping me out without asking for details; I hoped I'd be able to see him sometime tomorrow. Finally I wrote a long e-mail to Michelle telling her everything that had happened today. It was after midnight when I sent it and she still hadn't replied to my voicemail which agitated me even more.

"You want a drink to help you sleep?" asked Sharon.

"What are you offering?"

"Wine or vodka?"

"Vodka." I'm not really a vodka drinker, but I didn't think wine would really do the job the way I was feeling.

"You want anything with it?"

"No. I just want to sleep."

"Good luck with that."

She poured me about a hundred mils and a smaller measure for herself.

"I'm off to bed, do you want me to leave the bottle?"

CHAPTER 15

Despite the vodka I barely slept. All the plans for the rescue, and what could go wrong, whirled through my mind along with my fears for my mother and Michelle, keeping me awake through the night. I drank a bit more vodka to no avail. I thought about going in to talk to Sharon, but I didn't think she would appreciate being woken up and really there wasn't anything new to say.

I got up about six and had a shower. I brewed coffee then fired up my laptop and went into my e-mail. One message stood out; time stamped three thirty a.m. It was from Michelle and had a big red exclamation mark proclaiming its urgency. My stomach gave a little lurch at the sight of it.

'I went through the portal like you showed me and found my father. Tomorrow is midsummer. We have to get them out now!!!'

My stomach gave a stronger lurch. So that was why she hadn't picked up her voicemail. I felt relieved and scared at the same time; finally I knew the waiting was over and we had to act.

I made coffee for Sharon and went to wake her.

"Wow! Shit!" she said when I showed her the e-mail. "Hang on, we still have a bit of time. With the way time works over there, it doesn't have to be today."

"You're right." I thought about it a bit. "Tonight's meeting is the final briefing then and we go tomorrow."

I wondered what time of day Michelle had been there. If we went in during the day tomorrow we might hit night time over there which would be the best time to hit the stables.

"Better tell the army." I turned back to the keyboard and started typing a message to them. When I was done I had Sharon read it through.

"You'd better warn them to arrange to be gone for days," she said.

"Good catch." I added the warning to the message. "Anything else?"

"Whatever kit they were thinking about bringing, it has to appear tonight."

"I thought that would be obvious."

"Never hurts to spell it out."

I added the line and sent the message on its way, CCing Michelle so that she knew we were rolling. I'd call her later, I figured if she was sending e-mails at that time of the night then she'd be asleep now.

Sharon took her mobile and cigarettes and went outside. She only had time for one cigarette before she was back.

"Just lining up a couple of stab-jackets for tomorrow," she said. "Don't know if they'd stop a sword, but they're better than nothing."

I wouldn't fancy facing a gwasannath in any less than full plate armour but she was right; they'd be better than nothing.

"Anything else you can think of that would be useful to have along?" asked Sharon.

I remembered the gwasannath being scared off by Michelle's flashgun. "Some flashbombs, thunderflashes, or something similar would be good. I'm guessing a camera flash gun would get rejected by the portal."

"Thunderflashs are hard to get hold of at short notice, they have to be signed out by a senior officer, but there are a couple of fireworks shops in town."

Google found them within seconds. The nearest shop was only a few minutes' drive away down in Shirley, and they had a website that showed video clips of some of the fireworks.

"Let's have some breakfast then get down there as soon as they open."

They had a big selection of display fireworks, including some really tasty looking barrages which needed electronic ignition, but no bangers like I remember buying as a kid. We bought half a dozen repeating airbombs that should be good for a shock and awe assault; though they would tell everyone for miles that something was going down.

"Remind me to bring matches tomorrow," I said as we left the shop.

I got a text from Greg while Sharon was driving me up to the University, agreeing to meet up. I replied telling him to come to the coffee shop in the Union building and I'd meet him there.

Sharon dropped me by the bookshop in the main campus and went off to collect the stab-jackets and buy a dozen pickaxe handles. I walked into the half-full coffee shop and spotted Greg at a table immediately. I bought myself a coffee then joined him.

"What's going on mate?" he asked.

"I need to call in all my favours and then some."

"I got that. What do you need?"

"Non-magnetic weapons. Have you got anything that could be sharpened to make a long knife or a sword?"

He thought for a moment. "Yeah, can probably find you something. What for?"

"I thought you weren't going to ask."

"Yeah OK, but you got me interested now. How many do you need?"

"As many as you can lay your hands on."

"OK. I've got some titanium-tungsten turbine blades. Should be easy enough to put an edge on them and attach a handle. When do you need them?"

"Really soon, tomorrow morning at the latest."

"That soon?" He pulled a face. "OK, I can do that. You gonna tell me what you need them for? I mean swords? That's sounds dangerous."

"Yep." I nodded, trying not to think of just how dangerous.

"So what's going on? You don't need non-magnetic swords for helping in a police case."

"Well no. It isn't a police case, though Sharon is still part of it."

"So what is it?"

It was clear that Greg wasn't going to let this go. I took a mouthful of coffee and thought about what to say.

"How long have you known me?"

"Five years or so, why?"

"How many times have I bullshitted you about something important?"

"You haven't so far as I know. Why, are you about to tell me you have?"

"No. But I'm going to tell you about some seriously weird stuff, and I want you to remember my record before you say it's all bollocks."

"Ok. So what's going on?"

"You know the fires there's been and people going missing across the South recently?"

"No."

"Right." Greg never did read a paper or watch the news. "You know when the police turned up that Sunday morning after Sharon ended up in hospital?"

"Yeah."

"It all goes back to what happened then. A bunch of guys on horses turned up and charged into us. Since then they've been burning down houses out in the country and taking prisoners. I know where they come from, and I'm going to get the prisoners back tomorrow."

"Isn't this something the police should be handling?"

"Yes, but they don't believe me and I'm out of time. The prisoners will be killed tomorrow if I don't get them out."

"Right." I could hear the scepticism. "So where do these guys come from? Where are the prisoners?"

"They come from a parallel world. There are portals between here and there." I watched his face as he digested what I'd said. It was a bit like watching him take a mouthful of an unknown curry which turned out to be vindaloo. "Told you it was seriously weird."

"How come you know about these portals?" he said after about a minute.

"My dad is from over there."

"So it's like that book Chloe was crazy about?"

"Gordath Wood?" I'd bought Chloe the sequel for her

birthday last year; she'd read it in one night. "Pretty much."

Another pause for digestion. "Fuck! Is this for real?"

"Damn right it is. They've got my mum."

"Then I'm coming with you."

That was unexpected. "It could be dangerous. We might have to use those swords you're making."

"Yeah. But I need to see this. Besides, your mum's in bigger danger, and I know more about how to use a sword than you do."

That had to be true. To be honest I was glad he was coming along. "OK. I'm meeting the rest of the team later today. I'll e-mail you a map."

"Cool. I'd better get going if I'm going make the swords. See you later."

I could have hugged him, but finished my coffee and walked down to the lab; I had an idea for something else that might be worth taking with us. As soon as I got into the lab I logged on to my e-mail to send the meeting details to Greg and see if I had any replies from my volunteers.

To my relief they had all replied; a couple asking if they could bring more people with them. Another had some sets of plastic body armour made for motocross bikers. I still had an army.

Since there was nothing from Michelle, I assumed she wasn't awake yet and I decided to call her after lunch. I was itching to know how she had managed to get through the portal as well as what she had found there. There was an hour until the canteen opened, so I set about turning my idea into something useful.

I ended up calling her at half twelve. It took her a long time to answer, but any guilt I felt about waking her was washed away by her delight that it was me calling.

"Charlie. You got my message?"

"Yeah. We're going in tomorrow. That'll be in time, won't it? What time of day was it when you left?"

"No idea. It was daytime. Charlie, I saw my dad and he showed me where they're going to kill the prisoners. They're going to do it at sunset."

Sunset was much better news than dawn. "No they're not. We're going to get them out. How did you get there?"

"I used the gateway like you showed me. I remembered how it was between those two trees. I thought about my dad when I went through and it brought me out near the palace."

Smart girl. "So how did you find your father?"

"I sang his song and he came."

Doubly smart girl. "Did he show you where they're holding the prisoners?"

"No. We had to hide out in the woods. There were lots of patrols around looking for something."

"We've been over a few times recently. They must have noticed." Worth knowing there would be patrols around when we came through with the rescue party.

"Did your father say anything else about the prisoners or the ceremony?"

"No. We just talked about stuff, me and my mum. Hey! He did something so I can see the portals now."

"Right! That'll be useful tomorrow." I wondered what else she would learn she could do. "I'm meeting the volunteers at the gym at six. Will you be there?"

"Can't. Gotta work." I could hear the disappointment in her voice and wished I could do something to cheer her up. After tomorrow, seeing her could be pretty tricky with Dave the troll back in circulation. "What time are we going over tomorrow?"

"Early as I can get them there. We'll use the Netley Marsh portal. Can you meet us there? I'll call you when we hit the road."

"Okay. I'll see you tomorrow."

I went back to the lab and put some time into preparing the stuff to take with me. After I was done it didn't seem sensible to put on a reaction as I didn't know when I'd next be around. There was no sign of Prof, so I went through all my flasks of intermediates making sure they were properly labelled. After that, I started to prepare for the meeting, drawing a large map of the palace and grounds from what I could remember of my visit.

Sharon came to pick me up just after five. I filled a satchel with what I had prepared and came out to meet her by the University library.

"What's in the bag?" she asked.

I spread the mouth of the satchel that I'd slung at my side to show the flasks nestling in their bubblewrap.

"Trimethylaluminium and pinene in toluene. They'll spontaneously ignite in air."

"Oh! Nice!"

We joined the rush hour traffic heading out of town and reached the gym car park a little before six; some of the volunteers were already there, Greg and Chloe arrived about two minutes after us. I wasn't surprised to see Chloe, I'd have been more surprised if she hadn't come along.

By ten past six everyone in my army was present; all fifteen of them. I spread the map out on the bonnet of the Mini.

"Here's the situation. The prisoners are being held in the stable block on this side of the palace." I pointed to the map where the stables were circled in yellow highlighter. "This is where our gateway is." Highlighted in green. "We have to get from there, to the stables, take out the guards then get back with the prisoners. We probably can't bring them straight out. Our inside man will need to work with them first. Has anyone got experience doing anything like this before? I'm happy to hear any suggestions of how we should do it?"

"How many guards and where are they?" asked the very large guy with the quiet voice.

"One at each entrance, plus two circling the building. There are patrols in the palace grounds too."

"How far away and how strong is their back-up?" said another guy.

"I don't know," I said. "They do have cavalry, but I don't know how close they are."

"Sounds like we need to hit 'em fast, then get out even faster before the back-up arrives," said Sharon. "I hope your inside man works fast."

"We'll need to neutralise those wandering patrols," said the heavily-tattooed guy I remembered from the first meeting. "They could really slow us down on the way out."

"Those patrols are mostly one guy plus a bunch of apes, or just apes," I said. "They're fast and strong but not smart. If they get confused they're more likely to run than stand and fight. We've got fireworks and other stuff that should scare the shit out of them."

"Good. So we neutralise them. Then we just charge the guards at the stable block," said tattooed guy. "We'll outnumber them so they'll either leg it or get hurt."

"What happens if the fireworks don't scare 'em?" asked another guy.

"Then you get to use the swords," I said. "And find out how good the stab-jackets are."

"What do we do about our own casualties?" asked Greg.

"We bring them back," I said. "Anyone got first aid training?"

Chloe stuck her hand up as did one of the bouncers.

"What about fatalities?" said Greg. The group went quiet.

"We've got to recognise the possibility," Sharon said. She looked around at the group. "I suggest everyone writes a letter to be opened in the event of them not coming back saying that they knew the risks and came along of their own free will. Otherwise people could end up in court, like Charlie."

I was suddenly very much in favour of the idea. "What does everyone else think? We're all adults here. What we're going to do is vitally important, but it would be crazy to deny the risks."

More silence, then Greg spoke. "I'll write a letter."

"Me too," said Chloe.

There was a general murmur of assent through the group.

"Okay," I said. "Write your letters and bring them with you tomorrow. Now what else are you bringing?"

"I've got seven titanium-tungsten short swords," said Greg.

"Who's got experience of handling a sword," I asked. No one except Greg; not really a surprise.

"Okay. Sort out between you who should have them," I said. I rather fancied taking one myself, but I couldn't carry it and my bag of surprises. "We've got pickaxe handles for everyone else. Anyone got a bow?"

No one apparently which was a shame; we could have done with the advantage.

"How many stab-jackets have we got?"

Enough to go around it appeared once a couple of the

swordsmen had taken the motocross body armour.

"What about helmets and stuff?"

"Wouldn't bother with helmets unless you're used to them," said Greg. "Shin and forearm protection would be what I'd bring."

"Are we doing this in daylight?" asked someone else.

"Not by choice," I said. "But it depends what time it is when we get there."

"What are we using for light if we're doing this at night?"

I thought for a moment. "We could bring some lanterns, but the palace lights up the whole area. There'll be enough light to see where you're going."

"When are we going in?" asked Greg.

"What do people think?" I said. "Tomorrow morning? Who's got a car?"

Lots of hands raised.

"Okay, car owners. I've got maps." I held up a bunch of sheets I'd printed from Google Maps. "Look around and sort out lifts for anyone who needs them. What time can you get out to Netley Marsh?"

We agreed on eight in the morning though there were a number who wanted to go immediately. I reckoned that leaving it until tomorrow morning gave us a better chance of hitting darkness, and if we went earlier we'd just be sitting around waiting for it to get dark.

We had more debate about tactics after that: should we split off a team to run a diversion for the guards' response, when should we deploy the fireworks and similar stuff. I also reminded them that they should expect to be gone for several days due to the flow of time over there.

"There's one more thing we need to discuss," said Greg. "Are you the only person who can use this gateway? 'Cos if you are, we can't risk you getting hurt."

That silenced me for a moment. I didn't know if the portal would work for just anyone and if it wouldn't, he was right. Then I remembered Michelle.

"No. Michelle can use it. We'll leave her at the gateway with a couple of guards." Which I was pretty sure she wouldn't be happy with, but the logic was inescapable. "If anything happens to me, she'll get you back."

"Good. That makes me feel better," he said.

"Any more questions?" I asked the group.

"You know we'll be famous if we pull it off," said Chloe. "You particularly."

"Maybe. I wonder if the authorities are ready for the news that parallel worlds really exist?"

She smiled. "Going be hard for them to stop it getting out these days."

"Yeah. Maybe. Worry about that when we've made it back."

"Is that it, Charlie?" asked Warren. "I'll see you tomorrow morning then." He reached out a meaty hand to me. I shook it and was happy to find he was calm and relaxed about what we were about to do. It felt like a vote of confidence in me, a confidence I certainly didn't feel.

The army dispersed then; some of the guys heading into the gym, no doubt to move large lumps of metal around.

"What are you doing now?" asked Greg. "Is there somewhere to get a beer around here?"

"I need to get something to eat and then sleep." Now that the tension of the meeting was past I was really feeling my lack of sleep. "I'll see you tomorrow."

"Don't worry, Charlie," said Chloe. "I've got a really good feeling about this."

That didn't make me feel better.

"You handled that well, Charlie," said Sharon once we were in the Mini.

"You think so? I keep having this feeling that I've forgotten something. Wish we had someone along who'd done this before."

"But you haven't, so you've got to go with what you've got. I think you're doing fine under the circumstances."

"I wonder if people will think so afterwards?"

"Always easy to be wise after the event. I don't see what else we can do."

"Nor do I, but I'm still scared someone will die because I make a mistake."

"And if you do nothing they all die."

That didn't make me feel better either, but shut me up for a while.

"I've got the date through for my psych exam," Sharon said "It's on Friday. Be good to be back by then. "

Friday felt as far away as the moon. "Would simplify things a lot if we have the prisoners back by then. Your bosses won't be able to ignore them."

"Damn right."

We drove on in silence for a while.

"Do you want to get a takeaway?" she asked as we came through Millbrook.

"I suppose so." I wasn't really that hungry despite not having eaten since midday.

"What do you fancy? Indian?"

I ended up playing safe with a Chicken Korma; last thing I wanted was to have to fight my way into the Otherworld with a dodgy gut. I phoned Michelle while we were waiting for the takeaways to arrive. I told her how the meeting had gone and agreed to meet at the carpark in Netley Marsh next morning. I didn't mention the role I had set aside for her. I was pretty sure she was going to object and thought we should have the discussion face-to-face. I said goodnight and ended the call wishing I was staying the night with her.

CHAPTER 16

I barely slept and was awake before the alarm went off at six thirty. I had a quick shower and when I came out Sharon was sitting at the kitchen table eating toast. She was dressed in black, black jeans and black sweatshirt with her hair tied up. She looked good; dangerous and sexy at the same time.

"I like the ninja princess look," I said.

She smiled uncertainly as if unsure whether I was making fun of her.

"Gonna be night over there, isn't it?" she said. "I'm going for a cigarette, the kettle's boiled."

She got up and went to the stairs, taking her coffee with her. I made myself coffee and ate a bowl of Rice Krispies without appetite. Sharon was gone a long time; several cigarettes I guessed. I was about to go and look for her when she came back in.

"Time to go," she said and tossed me a box of matches.

We didn't talk on the way out to Netley Marsh; Sharon concentrated on driving and I sent Michelle a text to let her know we were on our way.

"You reckon everyone will turn up?" asked Sharon as we drove over the Redbridge flyover.

"Yeah. Hadn't occurred to me they wouldn't. Why?"

"It's dangerous. Some of them'll bottle it, others'll turn up pissed."

She was wrong; everyone was there by ten past eight and no one was drunk. Mostly they looked very businesslike dressed in black or army-style camo; with the added bulk of the stab-jackets they seemed huge. Michelle was all in black, though it made her look about fifteen.

I collected up their consent letters and put them in the glove box of Sharon's car along with our phones. We put on our stab-jackets as Greg handed out the swords, keeping one for himself. The stab-jacket was heavier than I expected and I felt awkward moving with it on.

"Just as well there're no dogwalkers around to see this," I said to Sharon as she adjusted my jacket. "They'd have the police out here for sure."

"I know a couple of people at Totton nick. I've dropped the word for them to keep an eye on the cars."

I called Michelle over to me while Sharon took the pickhandles out of the car and passed them round.

"Michelle. I need you to do a really important job today," I said, keeping my voice low to emphasise the seriousness of what I was saying. "When we've gone through, I need you to stay at the portal." I watched her face as I spoke; I knew she wouldn't be happy. I was right.

"But why?" she exclaimed. "I want to go with you."

"Because you're the only other person who can use the portal. If anything happens to me, you've got to get everyone back."

"Can't someone else do it?"

"No. There's only you and me."

She pouted, but shut up. I didn't think I'd heard the last of it.

Sharon put the rucksack containing the fireworks on her back. Then I led my little army down the valley to the portal, trying as I walked to adjust the stab-jacket to a more comfortable fit. I stopped just short of the softly glowing oval and turned to face them.

"This is it guys. When we go through we're in hostile territory so everyone keep quiet." I tried to keep my voice firm to give the impression I felt certain about what we were doing; not sure I succeeded. "First up I need two volunteers to stay by the portal with Michelle."

"No one moved.

"Two volunteers. This is important. You're guarding our escape route," I said. "Come on, I don't want to pick people."

Chloe and one other guy slowly raised their hands.

"Good," I said. "Right now we go. Most of you have done

this before so join hands, think of that shiny palace and don't let go."

I reached out a hand to Sharon; despite my focus on the palace her anxiety washed over me.

"Everyone ready?" I called. "Then let's go."

The chill touch of the portal rippled across me and the rushing wind of its magic blew Sharon's anxiety out of my mind. I pictured my father and the shining palace and walked forward.

We came out into darkness which was instantly a relief to me; we could get on with the job immediately. I brought the group a few yards from the portal and gathered them around me; the silver light of the palace was enough to see all their faces clearly. Greg grinned at me and gave me a thumbs-up.

"Right we're going in," I said, determined to sound decisive. "Follow me."

Leaving Michelle and her two guards, I led the group through the trees towards the light. We reached the edge of the trees, where the soft flute music was just audible and I called a halt.

"I need to call our inside man now, take five." I moved a few yards away from them and began my father's summoning song. I had barely sung it through once when he stepped out of the trees a few yards away and my anxiety reduced just a little.

"At last. I was waiting for you. I feared you were never coming," he said. He looked over at my team. "Could you muster no more?"

"Ran out of time. Did you know they took mother?"

He spat out an angry curse in his native tongue. "It does not surprise me." He cursed again. "He will pay for this. Let us be on our way."

"Have you spoken to the King?"

"He and the Queen are prepared and await my word."

"Good. Can you tell them to come to the portal now while we get the prisoners?"

"No. Not without going to them."

"Right. Can you get us to them now without us being seen?"

"Perhaps. There are patrols but we may avoid them."

"Can you conjure a glamour to hide us?"

"Not this many."

"Then we take our chances."

There was nothing but open grass between us and the palace, no cover at all. I took a few steps towards my team and waved them forward.

"If we work around that way..." My father pointed to the right wing of the palace. "We may approach by the kitchen garden. There is more cover there."

We did as he suggested; keeping just within the trees working our way around to where a gravel track approached the palace between neat rows of vegetable beds, leaving us a hundred yards or so to cover to reach the nearest shining building. We were halfway there when the patrol walked round the side of it.

One man, six gwasannath. The man stopped, his mouth open in surprise. The gwasannath charged. We were too spread out to form a line; the swordsmen ten yards behind me. The lead gwasannath bounded straight towards me club raised. I dropped my pickhandle, reached into my satchel and pulled out a flask, slipping off its bubblewrap sleeve.

I waited until the gwasannath was within five yards then hurled the flask. *I'm in a world of trouble if this doesn't work,* I thought as I threw it. The flask shattered on creature's chest. There was a woof, white flames covered its torso and head. It shrieked fit to wake the dead and clawed at its fur. The other gwasannath shrieked and scattered. Greg came past me at a run and ran the burning gwasannath through the chest with his turbine-blade sword. The shrieking stopped abruptly and the smell was truly sickening.

"Get the guard," I yelled. The rest of the swordsmen ran past me.

The guard turned to run but was tripped and disarmed within a dozen strides.

"Don't kill him," I said and turned to my father. "Can you put a compulsion on him to keep him quiet?"

My father just stared at me for a long moment, his mouth hanging open before he recovered himself.

"Of course," he said faintly.

He crouched over the guard and took his hand for a moment.

The guard stood up with a dazed expression on his face, walked over to the building and sat down with his back to the shining wall and lowered his head.

"He is going to sleep there until sunrise," said my father.

"What the fuck was that you hit it with?" asked Greg. "It really stinks."

"Homemade napalm. But those things stink anyway."

"Are you okay, Charlie?" asked Sharon.

"Yeah, fine. We need to get going. That row has probably woken the whole palace." I turned to my father. "Where's the stables from here?"

"Behind the palace." He pointed to the main building. "Over there."

"How many guards have they got round here?" asked Sharon.

"In all twenty men, more gwasannath."

"Right let's go," I said. "No point in being quiet, they know we're here."

We ran as a group, following my father around the palace outbuildings to the stable block expecting more guards to appear at any moment. We came around the corner of a building. In front of us, thirty yards away, three men stood before the wide double doors, two armed with spears, the third with a drawn sword in his hands. At the sight of us they backed up to the door shoulder to shoulder, weapons facing out outward.

"Stop!" I yelled as the swordsmen charged forward. They halted and spread in a semicircle facing the guards at about ten feet, swords raised.

I reached into my bag, drew out another flask and stepped inside the ring of swords. The guards stared steadily at me; they looked ready to die taking as many of us with them as they could. I threw the flask to the ground. The white fire flared and bloomed across the space between us.

"Tell them to drop their weapons or I'll burn them," I said to my father.

He spoke a few words of strange liquid speech. The guards looked at each other, then at me. I reached into the bag, took out another flask and raised my arm. The swordsman looked directly at me, challenge in his eyes. He was ready to die, but the man to his left wasn't, he dropped his spear and fell to his knees. The other spearman followed then the swordsman slowly lowered his blade.

"Right," I said. "Get them inside and let's get the prisoners sorted."

It was gloomy inside the stable but with the doors open there was enough silvery light to see by. I looked for mother, my stomach tight with fear that she wasn't here.

"Charlie!" She leapt up from the pile of straw she had been lying on and ran to me. "You made it."

"We've got to get out of here," I said after a long all-enveloping hug. "Jack's here to remove the compulsions."

She released me and I jumped up on a stall so the prisoners could all see me. They crowded around, demanding to know what was happening; I recognised Dave the troll and his mates. "My name's Charlie and we're here to take you home. We're not the police or the SAS, but we are getting you out of here. Who's ready to come?"

That quietened them.

"I want to, but I can't leave the building," said a haggard woman still wearing the blue fluffy dressing gown she'd had on when the raiders hit her home.

"We understand that," I said. "Come and talk to my father about it."

Jack took her by the hand and led her to a corner. I watched, wondering how long it would take to remove the compulsion. It seemed a long time before he let go of her and called the next person to him; a minute or two perhaps, but that is a long time when there are twenty or so people to treat.

I dispatched half a dozen scouts to give us warning of the guards' approach while the rest of us kept an eye on the captured soldiers and stood around silently urging Jack to hurry.

Minutes passed in silence as every one of us strained to hear the first sounds of the response we knew was coming. The group of treated prisoners grew, but Jack shook his head over two and they retreated to the shadows at the back of the building.

Dave and the troll squad were in the middle of the treatment queue. He kept looking at me as the queue advanced. I don't know what I expected when he walked over after Jack had finished with him, but it wasn't the meaty fist that smacked me in the face and dumped me on the floor.

"Your fucking fault we're here," he snarled and stalked back to his mates. Sharon and mother came over to see if I was alright.

"What the fuck was that about?" asked Sharon as she mopped at the blood from my nose with a tissue.

"He thinks it's down to me that he's here." My nose hurt a lot, but the pain destroyed any guilt I felt about shagging Michelle.

"How does that work then?"

"No idea." I spat out gobbets of blood and checked round my teeth with my tongue, all present and correct.

Half a lifetime later my nose had stopped bleeding, I had no nerves left and Jack was on his last patient when Greg ran in through the door with the scouts behind him.

"They're coming," he said.

"How many?" I asked.

"Twenty men plus a bunch of those hairy things."

"Time to go. Everyone out that way." I pointed to the door at the far end of the stable. The prisoners and my team ran for the doorway.

"You take them to the portal. Wait for me there," said Jack. "I'll bring the king.

"What about mum, and those two?" I pointed to the two prisoners sitting in the shadows.

"The compulsions are too strong, I cannot break them. Lord Faniel himself laid them."

"Can't we bring them anyway?"

"They would fight you, to force them would break their minds. Take those you have. Go to the portal. Now! I will bring the King."

"Go now, Charlie," said mother standing just beside him.

I ran for the door, there was no other choice. I just hoped mother would be alright. Jack would be well able to look after himself. I assumed he would put on a glamour to avoid the guards and wished I could. I caught up with the others and we legged it the most direct way towards the portal.

We made it about halfway across the lawn before our pursuers appeared behind us, the gwasannath whooping and shrieking when they saw us. I measured the distance with my eye; there was no doubt that they would catch us before we reached the portal.

"Sharon. Airbombs," I called.

She stopped running and took the rucksack off her back. We quickly planted a couple of the fireworks in the soft turf inclining them towards our pursuers, lit the touchpapers and ran.

The gwasannath were less than a hundred yards away when the first shell exploded with a brilliant flash and a shattering report. I turned to see the effect just as the second shell exploded. The gwasannath scattered in all directions dropping their clubs, screaming like demons. Another shell arched skyward, this one shrieking like the gwasannath before exploding.

Sharon grabbed my arm. "Come on. There's still the soldiers."

She was right, but they looked like they had stopped running and were advancing much more cautiously; wary perhaps of the new fire magic. We ran for the woods at the edge of the lawn, passing some of the prisoners who were labouring and our own folk who were assisting the strugglers.

At the fringe of the wood we planted and lit two more fireworks, launching the airbombs over the last few runners. We waited, watching the soldiers as the last of our people came past us, then retreated to the portal. Michelle had them lined up holding hands waiting for us.

"I've got to wait for the King." I said to Sharon. "When you get out to the other side call Mrs. Barrett. Tell her to tip off her friend that his VIP patient is incoming. Be good to have an ambulance waiting for him too."

"Will do. We'll probably have half the ambulances in Southampton out for these guys. See you back home."

I watched her go and join the end of the line and waved to them as they went through the portal. It was a strange thing to watch; a whole line of people vanishing into the glowing blue oval. I was relieved to see them go; they at least were safe.

I went back through the woods and found myself a place to hide between two bushes where I could watch the approach across the lawn. The soldiers advancing slowly towards me were all I could see. I hoped my father wasn't going to be long. I fingered the remaining flasks and fireworks and tried to project the image of a holly bush just like the one next to me.

The soldiers came past my hideout spread out in a skirmish line about fifty yards wide. The nearest soldier passed about ten yards away; I sat tight, gripping a flask and concentrating on looking like a holly bush in the silver light. There was a burst of shouting from some distance away. The soldiers broke into a run towards the noise, but the commotion quickly faded into silence. I stayed where I was scarcely daring to breathe.

"You have some talent, but they still should have seen you," said my father close beside me. I nearly pissed myself in surprise. He was suddenly standing right before me.

"I didn't see you coming."

"I should hope you did not."

I climbed out of my hiding place.

"Did everyone get away?" he asked.

"Yes, they're all gone through. How're things back at the palace?"

"Like an overturned ants' nest. Lord Faniel is most unhappy." He was unable to stifle his grin.

"Where's the King?"

"He is nearby. It is time for you to meet him. I can go no further from the palace."

He put two fingers in his mouth and produced a loud shrill whistle. The King appeared behind him, about ten yards away. I swear, I was looking straight at the spot and it was like he stepped out from behind a screen. *Makes sense, I guess. If he's the King, he's going to be pretty good at holding a glamour.* He was a big man, six six or more, and built like a second row with flowing dark hair and a close-cropped beard. Dressing in a flowing golden cloak and tunic, he certainly didn't look like a cardiac patient, but then I realised that this, too, was a glamour. A gorgeous woman appeared behind him, the Queen I presumed. Her glamour was damn good too; flowing white dress, long silver hair, face of a filmstar and a fabulous chest. She glowed softly as if she was back-lit. I wondered what they really looked like.

My father spoke to the King in that lilting bubbling speech, presumably saying something like 'this is my boy, he'll look after you from here'. The King looked at me and then put out his hand. I took it and got exactly what I expected; nothing. Then like the voice of God in my mind.

"We thank you, Charlie. You are valiant warrior. Lead and we will follow."

I turned to speak to my father, but he was already gone. I presumed he had recast his glamour to evade Lord Faniel's troops. He might only be feet away but I wasn't going to spot him.

We walked slowly through the woods in the silver light. The pace of the King, leaning on the Queen's arm as he walked, told me all I needed to know about the condition of his heart.

There were a handful of Lord Faniel's men around the portal who dropped to their knees the moment they saw the King. He barely acknowledged them as we made our stately way past them, his breath wheezing and rattling in his throat.

Don't have a heart attack before we get through, please. The chill touch of the portal was a relief, the rush of the wind in my mind soothing like the first mouthful of a well-earned beer. With the King's hand in mine, I focused on the car park at Netley Marsh and drew them forward.

We came out into daylight, sun dappling the forest floor, and someone yelling at us.

"Hey you. Police. Stand still." We stood still; it wasn't as if we were moving quickly or anything. A uniformed constable ran towards us and I could see others further away.

"I'm Charlie Somes." I yelled. "Is DS Wickens here?"

"Where did you come from?" The constable's eyes widened as he took in the King and Queen standing regally beside me. People headed towards us from all directions. Then I heard Sharon's voice.

"Charlie!" She ran towards us; two older plain-clothed men trailing behind her, one of them was DI Brown.

"You took your time." She stopped a couple of yards away. "This the King?"

"Yeah. Is there an ambulance for him? What day's it?"

"Thursday morning. There's an ambulance in the car park. Surgeon's waiting." She turned to the uniformed constable gawping at the Queen. "Get the paramedics up here pronto."

"You're Charlie Somes?" said the other plainclothes men. He looked about the same age as DI Brown but better dressed; his jacket was a better fit and his polished black shoes looked expensive.

"Yes."

"I'm Detective Superintendent Graham. This is all your doing?"

"Er mostly. I had help."

"So you wouldn't mind telling us about it?" His tone was soft, almost respectful. DI Brown's expression was studiedly neutral.

"Happy to, but I need to go to the hospital with this guy." I pointed at the King. "He's the key to ending the raids, he doesn't speak English. I'm the only person who can interpret."

"Someone else will have to go with him, I need answers now," Superintendent Graham said. His voice still soft but the intent behind it was rock hard.

"Can I have two minutes to explain stuff to him then?"

"Two minutes, not ten."

"I'll go and keep an eye on him sir," said Sharon.

"I'm sure you will, Sergeant." said DI Brown. Sharon glared at him but said nothing as he and Superintendent Graham walked off towards the car park.

"Where's Michelle?" she asked as soon as we were out of earshot of her bosses.

"Isn't she here? Didn't she bring you all through?"

"She went back. Didn't you see her? She said she was going to wait for you at the gateway."

"Oh shit!" I remembered the burst of shouting I'd heard while I waited for my father and the King and my brain froze. "They must've got her. Fuck, what're we gonna do?"

"Well you're not going back to get her. You're going to stick to the plan, get the King well and rely on him to fix it."

It made sense in a cold abstract way, but just thinking about Michelle held captive made my rational processes pack up and go down the pub.

The paramedics arrived carrying a collapsible wheelchair and several bags of gear.

"Where's the patient?" one of them asked.

I pointed to the King, there was a moment's hesitation before they unfolded the wheelchair and my thinking bits got back on the job.

"He doesn't speak English so I'm going to explain to him what's happening. If you need to communicate with him, hold his hand and he'll understand you."

The paramedic stared at me. "How's that work then?"

"It just does. Tell the surgeon to do it."

I turned to the King and tried to put my thoughts in order so that he would understand what the paramedics were doing. I reached out my hand to him; he looked at me for a moment then took it.

These men are healers. They will take you to the temple of healing. I pictured Southampton General for a moment. *Many strange and uncomfortable things may happen to you.* A memory of giving a blood sample. *Do not fight them. These are necessary to heal you. I will come to you when I can, but I must explain what has happened to my rulers.*

I watched his face to see his reaction, but the glamour hid any expression. There was a timelag before he spoke in my mind.

"If this is what must be, then I will go with them."

Have no fear, these are highly skilled men and they do this every day.

"I am a warrior. I have no fear." The glamour face smiled for a moment.

I turned back to the paramedic. "Hold out your hand."

He hesitated then reached out; I brought the King's hand to meet it. "Think clearly about the things you want to ask him."

I released the King's hand and held my breath until he

took the paramedic's hand. I watched the paramedic's face and almost laughed out loud at his expression when, I presume, the King spoke in his mind.

The King shuffled forward and awkwardly sat in the wheelchair; the queen came and stood beside him. The paramedic looked at me.

"OK. We'll take him from here," he said. He opened his case and began to connect the King up to the monitoring gear.

I bowed to the King then turned and walked back to where Sharon stood.

"He'll be OK," I said. "Let's go."

We walked back to the car park a couple of paces apart, aware of the eyes on us.

"I just don't understand why Michelle went back," I said. "There wasn't any reason to." I looked around and spotted her Polo parked in a corner.

Sharon shrugged. "No idea. She just did it, didn't talk about it."

I looked back across the forest at the gateway glowing softly blue feeling flat and dead tired. Right now there wasn't a damn thing I could do to help her except stick to the plan and hope.

I turned back to Sharon. "Guess I'd better not keep your boss waiting any longer then."

The car park was full of police cars and vans as well as the ambulance. DI Brown was sitting in a blue BMW 5 series, eating a bag of crisps, while Superintendent Graham walked around talking into his mobile. Sharon unlocked the Mini; I put the bag of firebombs carefully on the back seat then took off the stab-jacket with great relief.

We walked over to the BMW and waited while Superintendent Graham continued his call. DI Brown offered the crisps to Sharon and pointedly ignored me.

Superintendent Graham ended his call and snapped his phone shut.

"You are still suspended," he said to Sharon. "Go home and stay there. I don't want to see you around this investigation."

I was sure Sharon was going to argue back, but she bit her lip then said. "Yes boss. I'll see you later, Charlie."

She walked back to the Mini but didn't get in; instead she lit a cigarette and watched as the paramedics wheeled the King to the ambulance.

"You, get in," Superintendent Graham said to me.

I climbed into the back of the BMW. Superintendent Graham got into the driver's seat and started the engine.

The two policemen didn't talk on the way back into town so I had plenty of time to think about Michelle. The best scenario I could think of was that she was with my mother and the other two remaining hostages; there were plenty of other possibilities, all worse. I watched the suburban sprawl of Totton go by as I tried to understand why she'd gone back. The nearest I got was that it had something to do with me making her stay at the portal while we went to free the prisoners; that she felt she had to prove how useful she could be. Not much of a reason. I chewed on it all the way into town, but anything else I came up with made less sense. Sometime soon, I prayed, I'd get to ask her why.

They drove into the Civic Centre police station and parked up. Superintendent Graham disappeared to do important senior police officer things. DI Brown brought me in to the interview suite.

"Any chance of a coffee and bacon sandwich?" I asked. It was past midday and even my fucked-up time sense said it was lunchtime. "I'll buy my own."

No reply.

"Can I at least go to the toilet?"

"OK."

He escorted me down the corridor to the men's toilet and waited outside. I was just drying my hands when someone else walked in. I recognised him immediately; his face was burned into my brain even though I'd never met him. His reaction said he recognised me so I ducked out before he spoke. There would be another time to deal with him.

"You ready now then?" asked DI Brown when I came out into the corridor. "Let's get on with it."

We went back to the interview suite and he pointed out the camera on the wall. "This will be recorded, video and audio."

I sat down across the table from him, determined that his pissed-off attitude wouldn't get to me; there was too much at stake.

"How can I help you, Inspector?"

He scowled at me. "You could tell me where you recovered the missing persons from." He leaned forward and said quietly. "And don't give me any of this parallel worlds shit."

I took my time over answering. "I, and the people who came with me, recovered the missing persons from a place that exists beyond a gateway. They were being held captive there, and were about to be killed. No shit Inspector, just the truth."

He growled deep in his throat. "Where is this place? Is it near the Netley Marsh car park where you turned up?"

"It's not on any map. There's a gateway near the car park, that's what we used to get there."

"Tell me about it. Describe the building."

"They kept them in the stable block. It's part of the royal palace. It's all shiny white and silver. You can see it for miles."

Another growl. "How did you know where they were?"

"My father told me. He lives over there."

"And what's his connection with the people who took them?"

"He opposes them. They take their orders from the High Lord Faniel, he's the heir to the throne over there."

A growl, a pause and a deep intake of breath. "You brought twenty four people with you, did you see any more?"

"We had to leave some behind, including my mother...and one of our crew didn't make it back."

"Why did you leave them behind?"

"We couldn't break the compulsions on them, they were too strong."

"Compulsions?" He frowned deeply at me. "What are those?"

"Things they can do to make you obey them. Those people couldn't leave the building they were in. If we'd taken them out they'd have fought us to go back."

"What do you think's likely to happen to the people you left behind?"

"They'll be killed by Lord Faniel, just like he was going to do with the rest of them. And that's going to happen soon."

"How soon?"

"It's difficult to be exact. Time moves at a different rate over there. It's already the morning of midsummer's day there and the ceremony's at sunset. Couple of days, maybe."

He looked away and breathed heavily before turning back to me. "And why will they be killed?"

"As a sacrifice. To thank the gods who gave the land to the people over there. It's an old tradition that Lord Faniel is bringing back."

He suddenly thumped both fists on the table and surged to his feet, knocking over his chair. "I should nick you for wasting my time with this bullshit. What's your fucking game, Charlie? Eh?"

His eyes bulged and his face flushed red. I scooted backwards in my chair, afraid that he was going to grab me; I think he would have, but for the camera on the wall. He turned away from me and smacked the flat of his hand on the wall then left the room. I stayed in my chair, heart pounding, waiting for something else to happen.

My heartrate had just about returned to normal by the time DI Brown came back.

"Last chance, Charlie," he said, glaring down at me. "Tell me what's really going on and we'll forget about that fairy story stuff."

"Sorry Inspector. Can't help you. Go and check the statements I made before. Look at what the people I brought back are saying. It's all true. Just 'cos you don't like it that doesn't make it bullshit. Ask Sharon Wickens."

That annoyed him even more. "You leave her out of this. She's not well."

"That's bollocks." I stood up. "There's nothing wrong with her, and you know it. She just got stitched up by that spook Nigel." The memory of him sparked a pulse of anger. "What's wrong with you that you won't see it? She said you're a good copper, you'll follow the evidence. How much more do you need?"

I think he would have hit me then if it weren't for the camera but I didn't care; I'd burned a gwasannath and faced down an Otherkin swordsman today so he wasn't going to intimidate me.

"I think I'd like to go now. I'm not under arrest, am I? I can just go anytime I please, can't I?"

"You do yourself a favour and stay where you are," he growled then turned and stormed out banging the door shut; I heard the lock turn. I might not be under arrest but I clearly wasn't going anywhere.

I sat back down on my chair and waited for something to happen. I still had my phone and considered ordering a take-away pizza; I was hungry enough but thought that it might be taking the piss. More seriously, I thought about calling the student union office and getting them to sort me out with a lawyer. I called the main number, and was put through to the welfare office but the line was engaged. I hung up with the intention of trying again in a few minutes.

I never did make the call because Superintendent Graham and another, older, plainclothes officer came in just after I put my phone away.

"I want to ask you about the missing people." He picked up the tumbled chair and sat down, his voice still soft and reasonable. "You told DI Brown you'd seen them."

"That's right. We had to leave prisoners behind, including my mother. One of our crew is missing too." A cold arrow of anxiety stabbed me in the stomach at the reminder.

"I see, and do you have reason to think they're in danger?"

"Yes. I think they're going to be killed within a couple of days."

"Why do you think that?"

"Because the guy in charge over there was building this up to be a big spectacle to celebrate the start of his rule. He's been humiliated by us taking most of the prisoners back, so he's going to make sure it goes ahead with those he has left."

"And when will that be?"

"The ceremony was planned for sunset on midsummer's day. It was early midsummer's day morning when we pulled them out. I reckon we've got a couple of days at most."

"What about the people you brought with you, the man who went to hospital? Where does he fit into this?"

"He's the King, but he's too weak to control his son, who's the one causing all the shit. Once he's got his bypass, he should be able to get control back."

"And your plan was to take him back to do that?" Still calm and reasonable, nothing of what he'd heard seemed to have disturbed him.

"Yes. He should be getting his operation now; he ought to be fit to travel tomorrow." *And there's the invitation to fuck up my plans and get the hostages killed.*

"Will he be able to get the hostages released unharmed?"

"I don't know. Maybe. He's the best hope we've got."

Superintendent Graham stroked his chin and looked at me, his grey eyes apparently focused on something a long way behind me.

"What's your view on this, Don?" He asked the older plain clothes guy.

"I don't see that we have a choice."

"My thought exactly," said Superintendent Graham. His focus returned to me. "Is there anything we can help you with to get these people back?"

It is possible my mouth dropped open and stayed that way for a few seconds.

"Excuse me? Ten minutes ago your DI was threatening to nick me for wasting police time. Now you're asking me if there's anything I need?"

"I can only apologise for that." Superintendent Graham spread his hands. "In my position I have to take a wider view of events."

"Nothing to do with the statements that the people I brought back have made?"

"I can't comment on what may be in their statements. The most important thing for us is the safety of the people still missing. You're the only person who offers us any chance of getting them back. So, is there anything you need?"

"That only chance is completely dependent on the King.

If he comes through the bypass operation OK, then I could do with some serious guys to look after him on the trip back. We got lucky last time, they weren't expecting us. It'll be much harder going back a second time."

"That we may be able to help with, anything else?"

"They'll need a special kit. You can't take iron through the gateway, so no guns unless they're ceramic.

"I'll pass that on. Anything else?"

"Can't think of anything right now. Do you know how the king is?"

"No. But I'll get someone to find out. You want to go in tomorrow if he's fit?"

"I'd go now if he was fit." Damn right I would; I wanted Michelle safely out of Lord Faniel's reach as soon as possible.

"I'd like to send one of my officers with you as an observer, is that possible?"

"No problem." Then I added just for mischief. "How about DI Brown? No-one could accuse him of being gullible and easily influenced."

Superintendent Graham glanced at the other guy who nodded in reply.

"Possibly. If there's nothing else, I think we're finished here." He stood up. "Are your contact details in the system?"

"They should be, but I can give you them again."

"Come with me and we'll check now, then you can go."

I followed him out of the interview room, down the corridor to the front desk. While he checked my contact details on the database, he had the desk sergeant call to check on the King. I updated my address from Arnold Road to Sharon's flat while the sergeant spoke to the hospital.

"They're operating on him now, sir," said the sergeant. Which was good news; I'd been right about his heart condition. Now the chances were better that he'd be fit to rule again and put Lord Faniel back in his box. I looked at my watch—ten past four. With luck he'd be done soon; then after a good night's sleep we could get him back through the gateway.

"Then he'll probably be out tomorrow," said Superintendent Graham, echoing my thoughts. "We'll work on the basis that you're going in tomorrow, Mr. Somes. Is that alright with you?"

"Yeah. Soon as we can."

"Call me in the morning on this number and I'll tell you the arrangements." He passed me a card. "See you tomorrow." He turned and walked away, pulling out his mobile and starting his next conversion before he reached the door.

I called Sharon when I got out of the police station. She said she would come and get me, so I went and sat in the park to wait for her. I suppose I should have been happy with the outcome of the day. After all we'd got the King, Queen and most of the prisoners out unharmed and finally I had some level of official recognition and backing, but the truth was I was too worried about mother and Michelle to feel pleased. There was a significant chance that Lord Faniel would be pissed-off enough to just kill Michelle immediately, especially as she is a half-breed, and that scared the shit out of me.

Sharon turned up after about fifteen minutes.

"You want to eat in town, or go back to mine?" She smelt of cigarettes; couldn't say I blamed her. If I smoked I would probably have gone through a pack today.

"I'm knackered. Let's go home and get a takeaway."

"They give you a tough time? Who did you have?"

"Your boss first, and he didn't buy a word of it. Really pissed him off. He nearly lost it. After he went I got Superintendent Graham and some other older guy. They were a lot more reasonable, but then I reckon they'd just come from reading the prisoners' statements."

"Who was the other guy?" We started to walk towards Grosvenor Square where she had parked.

"Don't know, he didn't say much. Superintendent Graham called him Don at one point."

"That could be the ACC." She must have noticed my confusion with the acronym. "Assistant Chief Constable."

"Ah right."

"So what did they say?"

"Wanted to know about the missing people, the ones we didn't manage to get out. I told him about the plan with the

King to get them out before Lord Faniel kills them. He asked if there was anything I needed."

"Did you ask for anything?"

"Yeah, professional backup."

"What did they offer you? Half a dozen hard men from Hereford in an unmarked minibus?"

"Maybe. You ever worked with them?"

"No. I'm just guessing."

"There was one other nice thing. Your boss, DI Brown is coming with us."

"What! Fuck! You sure?"

"They liked the idea when I suggested it. Does he get to say no when the superintendent thinks it's a good idea?"

She grinned. "He'd need a very good reason."

"I saw your mate DI Scott too."

"Really? Where? What did he say?"

"It was in the gents. I didn't speak to him, but I'm sure he recognised me. How could he know me?"

"You were videoed when I first questioned you. That's linked to your file. It would be easy for him to view it."

"Would you be able to find out who had accessed the file?"

Sharon thought for a moment. "Don't know. Maybe. I'd have to ask the IT team."

"It would be a bit more proof if he had."

"Yeah, it would." She paused. "I going to have to talk to him, then I'll decide if I'm going to make it official. But not before we've got the King back home." She shook her head. "I don't want to believe he's a bad copper. I mean we've got history, but I don't think my judgement is that bad."

We reached Mini and got in. Just then my phone rang. I pulled it out and didn't recognise the number.

I did recognise the voice though. "Mister Somes. This is Alice Barrett. My husband has just arrived home and I owe you my deepest thanks. I must admit that I doubted you and for that I humbly apologise."

"That's OK, I'm just glad he's back. Is he alright?"

"He's physically unharmed, but he's had a rough time. It'll take a while I think. Alexander says your patient is doing well."

"That's good to know, thank you."

"No. Thank you, Mister Somes, from the bottom of my heart. If there's ever anything I can do to help you, please don't hesitate to ask." She ended the call and I wondered if I'd ever have the nerve to call that favour in.

"Who was that?" asked Sharon as we pulled out into Bedford Place.

"Alice Barrett. Thanking me for getting her husband back home. She said the King's doing well."

"Good. Be all kinds of shit if he died over here."

"I don't even want to think about how big a fuck-up that could be." I closed my eyes to try to banish the thought; it didn't work.

"So what do you want for a takeaway?" asked Sharon when we pulled up outside her place. "I fancy pizza."

"Works for me." Except it didn't really; I should have been ravenous, but thinking about mother and Michelle had stolen my appetite. Sharon had the number for pizza delivery stored on her phone and had made the order before we got indoors.

"I got two because I know what you're like," she said as she opened the door. I hoped the scent of them would reignite my hunger; otherwise they'd be breakfast tomorrow. "Will I put the kettle on, or do you want a drink?"

"Drink." No question.

"Thought so. Wine or vodka?"

"Wine. Can't afford to get too pissed if I'm going back through the portal tomorrow." Sad but true; I felt like getting completed blasted, anything to quiet my thoughts.

Sharon was opening a bottle of Chilean red when the doorbell rang.

"I'll get that," I called, expecting it to be the pizza delivery.

It wasn't. It was DI Scott.

"What the fuck are you doing here?" he asked.

It took me a couple of seconds to reply. "I'm staying with Sharon for a bit."

"Is that the pizzas?" called Sharon from inside.

"No. It's your mate DI Scott," I replied.

A moment later she was beside me. "Evening, Mike. Wasn't expecting to see you. Want to come in?"

I stood aside and let him in.

"So what did you want to talk about, Mike?" asked Sharon once we were inside.

"I…er…just wanted to see you. Heard you had a good result today." He didn't sound convincing.

"I'm touched," said Sharon. "'Specially since you didn't come and see me when I got suspended." She paused. "How about we talk about Pete Murphy?"

"Name means nothing to me." That sounded stronger.

"Really? Cos he's the reason Charlie is staying here. You see a little while ago, I starting asking questions about Pete Murphy, then a couple of days later Charlie gets grabbed off the street by Pete's crew. Coincidence would you say?"

"What's this got to do with me?"

"Charlie got a call just before he was grabbed, and you were the only other person who had his phone number."

"So?"

He sounded sufficiently confident. So I thought I'd step in, this after all was the guy who had most likely tried to get me killed.

"So you won't mind if I read you." I stepped towards him, reaching out a hand.

"No!" he said.

He turned away from me. "I'm going."

Sharon moved to block his way to the door.

"No, you're not," she said.

He glared at her and for a moment I thought it was going to get physical.

"Here's how it is, Mike," said Sharon. "Either you talk to us and let Charlie read you, or you can talk to the Professional Standards team. Your choice."

He went pale. "You keep your hands off me."

"Why don't you sit down?" said Sharon

He flopped on the sofa, head in his hands. We waited for him to look at us. When he didn't, Sharon said, "Why not start with why you're doing it?"

Eventually he lifted his head. His eyes were moist. "I honestly can't tell you."

"Why?" asked Sharon. "What's he got on you? Please tell me it isn't just money."

"Nothing. You don't understand. I don't know why I'm doing it."

"What?" said Sharon. "That makes no sense."

A light came on in my brain. "Oh yes it does. He's put a compulsion on you."

Sharon's mouth dropped slowly open.

"A what?" said DI Scott.

"A compulsion," I said. "Give me your hand."

"What are you going to do?" He pulled his hands back.

"I want to read you, take a look in your mind. Then maybe I can help you."

He slowly reached out a hand to me. I took it and his fear and pain washed over me. I focused on the image of Pete Murphy right at the front of his thoughts and reached for his memories of him. There were plenty, but some were out of reach as if they were behind walls of smoke and glass. I pushed at the walls, but they flowed away from me and darkened; the harder I pushed the more opaque they became.

I pulled back and released his hand. He stared at me with wide frightened eyes.

"Well?" said Sharon.

"Weird," I said. "Not like anyone else I've ever read."

"What's going on?" said DI Scott. "What's that fucking slag done to me?"

"I think he's put a compulsion on you," I said.

"What the fuck's that?"

"It's a mind trick," I said. "It makes you obey him."

"Bastard!" said DI Scott, his voice a hoarse whisper. "Is there anything you can do about it?"

"Me? No," I said. "But my father should be able to." Assuming he survives Lord Faniel's displeasure.

"Question is, what do you want us to do?" said Sharon. "If we can remove this compulsion will you help us go after Murphy?"

"God yes! Of course."

"Good choice," said Sharon.

"What are you going do?" asked DI Scott.

"Right now," said Sharon. "Offer you a glass of wine. You sound like you need one."

"Yeah, but after?"

"We have to get through the current shitstorm," said Sharon. "If we survive that, then we'll deal with Pete Murphy." She went to the cupboard for another wineglass, poured out the red and passed him a full glass. "Welcome back to the good guys' side."

The doorbell rang.

"Good timing." Sharon reached for her bag, took out her wallet and went to the door to collect the pizzas. Mike sat staring into his glass.

She came back with two boxes. "There's Double Pepperoni or Hawaiian Special. You eating Mike?"

He shook his head. "Look, I'm going to head off if that's OK with you. There's a lot I've got to get my head around."

"Fine by me," said Sharon. "But look, take some time off, you must be owed enough. Turn off your phone. Whatever you do, don't talk to Murphy because he can still control you. We'll talk about this again in a couple of days."

He stood up, his wine still untouched and Sharon showed him out. I heard them talking at the door but couldn't make out the words.

She came back, and took a large gulp of wine. "Thank Christ for that." She sat down. "I really didn't want to have to turn him in."

She opened the pizzas. "Which one do you want, Charlie?"

"Pepperoni." I still didn't feel hungry, but I knew I needed to eat.

She passed me the pizza and a large glass of wine and then said what I'd been thinking.

"So if Pete Murphy can put compulsions on people, does that mean he's at least part Otherkin?"

"I think he must be," I said. "But I don't really know. Just one more thing I need to learn about. I hope I get the chance."

Normally a pizza that size would be gone in under fifteen minutes, but tonight I only ate two slices in that time.

"Do you want to talk about it?" asked Sharon. There was

one slice left of her Hawaiian Special. "I know there's something wrong when you're off your food."

"I can't stop thinking about Michelle and what they might've done to her. Because she's half Otherkin they might treat her worse than the others. They could kill her."

"Nothing we can do about it before tomorrow," she said softly.

"I know, but I keep thinking I should have done something to stop her from going back."

"How could you? You weren't there. You know, I reckon the real reason she went back was to get away from that gorilla of a boyfriend. He was on at her as soon as they came through."

"Really?" I could see that, but it did nothing to diminish my worries about what had happened to her. "I still feel responsible though."

"But you're not. It was her choice. She signed a disclaimer same as everybody else."

"I guess. I'm just so worried about what I'm going to find over there tomorrow."

"Worrying about that won't change it."

She leaned forward. "You gonna eat that pizza then?" She reached for a slice of the Double Pepperoni.

"Have some." I refilled my wine glass and took the last slice of Hawaiian Special.

CHAPTER 17

Despite the red wine, I slept poorly; thoughts of what I would find on the other side tumbling and looping in my mind. I got up just before 6:00 A.M., had a shower, made coffee, and wondered what time to call Superintendent Graham as Sharon slept happily on. I watched a bit of breakfast TV, which reminded me why I never watch it, then fired up my laptop and went into my e-mail. There were a bunch of messages from my volunteers all saying pretty much the same thing; how they'd had a fascinating time, hoped the prisoners were well and they wanted to go over there again. If I got the king back home then maybe that could happen; if not, the Otherworld would be closed to us for the next few hundred years.

I pissed around surfing the net, trying to find anything to distract me from thinking about what I'd find over there. I hated the waiting; knowing that what lay before me would be life-changing and utterly unavoidable. Yet I was terrified of walking into it. It was worse than the morning of my first final exam.

I called Superintendent Graham about half eight, expecting to get voicemail or nothing, but he picked up straight away.

"The King should be coming out of hospital this morning after the surgeon has a look at him. That should be about ten. I'll send a car for you."

I went to wake Sharon and tell her what the plan was and found her awake.

"How long have you been up?" she asked.

"Couple of hours, didn't sleep much. Car's picking me up at ten."

"You eaten anything?"

"No. Just coffee."

"Eat something. You'll need it."

I made more coffee and ate half a bowl of cereal while Sharon showered. The minutes crept by and I nearly started smoking three times. The car turned up to collect me just as Sharon made a third pot of coffee.

"Have you got everything?" asked Sharon. "What about your firebombs?"

She was right; they were still in the Mini. "Won't the SAS guys have a better kit?"

"If they turn up."

Right again. I retrieved the bag with the last two flasks and got into the unmarked car with a driver I didn't recognise.

"Text me when you get back to this side," Sharon said, and then was gone.

The driver conveyed me silently and efficiently through the traffic out to Netley Marsh. There was plenty of activity in the car park when we got there. Superintendent Graham was talking on his mobile but gave me a wave of acknowledgement. DI Brown scowled at me from the front seat of a car where he sat eating a bacon roll. DC Wilson beside him looked no more pleased to see me. I got out of the car and stood in the sunshine feeling a little lost as everyone around me made busy.

I was texting Sharon when someone called my name.

"Charlie Somes?" The voice was familiar.

"Yeah. I'm Charlie." I turned. Nigel, the government spook, was standing there with a stocky man wearing dark combat fatigues.

"This is Steve," said Nigel. "He and his team will be going with you. Can you tell them everything they need to know about what they're facing?"

"I can try." There were other things I wanted to discuss with Nigel but now was not the time. "I've been a handful of times. I guess that makes me the expert."

"Great. Come and tell us about it," said Steve, he sounded like he was from Yorkshire. "We've got a brew on."

Nigel stayed with Superintendent Graham and I followed Steve to a plain white minibus parked in the corner of the car park. Three men dressed in similar dark fatigues sat around a portable stove on which a kettle steamed. What were they? SAS, Marines? Did it matter so long as they knew what they were doing?

"Geordie, Bonzo and Jimmy, this is Charlie. He's our local expert."

I was offered a seat, handed a large mug of hot tea and then the questions began. What was the layout of the palace? How many guards? What were they armed with?

I answered as best I could; reassured by their air of solid competence. If anything went wrong these guys could handle it.

"You know you can't bring anything iron with you, don't you?" I said. "That probably means anything magnetic."

"They said," said Geordie, the Tyneside accent distinct. "That's why we brought these." He opened a pocket on his pack and pulled out a dagger with a black nine-inch blade.

"Ceramic," he said. "Sharper'n steel and non-magnetic. Bomb disposal lads use 'em."

"Impressive. I could've done with these," I said. "We made swords from some experimental turbine blades."

"They work for you?" asked Jimmy.

"Well enough. Didn't have to use 'em much. Never tested them against the bronze swords they use over there."

"We brought some of these lads too," said Geordie. He opened another pouch and took out a black cylinder with metal cap and ring on top; it just about covered his palm. "Concussion grenade, fibre body, 8 ounces of TNT. Cap and firing mechanism're aluminium alloy."

"Hope you brought plenty," I said.

"Is there anything else we haven't covered?" asked Steve.

"Keep hold of me when we're going through the portal. If you let go it might take you somewhere else, and I won't be able to find you. When we get there just remember you can't believe a lot of what you see. They're really good at illusions, and they can do things to your mind so don't let any of them touch you skin to skin."

A black five-series BMW drove in to the car park.

"This looks like what we've been waiting for," said Steve. The black-clad men stood up and started strapping on their gear.

Don, the assistant chief constable, got out of the front passenger door and opened the rear door. The Queen, still clad in shining white, stepped out.

"Fucking look at that," said Bonzo, looking at the Queen. "Wouldn't mind a bit."

"Fuckin' right," said Jimmy.

"Perfect example of what I told you," I said. "You can't believe what you see, it's all illusion. I don't know what she really looks like, but I'll bet any money it's not like that."

I didn't hear his reply because my attention was taken by the scrawny little bloke with scraggy grey hair who got out of the car behind the Queen. He took her arm and I realised it was the King; the King without his glamour.

I caught his eye and he summoned me with a tilt of his head. I walked over to him still stunned by the reality of his appearance. The Queen no longer glowed but otherwise her glamour was still strong. To my surprise she reached out a hand to me.

"He is renewed." Her voice in my mind was soft as a summer breeze when I took her hand. "He thanks you for this renewal though his power is gone."

I thought for a moment about what he had gone through yesterday; presumably he'd spent several hours in close proximity to either an MRI magnet or an X-ray machine. Both of those were massive lumps of iron, maybe they had depleted his magic and it would return when he was back the other side.

"I pray it is so," said the Queen.

Superintendent Graham walked up to us, followed by DI Brown and DC Wilson.

"Everything is ready," he said and beckoned over Steve and his black-clad team.

"These men are our guards, they will come with us," I said to the Queen.

She looked at DI Brown, dressed in a black rugby shirt and brown trousers, looking even bulkier than usual in body armour. There was a moment's pause before "very well, let us go" drifted through my mind. She released my hand and turned back to the King.

I looked around for somewhere to leave my phone. Nowhere offered an obvious option, so I held it out to Superintendent Graham.

"Look after this, can you?"

He looked surprised.

"Can't take it through the portal," I said. "And I've got nowhere to leave it."

He didn't answer for a moment as if thinking about it, then reached out his hand. "I'll look after it. Are you ready to go?"

"Yes. I just hope we're in time."

"Any idea how long you'll be?"

"Not really. Based on previous visits it could be two or three days."

He nodded. "There'll be someone at this site permanently until you get back."

I gathered up my team and led them to the portal followed by Superintendent Graham and a group of spectators. I started out slowly to allow for the King's pace but it wasn't necessary; he was moving purposefully with no sign of discomfort. I stopped beside the portal and held out a hand to the Queen.

"Everyone join hands," I said. "It'll be cold and dark for a few moments. Keep hold, and keep walking until we get to the other side."

I reached out my other hand to Steve; he took it and his calm excitement washed through my mind for a moment before I pushed it off to a corner. After a check that everyone was joined up, I filled my mind with my memory of the palace and stepped into the portal. The cold darkness swallowed me; its wild wind filled with voices rushing through my head for what seemed longer than before as I towed the team forward.

To my great relief I stepped out into daylight though the sun, just visible through the trees, was low in the sky. I let go of Steve, took a lungful of sweet air and felt the lift as I turned to watch the others emerge from the gateway. DI Brown was looking around with his usual scowl as if trying to figure out what stunt had been pulled on him. I was going to say 'welcome to the other side, Inspector, but I didn't get the chance.

They hit us with no warning. A horn blew and a dozen or so soldiers with bronze swords were right in front of us; it must have been a concealment spell of some kind. They charged us, screaming war cries, from about twenty yards away.

The black team moved instantly. A concussion grenade boomed and disrupted the body of the charge, felling a handful. Ceramic knives in hand they engaged the first Otherkin soldiers. That stopped about half of them. The rest bypassed the fight and, screaming madly, came straight for us.

Holding my breath, ears ringing from the grenade, I reached into my bag and gripped a flask, looking for a target. Two swordsmen ran at me, blades raised. The first one took a faceful of firebomb at the distance of three yards. He tried to bat it away with his sword, missed and it set his whole head alight. He screamed like the end of the world. I dropped my bag and dived for his mate's knees, trying to bring him down and then make skin contact. His knee caught me in the side of the head and everything went sideways for a moment.

I saw his hand gripping his sword above me and held my breath anticipating his strike. A pale silver hand reached out and seized his. Time stood still then he dropped the sword and slumped to the ground beside me. The silver hand reached down and caught my arm. I climbed to my knees, head spinning. The Queen released me and instantly confronted another soldier who charged at us.

The Queen spoke a few brief liquid phrases, something along the lines of 'don't you know who I am?' I guess. The soldier dropped his sword and knelt before her and I remembered to breathe.

The Queen spread her arms wide before her, there was a brilliant silver-white flash and her voice filled my ears though I didn't understand the words. The fighting stopped as the surviving Otherkin soldiers stepped back and lowered their swords, staring at her.

The black team crouched in back-to-back pairs surrounded by half a dozen bodies. Geordie was bleeding heavily from his scalp, but his knife was still in his hand waiting for more business as he glared at the retreating soldiers. Beyond them DI Brown knelt over DC Wilson who was face down in the leaf litter.

The King strode up to join the Queen from beside the gateway where he'd stood ready to flee back into the cold darkness. He called out to the soldiers and, after a moment, one of them came forward to join the one kneeling before the Queen. Judging by his fancy bronze breastplate he may have been their leader. He held out his sword, hilt first, to the King, dropped to his knees and bowed his head.

The king took the sword and spoke several phrases, declaiming them so that all the Otherkin could hear him, then executed the kneeling soldier with downward thrust through his neck. He died without sound, just fell forward on his face; there wasn't even much blood.

I nearly pissed myself in surprise.

The black team guys sheathed their knives. Steve looked at me.

"You OK?"

"Yeah." I stood up and my head swam alarmingly for a moment but it passed. I went to pick up my bag and followed Steve over to DI Brown and DC Wilson.

"Should kill the lot of them," said DI Brown, his face hard as a beach pebble.

"Jimmy. Medikit." Steve called.

"No point," said DI Brown. "He's a goner."

I looked down at DC Wilson; he wasn't moving and the grass around him was red. My head swam again, I stumbled and Steve caught me.

"You sure you're OK?" he asked.

"Yeah. I just got a bang on the head."

He looked at me through narrowed eyes. "Your pupils are OK. You tell me straight away if you feel sick or sleepy or get a bad headache."

"Okay."

"Can you march? How far's the objective?"

"Under a mile."

He looked up at the sinking sun. "Gonna be tight. Right lads, time to move."

I looked at DC Wilson's body. "What are we going to do with him?"

"Leave him. He ain't going anywhere. We'll pick him up on the way back."

The King must have caught the sense of my question because he spoke a couple of brisk phrases to the soldiers. Four of them came over and picked DC Wilson up between them and stood ready to follow us. DI Brown glared at them as if he could kill them all bare-handed but said nothing.

The King and Queen led us towards the palace, the black team flanking them. Two of them weren't moving freely, though it didn't slow them as we marched briskly through the trees.

"That's fucking amazing," said Jimmy when the palace came in view, the walls shining gold rather than silver and the soft music of flutes replaced by triumphant trumpets.

"Illusion," I said. "It's all a glamour, a spell. Just like CGI."

"Yeah. Right. Fucking amazing though."

"Amazing, but not real."

We walked straight toward the palace across the lawn with no attempt at concealment, my head clearing as we went; the power of the place working its healing magic maybe. The blaring trumpets grew steadily louder, the sinking sun sending our long shadows back towards the woods. I wanted to shout at them to hurry, to run but didn't; the King was moving pretty well for a guy who'd had a bypass less than twenty four hours ago.

Two hundred yards short of the palace another, larger squad of Otherkin soldiers appeared from the outbuildings and advanced towards us, spears at the ready. Concussion grenades appeared in the hands of the black team, I gripped my last firebomb.

The Queen took my hand for a moment.

"We will deal with this," she whispered in my mind and walked towards them, the King at her side. There was a short discussion. Then the soldiers fell in behind us as we continued. Instead of going around the side of the palace as I had with Jack, we marched straight up to a grand entranceway. The guards took one look at the Queen, saluted and stood aside. We passed through the palace; all glowing golden walls and floors, but each room looked the same, like a painting on glass with no depth.

We emerged onto the wide grass plain, the hoofprints in the turf showing it had lately been the exercise area for the King's cavalry. Here the trumpets were mercifully silent and I could hear the buzz of an excited crowd. The sun was sinking behind a cloudbank just above the horizon; we had maybe fifteen minutes of daylight left.

At the edge of the parade ground the land fell away and nature, or man, had constructed a wide shallow amphitheatre open to the west. Most of the population of the place, several thousand strong, must have been there on the slopes. The folk I could see looked pretty ordinary and plainly dressed, beards were in fashion. Presumably the great and powerful were sitting at the front, all glamoured up.

The King led us down a stairway at the side, a thousand pairs of eyes following us. From the top of the stair I could see the wide flat stage area. Five tall stakes had been driven into the ground, tied to them with their arms above their heads were five figures. The smallest was Michelle. I could have cried in relief at the sight of her. Beside her was mother, then Jack. The other two I did not recognise. They must be the prisoners whose compulsions Jack had failed to break.

Beyond the stakes a group of men clad in shining golden robes stood facing the setting sun. It wasn't hard to figure which one was Lord Faniel; he was about seven feet tall and crowned with golden flames.

We followed the King down the stairs and out onto the stage. Lord Faniel and his golden mates ignored us until the King spoke in loud voice that silenced the buzz of the crowd. Lord Faniel turned instantly and strode across the stage to his father, yelling at him. The King stood his ground yelling back and the two of them ended up toe to toe. I moved quietly towards the stake where Michelle hung as they argued. She smiled weakly as I approached.

"Charlie, you made it," she said so quietly I could barely hear. She was very pale, but looked otherwise unhurt.

"We'll have you out of here as soon as the King takes control," I said.

The Queen and the black team moved up to flank the King as the slanging match continued. The gold-clad Otherkin came up behind Lord Faniel, bronze short swords in their hands. I reached into my bag for a flask and waited for the physicals to kick off.

Wasn't long to wait; Lord Faniel suddenly grabbed his father's wrists and yelled an order over his shoulder. Eight gold-clad Otherkin rushed forward and the black team met them head on.

Lord Faniel released his father who stood frozen like a statue, a compulsion I guess, and turned to face me as I stood in front of Michelle. He drew a sword at least a foot longer than the ones his guards carried, its edge flickering with golden flame and advanced on me.

He was five yards from me when DI Brown tackled him. Like the rugby player he had been, he dived for Lord Faniel's knees and missed. There was a flicker like a poorly edited film, for a moment Lord Faniel was a foot to the side, then he was back in front of me. DI Brown picked himself up and charged again. There was a second flicker, Lord Faniel was a foot to the side for a moment and this time he swung catching DI Brown behind the ear with the hilt of his sword. DI Brown hit the ground and stayed there.

Time slowed as Lord Faniel turned back to face me and lifted his sword above his head. I clutched a flask in my right hand and raised my arm ready to throw. The sun burst through the cloudbank; shining in Lord Faniel's eyes it slowed his advance momentarily and threw long shadows into the front rows of the crowd. I stared at him; eyes wide, mouth open. A shadow started about two feet to the left of where he stood but he himself cast none. He stepped forward and the shadow moved with him.

I held my breath and threw the flask at the base of the shadow. It burst and the white fire blossomed. The great golden warrior vanished, replaced by a short guy with scruffy long brown hair and his lower legs on fire. He screamed long and high, dropped his sword and tried to beat out the flames with his hands.

I was happy to let him cook; he'd started this shit so he'd earned some pain. The Queen thought differently. She ran to him, pushed him over and rolled him in his own cloak to quench the flames then cradled him in her arms. His cries ended the fight between his guards and the black team; two guards lay bleeding on the turf and the black team stood back to back facing the rest.

People surged onto the stage from the crowd, to surround the King and disarm the guards. I turned to Michelle and tried to untie her but my hands were shaking too much.

"Charlie," she whispered as I struggled with the cord that bound her.

"Allow me." Steve leaned over me and sliced through her bonds and she collapsed into my arms. I caught her and lowered her gently to the ground then buried my face in her hair and cried for sheer relief.

I don't know how long I stayed like that until someone touched me on the shoulder. I looked up into the battered face of Jack; the whole left side of his face was swollen, the eye closed and purple, a track of dried blood ran from the corner of his mouth down his chin. Mother stood just behind him.

"Are you alright, Charlie?" she asked.

"I'm fine," I said. "You alright?"

She nodded in reply.

"The King would speak with you," Jack said, the words distorted by his broken lips. "I will take her."

As I lifted Michelle her eyes opened.

"I love you, Charlie," she whispered. "Take me home."

"Soon baby," I whispered back. She was so light that it was no strain for me to pick her up and pass her over.

The King was still standing in exactly the same place with a crowd of Otherkin milling around him, most wearing a glamour. They made way for me as I approached him and he reached a hand to me. I took it and he spoke in my mind.

"I am deeply in your debt." Not as god-like as when he first spoke to me, a reflection I guessed of his weakened magic.

"My strength returns with every breath I take. I am renewed by your people's magic."

A small part of me was pleased that my theory about iron depleting magic appeared true.

"Your world has much iron. You could be strong if you came here. You could be one of the Great."

I thought then about Lord Faniel with his feet on fire; he seemed the kind of guy who would hold a grudge.

There was not a shred of sympathy in his reply. "He must learn the consequences of his actions and to obey his father."

Lord Faniel was in for a hard time then, which he richly deserved in my opinion.

"I have been neglectful of duties with him. It is my error. Please accept my deepest apologies."

I accepted, even though I felt I couldn't speak for all those who had been affected.

"Some of your people have suffered hurt." He looked over at DI Brown who was lying on the turf beside the black team and the other two prisoners. "For that, too, I apologise and I offer the assistance of the Great in returning you to your world. I regret that I cannot do it myself at this time."

I accepted his offer; right now it seemed like a long walk to the portal. Neither Michelle nor DI Brown looked in good enough shape for it and I really wanted to go home.

"I hope you will come back to visit soon. There is much I would learn about your world." The King released my hand with a smile. He turned to a couple of the glamour wearers nearby and spoke a few phrases in their strange lilting speech. They strode forward, chivvied people away and cleared an area of grass then beckoned me to them.

"Steve," I called. "We're leaving."

The black team got up immediately, supporting the bloodied DI Brown between them and walked over with the other two prisoners. Bonzo was limping heavily and Jimmy held his right arm immobile across his chest, Geordie's face and neck were completely blood-soaked from his scalp wound though he moved freely.

Jack half-carried Michelle over to join me, my mother just

behind him. I took Michelle from him and put an arm around her. She leaned heavily in to me; I think she would have fallen without support.

"I will come when I can. There is much to be done here." He said to mother. "I would have you see this land when it is at peace."

She put her arms around him and kissed him then turned to me.

"Let's go home," she said.

Jack smiled at me, lopsidedly because of the swelling, and reached out to take my hand.

"You have done great things my son. I am proud of you." His voice spoke within my mind. "Take care of your sister. It is good to see my children together."

There was no time to ask him what he meant because the two Glamour wearers spoke some phrase aloud. There was loud crack and a smell of ozone and a gateway opened right there before us. We didn't have to move, it swept right over us. The arena, the King and all the Otherkin vanished in a grey swirl and then we were back in the woods in Netley Marsh with a thin Hampshire rain falling on us.

Uniformed police officers came running. I remembered how the raiders had emerged from the portal and wondered if we had also reappeared with a flash like a lightning stroke.

"We're home," I whispered to Michelle. She clung to me and made a little sound halfway between a sigh and a sob. It didn't matter who she was right then; I loved her and she needed me. I held her tight until a paramedic insisted on taking her from me because she was in shock and couldn't stand unaided. Mother was whisked away too for a check-up and to give a statement. Then a uniformed sergeant grabbed me to say DI Brown wanted to talk to me.

DI Brown was lying on a stretcher in the back of an ambulance looking very pale and with a surgical collar around his neck.

"Inspector Brown?" I said as I climbed into the ambulance.

"Don't sit up," said the paramedic who was applying a dressing to the bloodied side of his head.

"I wanted to apologise, Charlie," DI Brown said, his voice a quiet croak. "I got you all wrong. I didn't want to believe what the evidence was telling me. I broke my own rule."

"Got there in the end though," I said feeling awkward about the conversation.

"Yeah, well. Good thing I've got a thick head."

"I wasn't going to say that."

"No? I owe you a lot of beer when they let me out."

"Look forward to it." Bit of a lie.

The paramedic was glaring at me as if to say visiting time was over.

"I'll be back to claim my beers, you just get well," I said and stepped out of the ambulance.

I walked away feeling suddenly tired and flat. I wanted a warm bath, a few beers and time to get my head around what had happened to my life and what I was going to do about Michelle. I didn't think that was going to be soon with another round of questions and statements clearly heading rapidly in my direction in the person of the uniformed sergeant.

I remembered my promise to text Sharon and wondered where Superintendent Graham had put my mobile. I hoped he hadn't lost it; if you can't trust a copper with your phone, who can you trust?

About the Author

Martin Owton was born in Southampton and grew up in the shadow of the Fawley oil refinery, he studied for a PhD in Synthetic Chemistry at the University of Southampton but there the similarity with his characters ends. He now lives in Surrey working as a drug designer for a major pharma company, and is a cancer survivor. He is the author of the non-epic Sword & Sorcery Nandor Tales novels Exile (mybook.to/ExileOwton) & Nandor (mybook.to/NandorOwton).

His website is at http://martinowton.com

CROSSROAD
PRESS

Printed in Great Britain
by Amazon